Praise for *The*

"Fisher balances emotional ... fun ice cream–making tips), all while keeping up a breezy pace. This delights."

Publishers Weekly

"Original, memorable, and a fun read from first page to last, *The Secret to Happiness* showcases author Suzanne Woods Fisher's natural flair for originality and the kind of deftly scripted and narrative-driven storytelling style that keeps her readers' rapt and entertained attention from cover to cover."

Midwest Book Review

"This is a story that embraces second chances, self-realization, and romance. *The Secret to Happiness* is a pleasure to read. Highly recommended."

Fresh Fiction

Praise for *The Sweet Life*

"This deliciously concocted novel is a charming start to a sure-to-satisfy series."

Booklist

"Restoration and reawakened dreams gather in Suzanne Woods Fisher's Christian romance novel *The Sweet Life*."

Foreword Reviews

"This is a clean contemporary story that will give many readers the feels. Such a fun summer read!"

Write-Read-Life

"*The Sweet Life* is a wonderful beach read, set at the Cape, with lots of ice cream sprinkled throughout. Nothing could be better on a hot summer day!"

Romance Junkies

LOVE *on a* WHIM

Novels by Suzanne Woods Fisher

CAPE COD CREAMERY · 3

LOVE *on a* WHIM

SUZANNE WOODS FISHER

Revell

a division of Baker Publishing Group
Grand Rapids, Michigan

Published by Revell
a division of Baker Publishing Group
Grand Rapids, Michigan
RevellBooks.com

Printed in the United States of America

Library of Congress Cataloging-in-Publication Data
Names: Fisher, Suzanne Woods, author.
Title: Love on a whim / Suzanne Woods Fisher.
Description: Grand Rapids, Michigan : Revell, a division of Baker Publishing Group,
    2024. | Series: Cape Cod Creamery ; 3
Identifiers: LCCN 2023035448 | ISBN 9780800739492 (paper) | ISBN 9780800745868
    (casebound) | ISBN 9781493445530 (ebook)
Subjects: LCGFT: Christian fiction. | Romance fiction. | Novels.
Classification: LCC PS3606.I78 L68 2024 | DDC 813/.6—dc23/eng/202300703
LC record available at https://lccn.loc.gov/2023035448

Scripture quotations are from the New King James Version®. Copyright © 1982 by Thomas Nelson. Used by permission. All rights reserved.

This book is a work of fiction. Names, characters, places, and incidents are the product of the author's imagination or are used fictitiously. Any resemblance to actual events, locales, or persons, living or dead, is coincidental.

Cover credit: photograph of sailboat at sunset by © Evelina Kremsdorf / Trevillion Images

Author is represented by Joyce A. Hart.

Emojis are from the open-source library OpenMoji (https://openmoji.org/) under the Creative Commons license CC BY-SA 4.0 (https://creativecommons.org/licenses/by-sa/4.0/legalcode)

24   25   26   27   28   29   30   7   6   5   4   3   2   1

Cast of Characters

Brynn Haywood (age 30), longtime friend of Dawn's, civil engineer who secretly longs to be a full-time baker.

Marnie Dixon (a woman of a certain age), mother to Dawn, co-owner of the Main Street Creamery; known for spontaneity and creativity.

Dawn Dixon Collins (age 30), daughter to Marnie, wife to Kevin, co-owner of the Main Street Creamery (she's the ice cream maker) and part-time CPA for Kevin's historical preservation construction company; known for being an exceptional planner.

Kevin Collins (age 30), husband to Dawn, preservationist architect, co-owner of a construction company.

Lincoln Hayes (age sixtysomething), retired Chatham resident, permanent volunteer for charitable causes, lover of ice cream, friend to all; silent partner of Kevin's historical preservation construction company. Has two adult children, Ashleigh and Bear.

Ashleigh Hayes (age 32), daughter to Lincoln, twin to Bear.

Bear Hayes (age 32), son to Lincoln, twin to Ashleigh.

Callie Dixon Bianco (30), wife to Bruno, stepmother to Leo the Cowboy, professional chef and owner of the Intuitive Cooking School. During shoulder seasons and winter, she helps out at the Main Street Creamery. Known for her exuberance and expertise in all things food related.

Leo the Cowboy (age 7), son to Bruno Bianco, lover of any and all ice cream.

Bruno Bianco (midthirties), father to Leo, husband to Callie, professor at the 4Cs (Cape Cod Community College), author of *The Secret to Happiness*.

Mrs. Nickerson-Eldredge (age seventysomething), Chatham resident born and bred, chair of the Historical Commission. Considers herself to be the guardian of Chatham.

Nanette (age seventysomething), Chatham resident, runs a T-shirt shop. Self-appointed town crier of Chatham.

Maeve Grayson (age mid-sixties), Marnie's best friend from Needham, Massachusetts. Married to Paul Grayson of the Three Sisters Island series. Marnie and Maeve text a lot. Quite a lot.

Deidre Klassen (won't reveal age), considered by many (herself included) to be the *best* wedding planner on the Cape. Possibly in all New England.

T. D. (TD) DeLima (midthirties), twenty-four-hour husband to Brynn Haywood. Not much is known about him. Not at first, anyway.

Glossary
of Ice Cream Making

add-ins—premade food products that are mixed into ice cream base

artisan—a skilled worker in a trade that involves making things by hand

barrel—opening of the ice cream machine to allow ice cream to slide out

base—egg-dairy-sugar mixture that is the main ingredient in all ice cream products

curing—usually a twenty-four-hour period to allow the flavors in the ice cream base to blend and mature

custard—base for ice cream products if it includes eggs

dasher—churning tool of the ice cream machine, also known as beater

frozen custard—has more egg and less air than regular ice cream, making it both rich and dense. Popular on the East Coast and in the Midwest.

frozen yogurt or Froyo—contains less fat than regular ice cream. Popular on the West Coast. Perceived as a healthier option, though sugary toppings are usually piled on it.

gelato—Italian style ice cream

overrun—air pumped into each batch of product (varies dramatically)

pasteurization—the process of involving heat to sterilize a product, destroying microorganisms, to make it safe for consumption

prepackaged base—ice cream base from a dairy that is premade and prepasteurized

soft-serve machine—injects air into the liquid cream mix to get the right consistency

Eat ice cream. Read books. Be happy.

—author Carew Papritz

Chapter
ONE

Breakup: An excuse to eat ice cream no matter the weather.

—Unknown

Sunday morning, June 26

Fingers hovering over the phone, Brynn Haywood hesitated before texting her best friend. Was Dawn the right person to go to? Brynn had met Dawn as a freshman in college, and she'd never known her to do anything wrong, stupid, embarrassing, or rash. All those adjectives could describe the last twenty-four hours in Brynn's life. Add to the list mortifying, humiliating, impulsive. What happened last night was, by far, the worst thing she'd ever done, so out of character. So shameful.

How would Dawn react? From the start of college, Brynn and Dawn had been dubbed the Sensible Sisters. They never did anything crazy, nothing close to foolish or irresponsible. Their majors, and then careers—Dawn was a CPA, Brynn was a civil engineer—reflected their rational, logical, left-brain-dominant personalities.

Then came last night. Brynn had committed a regrettable, out-of-character, reckless act.

How to untangle it? How to make it all go away? She needed help. Desperately.

Brynn looked up from her phone to see why the long, snaking line to get through TSA was barely moving. Only one TSA agent was checking IDs and boarding passes, and he looked as old as Methuselah. Behind him, only one screening machine was open. She blew out an exasperated puff of air and looked down at her phone. She needed Dawn's help.

Brynn
Something terrible has happened.

Dawn
What? Are you OK?

Barely OK.

I'll call.

No! Don't call.

If Brynn were to hear Dawn's voice, if she had to try to explain herself, she would burst into tears. And once the tears started, they'd never stop.

I just can't talk. I can hardly think straight.

Where are you?

Standing in a TSA line.

Airport? Change your ticket and come to Cape Cod.

But . . .

Don't overthink. Just come! We'll sort it all out.

Not this time, Brynn thought. This wasn't something that could be easily sorted out. A knot of helplessness clogged her throat until she felt as if she was struggling to breathe. Almost shaking, she stepped out of the interminably long TSA line to rush back to the ticket counter. There, she switched her flight to Boston to a flight that would go straight into Hyannis on the Cape.

She knew she was running away from her problem. She knew that what happened last night would require some legal action, but all she could think about was escaping to the beach. She felt an almost frantic longing to face the ocean, to hear the crash of the waves against the shore. To sense their eternally soothing reminder that everything was going to be okay.

She squeezed her eyes shut, defeated. She had absolutely no idea how to get back to okay.

●　●　●

When Dawn picked Brynn up at the airport, it was obvious something was seriously wrong. Brynn always looked like she'd stepped right out of *Vogue* magazine, even on a sleepy Sunday morning in a college dorm. She sent her blue jeans to the dry cleaners. She leather-conditioned her purse and shoes. And her personal grooming was impeccable: French-manicured nails; long, straight dark hair, cut every six weeks; bangs trimmed every three weeks; makeup perfectly applied. Even the wings on her eyeliner looked professional.

But this girl? She was unrecognizable as the Brynn whom Dawn had roomed with all through college and into their mid-twenties. Brynn had no makeup on, or if she did, it had been washed away with tears. Her hair was pulled into a messy bun, and it wasn't the stylish kind of messy. Her socks were mismatched, her T-shirt had a coffee stain, and her beautiful dark doe eyes were puffy and red.

Dawn couldn't imagine what had happened to her. Brynn

was a civil engineer who worked with tough construction types. Somehow, as small and slender and feminine as she was, she'd always been able to handle them well. No one dared to push her around or hit on her. But looking at her, Dawn worried that someone had hurt her, had taken advantage of her, and that worry made her stomach turn over. Then flip back. Brynn was one of Dawn's most beloved persons in the world. She was the sister she'd never had. Brynn's parents had divorced, several times, and were absent more than present. Since the age of eighteen, she'd spent every holiday with the Dixons. If anyone had laid a hand on her, Dawn would hunt him down and—

Hold it. She was letting her imagination run wild with dreadful possibilities. Dawn didn't see any bruises, any signs of physical injury. Still . . . *something* terrible had happened to Brynn.

Earlier, on the drive to the airport, Dawn had promised herself that she would let Brynn talk when she was good and ready. So as hard as it was to stay silent, Dawn held her tongue. She hugged Brynn, opened the car door to help her in, put her suitcase in the back, and drove away from the small Hyannis airport—all done wordlessly.

In Yarmouth, as Dawn flipped on the blinker to turn onto Highway 6, Brynn finally spoke. "Could we go to the beach first? I don't think I can face anyone right now. Especially your mom."

Dawn flashed her a sympathetic smile. "You bet." She knew of a quiet beach in Chatham that wouldn't be overrun with children and dogs. July was the most crowded time on the Cape and today was a picture-perfect day. The population of Chatham swelled fourfold in the summer. Good for an ice cream shop, not so good if you were trying to find a quiet spot on the beach to sob your eyes out.

Dawn knew all about *that*. A few years ago, she'd come to Cape Cod to nurse a broken heart. Her fiancé, Kevin, had broken off their engagement just weeks before the wedding. Dawn had felt the same desperate longing to sit on a beach and watch the waves come in, to absorb the tranquil sounds of the ocean. Vast and mysterious, yet calming and soothing. Time healed her heartbreak, aided by her mother's impetuous purchase of a run-down ice cream shop. And somehow, both time plus the dire needs of the ice cream shop brought Kevin back into her life. Two years later, they had worked through their problems and were happily married. So happily that they'd been trying to start a family.

Trying . . . without success . . . for six months. She hadn't found the right moment to tell Kevin that she'd made an appointment with a fertility specialist. Her mom had trouble conceiving, and she'd always had a dread that infertility might be a problem for her too. Because of that niggling fear, she didn't want to let any more precious time slip away.

Brynn sniffed, wiping her nose with her sleeve (soooo unlike her), and Dawn rummaged one hand through her purse to find a tissue packet to hand to her. When she saw the sign for Harwich, she exited onto Pleasant Lake Avenue, then drove along Queen Anne Road to 137, turning onto Route 28, until she reached Forest Beach Road in South Chatham. The road ended at the beach, facing Nantucket Sound. A lovely, overlooked spot.

Most people assumed that Cape Cod beaches were one long sandy strip, one wide ribbon. Just the opposite. The beaches were narrow strands, separated from each other by inlets, ponds, bays, jutting dunes covered in wild roses. More like a chunky necklace than a wide ribbon.

Dawn parked the car along the side of the lane, and the two walked down to the beach. She let Brynn decide where to plop down. A few people clustered on the beach but no children, no leashless dogs, and the tide was heading out. About a third of the way down, Brynn dropped to her knees. Dawn followed her lead, then crossed her legs, settled into the sand, and patiently waited. She breathed in the salt-scented air, watched the waves as they crashed, admired a bobbing sailboat in the distance, looked at the seagulls circling overhead, noticed the angle of the sun, and counted a few puffy clouds floating in the sky. Waiting, waiting, waiting for Brynn to start opening up. Dawn had never been good at waiting. She lasted a full two minutes before turning to Brynn. "Okay, spill it. What in the world happened to you?"

Eyes squeezed shut, Brynn tensed up, and suddenly, the dam broke. Big, choking sobs. Shoulder-shaking gasps. Struggling breaths. Dawn rubbed her back in circles and let her cry it out. In between sobs, Brynn mumbled something.

"You did *what*?" Too harsh. Dawn had triggered another crying jag.

When that jag ebbed, Brynn repeated herself, more clearly.

Dawn's mind could hardly grasp what Brynn was trying to tell her. She leaned back, elbows digging into the sand, gobsmacked. "You got *married* . . . to a stranger?"

●　●　●

Dawn
Brynn has come for a visit. Can she stay in my old room at the Creamery?

Mom
What? Now? The 4th of July week? It's the busiest time at the Cape! The ice cream shop needs our full attention.

Not to worry. You'll hardly know she's there.

How long does she plan to stay?

Hmm. Not sure. She just needs a place to crash for a while. Her life has just become a little bit . . . complicated.

Chapter
TWO

It's never too early for ice cream.
—Michael Scott, character
from TV's *The Office*

Crash was an apt word for Dawn to have used. Funny, that. It's exactly how Marnie felt when Dawn texted to please prepare the extra bedroom for Brynn's unexpected visit. Like someone had crashed into her life.

It had been only a few months since Marnie had the upstairs Creamery all to herself. Dawn had moved out over a year ago, right after she and Kevin married. Callie, after marrying Bruno in early spring, was now living in his house with his son, Leo. Dawn and Callie had been concerned about how Marnie might handle living alone, so she tried her best to seem melancholy on the actual moving-out day. Really tried. Inside, she was dancing a jig. She didn't have to share the bathroom. She could leave her bed unmade if she felt like it. She could spread her stuff into the spare bedroom. She had a vision of establishing a craft room—long tables on both walls. Perhaps a reading nook by the window.

Or maybe a stylish home office? She wasn't sure. All she knew was that her lovely expectations of solitude and space had just been put on ice for an indefinite period because Brynn needed a place to crash.

As for why Brynn was arriving at the Creamery out of the blue (so unlike her! She was a planner like Dawn. Nothing ever happened spontaneously in those two girls' lives)—that was apparently top-secret information. Marnie's classification level didn't seem to reach that high.

Yes, Marnie enjoyed Brynn very much, but she couldn't have picked a worse week in the entire year to come to the Cape for a visit. High season meant Chatham's local population of 6,500 grew to over 25,000. These summer months made it possible for local retailers like the Main Street Creamery to survive the winter. So when Marnie received Dawn's text asking her to clear out the spare bedroom, her first response was to text back *No way. Impossible. Any week but this week.*

She didn't send that text. She'd like to think she was responding to a prompting of caution by the Holy Spirit, but the truth was that she had been distracted in the middle of writing that text by a customer.

And then, for the first time all day, there came a lull in the store. Marnie had been working the counter all afternoon without a break. Two minutes passed without a customer, then five, then ten. Marnie looked up at the ceiling. "Lord . . . I get the feeling that you want me to go clear out that room for Brynn." So she did, and even had time to change the sheets. No sooner had she smoothed the bedspread than the door chimes rang downstairs. The swarm of customers had begun again. And Marnie was at the counter again, scooping ice cream, solo.

Marnie, Dawn, and Callie were supposed to be sharing the load at the Creamery this summer, but it wasn't turning out that way. Callie's Intuitive Cooking School had just opened and needed all her attention. Both Marnie and Dawn had encouraged

Callie to go ahead and seek all the business she could while the summer crowds were here. Soon enough, the crowds would disappear. If Callie didn't get some momentum in July and August, the cooking school might not have a second summer.

But Dawn's life had also notched up in busyness. She still made all the ice cream for the shop, but Kevin needed help with accounting to keep his historical restoration business on track. With both Callie and Dawn juggling other responsibilities, important ones, most of the dailiness of the ice cream shop landed on Marnie's shoulders. It had been nearly impossible to find summer help—the service industry was desperate to find workers. Waiting tables brought in much more income than scooping ice cream, even for teenagers.

Brynn. Hmm. A smile tugged at the corners of Marnie's mouth. Maybe Brynn would be willing to help out with customers at the Creamery during this holiday week. She remembered how overwhelming the last Fourth of July weekend was—a line of customers out the door, all day long. It was wonderful. Immensely profitable. And thoroughly exhausting.

Brynn might be an answer to an unspoken prayer.

And Marnie was deeply fond of Brynn. She'd known her since Dawn's freshman year in college. She'd watched her mature into an accomplished young woman. She'd always thought Brynn had an interesting combination of traits. Like Dawn, she was an only child, serious and focused. Unlike Dawn, Brynn liked to talk. To laugh. Like Dawn, she was an überplanner. Unlike Dawn, she saw the best in others. Brynn could spin very serious issues into something funny. One example was how she spoke of her wacky parents, who married and divorced and married again with regular frequency. "You have to admire their optimism," Brynn had once told Marnie. "Each time they marry, they're absolutely, positively convinced that this is the one that will last." The others, she said, were just practice marriages.

Dawn said Brynn needed a place to crash *for a while*. Marnie took in a deep breath. As much as she loved Brynn, and even thought of her as family, she couldn't help but wonder just how long *a while* might mean. She had one of those bone-deep feelings that it could mean a very long time.

• • •

Saying it all out loud to Dawn, Brynn thought, made last night's fall from grace seem completely reckless and foolish and stupid. And it was! But not in the way it sounded. "It just sounds so . . . trite. So cliché. You know . . . we happened to be in Las Vegas at a boring conference, met, felt a spark . . . and got carried away."

"You're not trite, Brynn." Dawn squinted. "Unless you were married by an Elvis impersonator. *That* would be trite."

"I didn't pay any attention to the preacher. I was too busy caught up with staring into TD's eyes." Oh gag. That did sound trite.

"TD? That's his name?"

Brynn nodded. "T. D. DeLima."

"And where does he live?"

"Boston."

She glanced up. "What do his initials stand for?"

Brynn opened her mouth to say, but then she realized she didn't know. She hadn't asked. How mortifying that she didn't even know this man's full name. Her husband! Her twenty-four-hour husband.

Now she was starting to think that maybe she'd suffered a stroke. Pieces of her brain had gone missing. Her logic, mostly. Her clearheadedness. Her cool detachment. But she couldn't imagine what kind of stroke would lead her to make such an impulsive decision. Didn't strokes usually incapacitate you? Being with TD did not feel like Brynn had been incapacitated. Just the opposite. When she was with him, she had felt fully alive, fully herself, every single part of her, for the first time in her life.

22

Dawn sat cross-legged on the sand while Brynn hugged her knees. "So, I'm guessing alcohol was involved?"

Brynn shook her head firmly. "No. Not really."

"You know you have a very low tolerance. You don't process alcohol well."

"So maybe I had a little more than I should have, but I wasn't drunk. Neither was TD."

Dawn looked unconvinced. "Maybe you should start at the beginning. So you met this guy at a conference in Las Vegas."

"It was the strangest feeling, Dawn. The moment I saw him, I felt struck by lightning. I always thought 'love at first sight' was such a cliché. But that's exactly how I felt. Like Cupid struck me with the arrow. My heart started racing, my palms got sweaty, I felt trembly all over. Then I got a whiff of his aftershave or soap or whatever and it nearly undid me. So strange! It was like he cast a spell on me." She paused, her chin resting on her knees. "What makes you feel that way about one person and not another? I mean, do you think it's fate? Or chemistry? Or sheer chance?"

"Let's hold that question for another day and try to stay on track. So you saw him and felt struck by lightning, and then . . ."

"Then, later that morning, he happened to sit next to me. He asked if I had a pen he could borrow and"—she lifted her palms in the air—"that was all it took. We couldn't stop talking. Finally we decided to skip the conference and go for a drive out to see the Hoover Dam."

"The Hoover Dam," Dawn said in a flat voice.

"Yes. We were both interested in how it was constructed. On the way there, we talked and talked and talked. About everything and nothing. Same thing on the way back to Las Vegas. The afternoon turned into evening . . . and then . . . we passed by a wedding chapel and . . . he asked me to marry him."

"So you got married." Dawn said it slowly, as if she couldn't believe it herself.

Brynn nodded.

"But in the morning, you ran away."

Brynn's arms wrapped around her knees again. Trembling, she felt as if she were trying to hold herself in one piece. "I woke up and saw him sleeping there and . . . the cold reality of what I'd done hit me. I completely panicked. TD was still sound asleep, so I just dressed and left."

Dawn's eyes went wide with surprise. "You didn't say good-bye?"

"I just left." Brynn's teeth were chattering, and she was shivering, though the hot sun beat down on them. She couldn't believe what she had done to this poor man. "I didn't leave a note. I don't even have his phone number."

Dawn whipped out her phone and started googling. "Lots and lots and lots of DeLimas in Boston. Big Portuguese population." She was quiet for a moment, then finally gave up googling. "Too many DeLimas, not enough information." Her eyes squeezed shut, thinking hard. "There's got to be another way to find him." Her eyes opened. "He was a conference attendee. We can track him down."

"How?"

"Um . . . we'll have to ask my cousin Callie. She knows all about hotel conferences."

"But then what?" Brynn could hear the rising hysteria in her voice, but she couldn't seem to stop it. "What do I do? What would I say?"

Dawn gave her a look like *Isn't it obvious?* "That you want to get your marriage annulled."

"I do?"

"Of course you do. Why else would you have panicked?"

Good point. "Annulled. Not divorced?"

"To be honest, I'm not sure. But we'll find out. One or the other."

"Right." Brynn covered her face with her hands. When she dropped them, she said, "You know what really bothers me? This

24

is the kind of thing my mother would do. Actually, she *has* done it. She met a guy on a plane and married him a couple of days later." She blew out a puff of air. "Unbelievable. I have become my mother."

Dawn nudged her with her elbow. "Don't think like that. Don't project. Let's just stay focused on this current crisis."

"Hard to ignore that I beat my mother's record. I married a guy I'd met only twelve hours earlier. At least she waited a few days."

"Which husband was that?"

"The last one."

"That's Jim?"

"Yep. Husband number five."

"Well, that one seemed to have stuck. Maybe this guy is your Jim."

Brynn gave her a look. "Dawn, I never wanted to be like my mom. I have tried to do everything the opposite of her. She's an artist. I'm an engineer. She hates to exercise. I run marathons. She doesn't cook. At. All. My number one hobby is to bake. If I'm not working or running, I'm baking." She turned to look at Dawn. "And I was never, ever, ever going to get divorced. That's why I've been so picky about dating. If I got any hint that a guy's got one foot out the door, I was done with him. And now look at me."

"It was just one night. One brief moment in time." Dawn shrugged, like it was no big deal, though she wasn't fooling Brynn. It was a very big deal. "So you were swept away by passion."

"By stupidity." But also by passion. Brynn couldn't deny there was something powerful between her and TD. She'd never felt about a man the way she'd felt about him, and he had told her the same thing. She felt the tension start to drain from her, her shoulders loosening their stiff hold. Maybe Dawn was right. It was just one night. One brief moment in time.

"Could the whole thing have been a setup? Was there a chance that he was out for your money?"

Brynn's shoulders stiffened again. It hadn't occurred to her that he could've had an ulterior motive. "I guess . . ." Her voice came reluctantly. "I guess I did mention my trust fund. But I also told him that I can't touch it until I'm thirty-five. Why would any man try to fake love for five years?"

"I wasn't thinking that he was faking anything. But I do wonder if he might try to tangle up the ending of your impulsive marriage by demanding big bucks."

Brynn regarded that thought gravely. The thing was, she was 99 percent sure that TD wasn't that kind of guy. His motives had seemed sincere. He spoke from the heart and she detected no reason to think he was lying. He was no liar. He didn't seem to care about money or status or ambition. Most guys she had met spent so much time trying to stress their significance, inevitably doing the opposite. TD was nothing like them.

At least, that's what she'd thought when she said "I do."

Dawn patted her on the back. "Brynn, this can be fixed. I'll ask Linc if he has a good divorce lawyer to recommend. He's super connected. He seems to know just about everybody in town."

"Who's Linc?"

"My mom's boyfriend. Lincoln Hayes. I'm sure I've mentioned him."

"You never said your mom had a boyfriend."

"Didn't I? I thought I told you. Well, they started out as friends and it's kind of morphed into a romance."

See? That's exactly how Brynn had thought she'd fall in love one day. First, the friendship. Then would come love. "Is he good to your mom?"

"Beyond good. Linc is absolutely wonderful."

Brynn smiled. Her first smile all day. "I'm glad. She deserves a good man."

"As do you." Dawn stretched out her legs and crossed one ankle over the other. "One mistake, Brynn. You're allowed to make mistakes. Hopefully, this one has no consequences."

No consequences? *Oh Dawn*, Brynn thought, making a production out of retying both her shoelaces so she could hide tears that were sliding down her face. *Dawn, can't you see? This mistake already does have consequences. You can't just wish away shame.*

● ● ●

Dawn
FYI Brynn has come to Chatham for a while.

Kevin
Here as in . . . our house?

No . . . she's staying at the Creamery.

Phew. Our house isn't livable for a guest.

Our house isn't livable for US.

Chapter
THREE

Ice cream has a way of curing most ailments.
—Lincoln Hayes

Love had come as a surprise to Marnie. She wasn't exactly sure when her friendship with Lincoln Hayes took a turn into romance, but there came a moment a while ago when she knew she loved him. She just knew, the way you knew the sun would rise today, tomorrow, and the day after that.

Widowed a few years now, she had never expected to fall in love with another man, especially one so very different from her late husband, Philip. But maybe some of that had to do with the fact that she had changed so much since Philip's passing. She was stronger, more independent, more resilient. Grief, for all its pain, had a way of doing that.

And Lincoln Hayes sounded like he was an entirely different man than the one he used to be. He described himself, up to the age of sixty, as insanely ambitious. He said he was on a "frantic sprint to nowhere" and his family had paid the price. He was the father of twins—a boy and a girl—and said he'd completely missed their childhood. He couldn't remember anything they had done. Not one Little League game, not a single piano recital. Work took all of him—time, energy, attention. After his kids moved on to college, his wife decided she wanted to move on too. She taped a note on the refrigerator to say she had left him and wanted a divorce. Amazingly, he once told Marnie, at the time he wasn't terribly bothered. He just dug in deeper to work.

It took a cancer diagnosis to shock Linc into all that he had missed in life. While he had certainly achieved wealth—though Marnie really had no idea of his net worth, nor did she care—it came at a steep cost. He had no one to call for a ride home from the hospital after his cancer surgery. No one. Not a family member, not a single friend. That moment became his wake-up call. He retired from work and decided to spend the rest of his life making up for the first sixty years.

Today, he still didn't have much of a relationship with his children, especially his son, but it wasn't for lack of effort. His children, Linc said, had gone from distant to angry. And that's where his son, nicknamed Bear, had stayed. Ashleigh, Linc's daughter, had gone from distant to angry and finally to accepting. She was softer-natured than Bear, Linc said. More forgiving.

Ashleigh had recently gotten engaged and asked her dad if she could have the wedding and reception this summer at his Chatham cottage. *Linc* called it a cottage. Marnie and Dawn thought of it as a grand mansion. Linc had been overjoyed when Ashleigh called to ask. To him, it meant that despite having a father who had played a very minor role in their lives, his children did have fond memories of their childhood. They'd spent every summer in Chatham with their mother and her parents while Linc traveled on business. After Linc's divorce, his ex-wife chose the Boston house and he took the Chatham one, hoping to lure his children back . . . to the beach, to their childhood, to him.

That was the point when Marnie met Linc. He called himself the 2.0 version of Lincoln Hayes. Linc 2.0 was completely invested in others, especially in finding ways to help them. Six days a week, he volunteered at charitable organizations. He made strong friendship ties with all kinds of people in all walks of life. He placed enormous value on others. It was impossible for Marnie to imagine Lincoln was once the husband, father, and friend he described himself to be—detached, distant, disinterested. If his assessment was objective, then he was truly a new man. To be honest, Marnie assumed he was being overly hard on himself. At least, she had thought so until lately.

A few weeks ago, Ashleigh had come to Chatham to meet in person with the Cape's premier wedding planner, Deidre Klassen, known for over-the-top, lavish events. Marnie had hoped Linc might have made an effort to introduce Ashleigh to her, even if that meant a quick drop-in to the Main Street Creamery. She was eager to meet Ashleigh yet felt that it was up to Linc to make it happen. But he didn't. In fact, he had seemed nervous about the visit. Linc didn't have much to say about it—only that he thought Ashleigh seemed pleased with the wedding planner's ideas. Linc had yet to meet Ashleigh's fiancé, Ryan.

That seemed unbelievable to Marnie. Philip, her late husband, had taken Dawn's boyfriend/future-husband Kevin under his wing like the son he'd never had. Then again, Philip had earned that role in his daughter's life. Linc, it seemed, had not.

The closer the wedding date loomed, the more often Marnie's thoughts drifted to Lincoln and his two children. She had a growing and intense curiosity about them. Whenever she asked Linc about them, what they were like or the kinds of things they were interested in, he would clam up. "Marnie," he would say, "I just don't know."

How could that be? It baffled Marnie. Linc had become a member of the Dixon family, sharing holidays, pitching in at the Creamery on busy summer evenings. He had a warm familiarity with each member—Marnie, Dawn and Kevin, Callie and Bruno. He was even a silent investor in Kevin's house restoration business and Callie's cooking school. He'd offered—they didn't ask—to help them start up their different businesses. It just felt strange to Marnie to know so little about Linc's children, to have never met them.

But tonight, that was finally going to change. The wedding week would kick off this evening. Ashleigh and Ryan had arrived in Chatham earlier this morning. Bear was driving down from Boston and going straight to the restaurant where Linc had made reservations for dinner. (Marnie wasn't sure about the ex-wife's arrival time and thought it best not to ask.) Linc had invited Marnie to have dinner with them before everything slipped into full gear. She answered calmly, but what she really wanted to do was to shout, "You'd better believe I would!"

She could hardly wait. The only thing that left her unsettled was the uncomfortable look on his face as he asked her to join them. Almost as if he was in some kind of pain, like a nagging toothache or a persistent stitch in his side.

Marnie checked the mirror one last time for a critical appraisal. She'd changed three times before she settled on the right outfit for tonight's dinner, and she still wasn't sure she'd picked the right one. She remembered reading a magazine article that said you should dress how you feel. So how did she feel? Flustered, anxious, nervous. Scratch *that* article's advice.

Her long hair—more white now than strawberry blond— didn't look quite the way she wanted it to, and she hadn't left enough time to iron her favorite blue linen sleeveless dress, but if she spent any more time fussing, she'd be late. Linc was never late. Looking in the mirror, she let out a defeated sigh. This would just have to do. She grabbed her purse, waved goodbye to Callie, who had volunteered to man the shop until Dawn arrived to relieve her, and hurried down Main Street.

Outside the restaurant, Lincoln was waiting for her to arrive. A smile started inside Marnie, anticipating the moment when he would spot her and his whole face would transform into a soft, tender look of love. Even Philip, as close as they'd been in their thirty-year marriage, had not looked at her the way Linc did. She thought it had to do with a late-in-life second chance at love. You just didn't take it for granted.

As expected, his eyes lit up as she approached, and he gave her a gentle kiss on her lips. "You look great."

She didn't, not really. Pretty good, but not great. "Are you all right?" She thought he looked tired, his face pale.

"I'm fine," he said, but he didn't seem fine. His eyes kept darting, drawn to something behind her. "Ashleigh and Ryan arrived earlier today and met with the wedding planner to finalize a few things."

"So, you finally met Ryan. Does he seem like a good match for Ashleigh?"

"I think so." Linc shrugged. "They seem very happy."

She was hoping he would elaborate, but his attention was fixed on the cars as they passed. She followed his gaze. "Who are you looking for?"

"My son." He glanced at his watch. "I'm sure traffic on the Six is heavy."

Yes, traffic was congested tonight. It was always heavy in July. Then she saw it again. That uncomfortable look on his face, like he felt a sharp jab. Something else was bothering Linc. She watched him, watching the cars go by. "Are you worried Bear won't show up?"

"Bear hasn't been back to Chatham in years and years. It used to be his favorite place." He pulled in a deep breath and looked up at the sky. "But for Ashleigh's sake, I think he'll be here."

"Tonight? Or for the wedding?"

He gave her a sideward glance. "That's the part I'm not sure about."

And suddenly Marnie understood that this wedding week would stir up difficult emotions for Linc. Full of reminders of how he had failed his family. She should have realized how loaded with feelings this week would be for him. "Here's some good news," she said, suddenly remembering it herself. "My adopted daughter has come to town. She's staying at the Creamery."

His eyebrows shot up. "Is there something you haven't told me?"

"She's not officially adopted. But in my heart, she's a Dixon. Do you remember Brynn? Dawn's best friend from college and post-college and everything in between."

"You've mentioned her, but I don't think I've ever met her."

"Oh, I forgot you haven't met her. She couldn't come to Dawn's wedding because of the ice storm. She's come to stay . . . for a while. I'm not sure of the details, but I think heartache is involved."

"Well, ice cream has a way of curing most ailments." With a sigh, he gave up searching the street for Bear and opened the restaurant's door. "Let's not keep Ashleigh and Ryan waiting."

Ashleigh was not at all what Marnie had expected, though she wasn't really sure what to expect. Here's what Lincoln had told her about Ashleigh: she was a pediatric speech pathologist, with a master's degree from Northwestern University. Rather intimidating credentials to Marnie, who hadn't gone to college. Marnie made ice cream for a living. Ashleigh helped children overcome severe language challenges for a living.

Here's what Lincoln didn't tell her: Ashleigh was warm and friendly, and laughed easily and often. Also, she was short and round.

Ryan worked in some kind of medical research that went way over Marnie's head. He was just as round as Ashleigh, and not much taller. They seemed to enjoy each other immensely, laughing and teasing each other, holding hands, and their relaxed comfort helped put Marnie at ease.

And then Bear arrived.

* * *

Maeve
Is tonight the night you finally go out to dinner to meet Lincoln's children?

Marnie
At the restaurant now, hiding in the women's bathroom.

Good, bad, or something in between?

Yes.

LOL! Hangeth thou in there. Linc is worth it.

Chapter
FOUR

They say ice cream is the best friend of summer.
—food editor Licia Granello

Brynn and Dawn stopped at a café for a quick bite to eat, then drove to the Creamery. They came through the kitchen door in the back and tiptoed straight upstairs, avoiding Dawn's exuberant cousin Callie, who was working the counter in the front room of the shop. Dawn made sure Brynn had everything she needed, then left her to go relieve Callie. "I'll be downstairs if you need anything," Dawn said. "Think about what you'd like to do next, and we can talk tomorrow."

What would Brynn like to do next? Try to forget about the last thirty-six hours, that's what. Brynn unzipped her suitcase and opened it. She had so much experience traveling for work that she had packing down to a science, especially after whittling her wardrobe to the capsule concept. Only twelve pieces, three colors—white and khaki and black—and every single item could coordinate with each other. Her suitcase was small, efficient, and compact, as was her entire life. After Dawn had moved out of their Boston apartment to live in Chatham, Brynn downsized to a studio. Everything in her life was small scale. Organized. Predictable.

Until a few days ago.

Taking clothes out of her suitcase to hang in the closet, Brynn decided she was glad she had come to Chatham. It was nice to forget about what had happened in Las Vegas, even if the mental and emotional respite lasted only a few moments at a time. Dawn's unflappable demeanor was just what Brynn needed. This could be fixed, Dawn kept saying. It could all be made to go away. She had snapped her fingers for effect, like a magic trick that made something vanish into thin air.

But could it? Could a marriage be dissolved all that easily?

Brynn wasn't so sure it would be quite so easy to undo as Dawn had made it sound. She'd know more after Dawn found a divorce lawyer to talk to.

Gag! A divorce lawyer. Someone Brynn never, ever, ever thought she'd need to talk to. She could just imagine how that conversation would play out:

"What is your husband's full name?"

"Um, well, I don't actually know. He goes by his initials."

"And where does he live?"

"Somewhere in Boston. But I, um, don't know his address."

"What does he do for a living?"

She imagined herself clearing her throat, stalling for time. Looking down at the tops of her shoes, avoiding eye contact with this imaginary divorce lawyer. "I'm not entirely sure about that either. I think he said he works at a law firm, and I'm sure it must have something to do with civil engineering. That's probably why he was at the Safety in the Workplace Conference in the first place. Sounds logical, don't you think?"

And the divorce lawyer would peer at her over his bifocals, astounded. "What *did* you talk about during your twenty-four-hour marriage?"

"What did we talk about?" So much! TD had a knack for by-passing the regular "So where did you grow up?" awkward first-date questions to jump right into the deep end with very thought-provoking questions. So unusual in a man, so remarkable. Talking deeply with him had been as easy as breathing air. "Everything. Absolutely everything. Just not specific things, like . . ."

"Where he lived. What he did."

"Yes. Exactly."

Gag! Double gag!

How in the world had she gotten herself into this bizarre situation? She tucked the empty suitcase into a corner of the closet, her mind rolling backward.

The first day of the Safety in the Workplace Conference had started off-kilter. She'd overslept because she'd been up late the night before finishing a project for work. On her way to the conference room in the hotel where she was staying, she had stopped to buy a coffee and croissant at a kiosk in the lobby. She was frantically scrounging through her purse for her wallet. She realized she must have left it in the hotel room, and as she started to apologize to the barista, a customer behind her reached around to hand the barista a ten-dollar bill. "It's on me," he said in a low-key way.

Brynn whirled around. The voice belonged to a face that could've been on the cover of *Gentleman's Quarterly*. Raven-black hair, a Roman nose, a strong square jaw, broad shoulders. Tall but not towering. A sharp dresser. He wore a crisp Tommy Bahama short-sleeved shirt tucked into neatly pressed khakis, finished off with sturdy leather boots reinforced for construction sites. But it was his eyes that captivated Brynn. Dark brown, almond shaped, rimmed by thick eyebrows. Those eyes of his radiated warmth and kindness. Shockingly handsome, yes, but Brynn had met plenty of handsome men in her work. What was so attractive about this man was the tender way he looked at her, as if there was no place else he'd rather be at that moment, no one else he'd rather be talking to.

They stared at each other for a long moment, neither one saying anything. The gap between their bodies was charged with electricity. "Thank you," she finally stammered, oddly breathless, a little tongue-tied by the star appeal of the man standing before her. He was feeling something too, she was almost sure of it. She thought she even saw his Adam's apple rise and fall, like he, too, was nervous.

"My pleasure," he said, smiling, revealing a dimple in a cheek. He dipped his chin—a chin with a cleft!—and headed off. About ten steps away, he pivoted, as if there was something else he wanted to say to her, but then he got an embarrassed look on his face and turned around again to head to wherever he was going. Brynn had wondered what he was going to say. Or ask. For her name? Her number? She'd wished he'd just said whatever was on his mind.

Downstairs, she heard the steady chimes of the Creamery's door as customers came in and out. So many customers! Dawn's ice cream shop was doing a brisk business. She felt proud of her friend. When Dawn had first told her she was leaving her CPA firm to move to Chatham and start an ice cream shop with her mom, Brynn had been convinced it was nothing more than a reaction to her broken engagement with Kevin. Two-plus years later, it was clear that Dawn had made a good—albeit radical—decision. She had made a nice life for herself.

Out of her makeup bag, Brynn took her toothbrush and toothpaste and went to the bathroom. As she squeezed the toothpaste onto the bristles, she noticed her hands were trembling. She took in a deep breath, trying to calm herself.

It was Dawn's accusing questions about TD's motives that had rattled her, and kept on niggling. She loved Dawn, but she didn't love her implication that TD was on the prowl for an easy meal ticket. Unless Brynn's man-radar was really off, he just hadn't struck her as a man who was hiding an ulterior motive.

This morning, it had pained her to walk out that door while

he was still asleep, literally caused her stomach to cramp in pain. But staying seemed far more terrifying.

She wondered how he had felt when he woke up and found out she had fled the scene. Was he relieved? Was he sorry? Had she hurt him?

She scrubbed her teeth, way too hard. Of course she had hurt him. Of course she had! Hadn't they talked at length about feeling neglected by their parents' endless quest for self-fulfillment? For happiness. For true love. How could she not have hurt him?

But then again, she was sure he regretted the impulsive wedding ceremony as much as she did.

She did, didn't she?

Absolutely. Yes. It was an absurd, foolish, idiotic thing to do. Even if TD *was* the most perfect man she'd ever met. Even if she did feel an indescribably powerful bond with him, an understanding, that she'd never known with anyone else, not even Dawn.

Brynn and TD had so much in common. Both came from broken homes and felt their parents had ruined every holiday for them forevermore. They talked about their dreams for the future, their hopes, their deepest fears.

TD told her that his greatest fear was to end up like his own dad. It sounded like his father had left the family long before his parents had an official divorce.

Brynn's greatest fear was that she would end up like her mother, who only wanted love and romance out of life. New husbands came in and out of her life like a revolving door.

And Brynn had done just what her mother did. She did! *I am turning into, Heaven save me, my mother.*

Gag. Triple gag.

Back in the small bedroom, she flopped on the bed with a *whoosh*. Lying on her back, she let her gaze sweep the little room. The Creamery was soooo much smaller, soooo much older than the Dixons' Needham house. That had been a typical suburban home in a friendly, middle-class neighborhood. Nothing fancy, not like Brynn's parents' ridiculous homes, over-the-top and empty. The Dixons' house was happy, full of friends, slightly chaotic, and noisy. The kind of house where you braced yourself before opening a closet because stuff might fall down on you.

It surprised Brynn that Marnie would have chosen Chatham, of all towns on the Cape, to settle down for what she called "Chapter Two." As in, life beyond a long marriage to Philip Dixon and then his untimely death. Brynn would have thought Marnie would prefer a more modest town, like Truro or Brewster or Orleans. As the saying went, there's Cape Cod, and then there's Chatham. It was the jewel of the Cape. At some point, she wanted to explore the town.

Tonight, Brynn was thankful for the solitude. She needed a hot bath, a good night's sleep, and time to think, all in that order. She pushed herself off the bed, grabbed her nightgown, and returned to the bathroom to fill the tub. As she slid down into the hot water and soapy bubbles, she forced herself to stop thinking about TD. She was too drained to work through any more thoughts, any more plans about what to do next. She tried to channel Dawn's matter-of-fact outlook on life. Everything could get fixed. Everything could get fixed. Everything could get fixed.

· · ·

Late that night, Marnie lay in bed, mulling over tonight's dinner. Bear, mostly. He resembled Lincoln in most every way—tall, lean, handsome—but not in the most important one: Lincoln was warm, Bear was cold. Ice cold. Not to Ashleigh and Ryan, but to his dad. To Marnie. As Linc introduced them, Marnie held out her hand to shake his. Bear examined her outstretched palm for five very long, uncomfortable seconds before accepting it. His eyes lifted to hers, studying her face as he shook her hand. She could sense the question running through his mind, as clearly as if he had said it aloud: *Why are you here?*

She glanced at the alarm clock next to her bed. Too late now to text her best friend, Maeve, to get her input. Marnie and Maeve went way back, having raised their families together in Needham, Massachusetts. Since the death of Marnie's husband, Philip, Maeve was the person who had known her better than anyone else in the world. Maeve's first husband had died early in their marriage, leaving her a widow with two small children. It was her faith, she always said, that got her through, and Marnie believed her. Maeve drew on her faith like it was a deep well with limitless water. She was the one who invited Marnie to attend a neighborhood Bible study, and then to join a church.

Maeve had remarried a year or so ago. Even though she'd moved to Maine, the two women kept up their friendship. They texted each other nearly daily and spoke on the phone at least once a week.

Marnie wondered if Maeve had ever received a cold shoulder from her husband Paul's three daughters. Probably not. Maeve and Paul had both been widowed, which created a different circumstance than divorce. Death left people bereaved. Divorce left people bitter.

Bear was definitely bitter.

All through dinner, he had hardly acknowledged Marnie. Afterward, walking Marnie back to the Creamery, Lincoln apologized. "Bear seemed particularly bothered about something."

Her eyebrows lifted. "Me."

"No, not you."

Definitely me. Especially after he learned that Marnie ran an ice cream shop. There was ridicule in those dark eyes of his. She saw it. She felt it.

"I'm sorry if he seemed rude to you."

"Not rude." Well, maybe a little rude. "Just . . . not welcoming."

"Nor to me. Not a single question. Did you notice?"

Marnie noticed. "But at least Bear came to Chatham. He's here for his sister. It's a start."

41

Lincoln stopped and gave her an affectionate look. "Thank you. That's a very kind way to sum it up. Yes, at least he's here." He looked up at the night sky, full of twinkling stars. "Did you happen to see how often he checked his phone?"

How could she not have noticed? It was like he was on high alert, expecting a call from the president himself.

"Maybe something was bothering him."

It was hard for Marnie to tell if Bear was bothered or preoccupied. Mostly, she thought he was preoccupied with himself. He had an Apple watch and was constantly lifting his wrist to see the latest notification. Very annoying, but Marnie observed the same behavior in customers at the ice cream shop. Mostly in the young, but even older customers were addicted to their phones. Like Pavlov's dog experiment, she thought. When their phone buzzed or rang, people started to drool.

"You're definitely coming to the wedding? You're not going to bail, are you?"

"Why would I bail on you?"

A sheepish look filled his eyes. "Because now you've met them."

"Ashleigh is lovely. Ryan seems nice."

"But then there's Bear . . ."

True. What rankled Marnie the most happened at the end, when Ashleigh turned to her dad and said, "I hope you've invited your local friends."

Linc had shifted in Marnie's direction and smiled. "She's my favorite local friend."

Bear's eyes went from his dad to Marnie and back to his dad. Not happily.

Now *that* was rude.

"Marnie . . . everything you saw in Bear tonight—arriving late, acting distracted, checking his phone during the meal, seeming preoccupied, showing little interest in others. That—" Linc looked away, paused, then turned to her to start again. "That was me, prior to my cancer diagnosis. Not so very long ago, what you saw in Bear tonight is what you would've seen in me."

Oh. Oh, oh, oh, oh.

● ● ●

Monday morning, June 27

Dawn clicked off her phone and stared at it in her palm.

"Something wrong?" Kevin had come into the kitchen to fix a pot of green tea. "Did Brynn finally hear from the Mister?"

She arched one eyebrow in a "don't start" way. She had told him about Brynn's twenty-four-hour marriage when she got home last night, and he was floored by it. He'd known Brynn nearly as long as he'd known Dawn. Very un-Brynn-like, he had said. "Nothing new from Brynn. Actually, that was Mom on the phone. She met Lincoln's two kids last night."

Kevin filled the teapot with water. "How'd it go?"

"I couldn't really tell. She seemed . . . vague."

He turned the burner on under the teapot and adjusted the flames. "How so?"

"I don't know. She said Linc's daughter, Ashleigh, was very nice. But then she hedged when I asked her about his son. She said she didn't think Bear liked her much." She squinted. "Who doesn't like Mom? Everyone loves her."

"Maybe the son isn't thrilled about his dad having a girlfriend."

Dawn made a face. "Good grief, he's not a child."

Kevin gave her a look. "Isn't his name Bear?"

"Good point." Nicknames were such a funny tradition. Before moving to Chatham, Dawn had worked as a CPA in a Boston firm. Her fifty-four-year-old boss went by the nickname Chip. Bear was better than Chip, but not much.

Dawn watched Kevin carefully measure the tea leaves into the infuser, snap it shut, and gently swirl it in the hot water. Very, very hot but not boiling. That wasn't good for the tea leaves. He wouldn't drink until five minutes had passed. There was a right way of doing things and a wrong way. This way, he believed, was the right way to make the perfect cup of tea.

Kevin was an architect, exacting in everything. As a trained CPA, Dawn shared a love of details with him, and mostly, it was a good trait to have in common, especially in their historical house preservation business. They'd bought three houses so far. The first one had been restored and sold to Callie, customized for her cooking school. The other two were under construction, which included the one they were currently living in. Progress was glacially, painfully slow, but they didn't make mistakes along the way as so many in their line of work did.

Chatham's Historical Association was legendary for resisting change. Kevin worked *with* the Historical Association instead of *against* them, and that attitude made all the difference as he applied for permits from the town of Chatham. Kevin said that most contractors drew up plans and then expected the Historical Association to green-light them, which, of course, they didn't. Kevin talked to the Historical Association before drawing up plans. So far, he had yet to be denied a permit. Two of his contractor friends were regularly denied permits at their first attempt.

So a love of details was a good quality for Kevin and Dawn to share in their marriage. They gave each other room to take the time needed to do something well, to avoid mistakes. But there was a stark difference in what drove their perfectionism. For Kevin, it was possibilities. He was an architect, a visionary, able to see past the flaws to envision the best in a historical building. In people too.

Dawn? Not so much. Her CPA brain searched for overlooked mistakes. That's what everybody wanted in a good accountant— someone trained to find errors that others had made. Most problems could be solved, as long as they were addressed and not ignored. If you ignored a problem, you'd regret it. And if you didn't, the Internal Revenue Service would help you regret it.

The kitchen timer went off at the five-minute mark. Kevin

poured two cups of tea and handed her one. She held the mug in her hands, avoiding his eyes. "So I've been thinking about making an appointment with a fertility specialist in Hyannis."

He sipped the tea, deliberately slow. "I thought we were settled on this. No interference for a year. We've only been trying to get pregnant for a few months—"

She glanced up. "Over six months. And I would hardly call having an initial consultation with a fertility specialist as interference."

"Dawn, you've never been a particularly patient person. But now you're letting anxiety and fear drive you."

Maybe. Maybe there was some truth to that. "I don't want to be naive, either. I've been doing everything I can to boost our chances. I'm exercising daily, I don't eat any sugar, I'm not drinking any alcohol, I'm trying to reduce stress. I track my bio clock each month. All the experts say that six months is a reasonable amount of time to try to get pregnant."

"It's been a busy six months too. Hardly a time of stress reduction. Buying this house, figuring out the plans, starting construction." He glanced around the kitchen—looking through the two-by-fours into the great room beyond. "I'm not sure a baby would want to come home to this."

She gasped. "Don't even say such a thing out loud."

"What?" Kevin coughed a laugh. "Now you're getting superstitious? Dawn, get a grip. You just can't control everything."

"Control?" Her eyes went wide. "How is this about control? I want to have a family. You said you did too. I thought we were on the same page."

"Of course I do. But I believe there will be a right time for a baby."

"And I believe that I won't be able to conceive without some help." There. She said it out loud.

He moved closer and gave her a gentle kiss on her neck. One side, then the other. "I'm willing to help."

She put her hands on his chest to push him back, gently, so that she could look him straight in the eye. "So you'll come to the appointment with me?"

"Not until we pass the one-year mark. In the meantime, I think we need to relax and"—he kissed her on the lips—"enjoy the process."

That was always his answer to her worries about infertility. Give it time. She couldn't seem to make him understand that, for a woman desperate to conceive, time was the enemy.

• • •

Brynn
Thinking of going on a long run at the beach tomorrow morning.

Dawn
Good for you! Pump those endorphins. Exercise works like magic.

Want to join me?

Nah, better skip it. I'm beat from scooping ice cream tonight.

Chapter
FIVE

Ice cream is cheaper than therapy.
—Anonymous

The next day, Brynn felt even more discouraged about life, especially after calling in sick to work (she *was* sick—she was certifiably mentally ill), and even more so after she came downstairs to the Creamery kitchen and Marnie handed her a cup of coffee. She didn't have to say a single word, not one! Brynn burst into tears. She had planned to go to the beach for a run but ended up sitting down at a little table in the ice cream shop and spilling the entire story, start to finish. Marnie listened in all the right places, watching her with concerned eyes, and then she said something that made everything worse, and better. Both.

"Is it possible that something deep inside, something instinctive, something bigger than yourself that can't be explained told you that you had found the man you wanted to spend the rest of your life with?"

What? Impossible! Illogical. "No! I just don't believe in . . . that kind of thing."

"What kind of thing do you think it is?"

Brynn took her time answering. "An instinctive response that could counteract logic and reason."

Marnie scrunched up her face. "I was talking about love."

Brynn shook her head. "Couldn't be love. I'm not saying that I wasn't attracted to this . . . man."

"Does he have a name?"

"T. D. DeLima. He goes by his initials."

"Don't you think that attraction is part of love? That maybe . . . it's the start?"

"Like . . . romantic chemistry?" Brynn pondered that thought. "I have read of theories about intense attraction rooted in chemicals. Yes. I would agree with that. High levels of dopamine and norepinephrine are released. There was definitely some kind of hormone magic going on. I'll grant you that."

"Maybe chemistry is the key that unlocks the door to love."

Brynn's eyebrows shot up. "Having chemistry with someone is hardly a good basis to make a permanent commitment."

Marnie sighed. "I'm trying to talk about the heart and you keep talking about the brain."

Brynn did her best to not look as appalled as she felt. "That's because the heart is not to be trusted."

Marnie's eyes went wide. "Brynn, I've never thought of you as a cynic."

"How could I not be cynical about love and marriage? Just look at my parents! They let their hearts lead them . . . right into disastrous, impulsive decisions. You know what their marital history is like! I cannot, will not, allow that to happen to me." She paused. "Even though I did." She covered her face with her hands and let out a deep breath. "However, Dawn is helping me undo this . . . mistake."

"How?"

"She's working on finding a lawyer to make it"—she waved her hands in the air—"disappear."

"Erased. Just like that." Marnie snapped her fingers.

"Yes, just exactly like that. Quickly. She's concerned that TD might have known I have a trust fund. That it was all a setup."

"A setup," Marnie echoed.

"Yes. A scam."

"So . . . this young man, whom you trusted in your gut, was a masterful actor who could cover up a sinister motive?"

"I . . . um . . . yes."

"Let me get this straight. This man created an elaborate scheme to snare you into having a shotgun wedding . . . just to raid your trust fund."

"Exactly that," Brynn said, nodding.

Marnie had a look on her face that read *Seriously?*

Yes, seriously. At least, Dawn was serious about that scenario. It had made sense to Brynn when Dawn said it.

"So you're telling me that you—an intelligent woman who has worked with all kinds of men in the world of construction and handled them well—you, of all people, were snookered by a con artist?"

Put that way, in the cold light of day, Brynn started to have doubts about Dawn's theory. If TD were a con artist, an actor, he had given a Broadway-level performance. She'd find out soon enough. Once the lawyers got involved, if TD had an ulterior motive, it would be evident. That's what Dawn had told her, anyway. "Dawn said your friend Lincoln knows everyone, and that he'll have someone to recommend, but that his son is getting married so she can't ask quite yet."

"His daughter. She's the one getting married this weekend. At Lincoln's cottage, which is really a mansion."

Frankly, it didn't matter to Brynn who was getting married. She had left finding the divorce lawyer to Dawn. She got up to head down to the beach, but Marnie put her hand up.

"Hold it a minute. Let me just run a different scenario by you. What if it wasn't a mistake?"

Brynn lowered herself back into the chair. "But it was."

"I'm not your mother, but I have known you for over a decade. I've seen how you make decisions. I can't help but think that there was something about this TD fellow that spoke to your heart. Something that caused you to override your determination to be so entirely dominated by your left brain. I just don't think you would have made a decision to marry someone unless you knew, deep, deep, deep in your heart, bone-deep, that this was the right man for you."

"No, no," Brynn said, a certain panic in her voice. "Not possible." Dawn was always complaining about her mom's hippy-dippy, juju advice. Now Brynn understood exactly what Dawn meant. Marnie's advice was not at all helpful. Completely contrary to Dawn's perspective. As much as Brynn appreciated Marnie, she never should have confided in her.

Marnie shrugged. "Just promise me you'll consider that scenario before you take any step to dissolve the marriage. Figure out why you did what you did. There's a reason."

"There is. I'm crazy."

Marnie smiled. "Crazy isn't always bad. I bought this ice cream shop on a whim. And look at all the goodness it's brought into our life."

Brynn didn't have an answer to *that*. Nor for her own version of crazy. "Honestly, I don't know why I did what I did."

"There's got to be a reason for it, Brynn. Maybe you've been suppressing a longing—"

"A longing?"

"For a change, maybe?" Marnie shrugged. "A different direction? I don't know. But you do. Deep down, you know the answer to that question."

But she didn't.

"And promise me that before you sign anything, you'll talk to TD."

"I don't even know how to find him!"

"You're a smart girl, Brynn. You can track him down." Marnie rose from the table in the main room and picked up their coffee cups. "So while you're staying with us—"

"I don't plan to stay for long. Just until this . . . situation gets sorted out."

"But while you're here, I could use help in the shop. In the summer, the shop is packed with customers from the moment it opens to closing time."

Brynn looked behind Marnie to see the cases of ice cream. Scooping ice cream, making people happy, sending them on their way. It would only require minor interactions with customers, probably reduced down to five words: *What can I get you?* Perfect. Just what she needed right now. Stay so busy she had no time to think. No time to think about what the future held.

A smile tugged at the corner of Brynn's mouth. Her second smile in the last twenty-four hours. Maybe she was going to be okay, after all. Maybe she wasn't ready for the loony bin. "I'll do it. You can count on me, Marnie. I'll help in any way I can."

So after a run on the beach to clear her mind, that's what Brynn did. All day Monday. Whatever Marnie needed to have done in the ice cream shop, she did. It was wonderful to not have to think so hard. Her job as a civil engineer required so much concentration. One tiny mistake could end in disaster. Not so much in an ice cream shop. Washing dishes, sweeping, removing empty ice cream containers and replacing them with full ones, scooping ice cream for customers—delightful manual labor that required a minimum of brain energy. Just what she needed today, because her brain was tired of thinking so much.

What her brain kept wanting to think about was TD. She thought back to the spark of connection they'd felt, back to when it ignited. He had sat next to her during the Safety in the Workplace Conference and kept whispering funny one-liners during the presentations. He wasn't being disrespectful or childish—

51

the talks really were that bad. Tedious. Elementary. Brynn had already decided not to return next year.

When a presenter started a slideshow about safety practices while building the Memorial Bridge at the Hoover Dam, TD leaned over to say, "I hear the bridge is really something to see."

"Really? I've never been. I might try to get out to it before I leave town."

After a few more minutes of the presenter's dull monotone, TD whispered, "Maybe we just go see it for ourselves." He rose and tipped his head toward the exit, hinting that she should follow him.

Brynn wasn't the type to skip out. She'd never missed a single college class, had never ditched a mind-numbing conference talk—but she knew she would follow him out. They were two magnets, drawn to each other by an invisible pull. Quietly, she went out to meet him in the entry area. He was waiting for her over by the large window and smiled when he saw her. "What do you say? Should we go check it out?"

She could get used to that smile. That face. That spontaneous lightheartedness. "But I don't even know you."

He held out his hand to introduce himself. "Friends call me TD." He grinned. "And I hope we'll be friends."

She shook his hand. "Brynn Haywood."

"I know. I noticed your name tag when we met at the coffee kiosk this morning." He leaned in a bit. "I made a point to sit next to you."

Oh? Brynn had felt a spiral of pleasure swirl through her. "Flattering, but it doesn't mean I should get in a car with you and dash off to the desert." They were both flirting, testing the edges of their attraction. Something was definitely happening between them. She could feel a twinge in the bottom of her stomach. She was thirty years old. She hadn't experienced much more than a passing interest in any man in a long time. And now, suddenly, she felt like every sense was on high alert.

He had tipped his head with a grin. "Let's review the facts. We are meeting as attendees of an OSHA conference called Safety in the Workplace. The people in that room are either safety professionals or deeply concerned about the protection of their employees. In my humble opinion, I don't think there's a single person at this conference whom you wouldn't be completely safe with in a car. And I'm asking you to leave the glitz of Las Vegas to go study the Memorial Bridge at the Hoover Dam. Only a like-minded soul would geek out at an engineering marvel."

He leaned even closer to her, so close she could smell his aftershave. "Do I really seem like someone you shouldn't get in a car with? Trust your gut, Brynn Haywood. You probably know more about me than you think you do."

He was right about *that*. Sitting beside him all morning, she'd already figured out a number of things. Despite his whispered one-liners, he had taken notes during the lectures, easily capturing the highlights. His penmanship was all caps, indicating he had some training in engineering or architecture. He wrote in bullet points, which always struck her as evidence of a clear, organized mind. His clothing was quite fashionable, hinting of good taste and a solid income.

But was he someone she could trust? She looked at him. Really looked. Past his obviously handsome looks to study his eyes at close range . . . dark brown, vulnerable eyes. Tender eyes. In them, she saw no guile, no harm. Her gut said yes.

She smiled. "Then let's go."

And that's how their relationship had begun.

All throughout Monday at the Creamery, Brynn kept thinking she saw TD. Absurd, she knew, but practically every male customer who came into the shop reminded her of him in one way or another. His raven-black hair that curled around the nape of his neck, the cleft in his chin, the olive tones in his skin, his long, tapered fingers. Once, she looked out the window and could have sworn she saw him strolling down the sidewalk. She dropped the ice cream scooper, mid-scoop, and bolted outside, calling out his name. The man turned to her, confused. Not TD. Not even close. This man's face was covered with piercings. Eyebrows, nose, lips, tongue.

Another time, when she was elbow deep in a sink full of soapy dishes in the kitchen of the Creamery, she thought she heard his deep voice ordering an ice cream cone from Marnie in the other room. She froze, then forced herself to shake off that thought. She couldn't stop thinking about him. She was obsessed.

A giant wave of uncertainty washed over her. Marnie's remarks were unsettling. Dawn's advice, completely opposite of her mom's, was equally disturbing.

A lawyer wasn't the only thing she needed. She needed a psychiatrist.

• • •

Marnie was thankful for Brynn's help, especially for this week of all weeks. Chatham was filling with tourists, strolling up and down Main Street, covering the beaches with umbrellas and towels and sand toys. For a destination beach town, this particular holiday week was the golden time for retailers and restaurants.

During the months of April, May, and June, as Chatham's population started to bloom again after a long cold winter, Marnie and Dawn had spelled each other throughout the days—one handled the customers at the counter while the other worked in the small galley kitchen. Today, the busiest day of the year so far, Brynn's help allowed Dawn to stay focused on making ice cream, and it made all the difference. The freezer was fully stocked, ready for the next few days.

That hadn't been the case in the last two weeks of June, as the shop's foot traffic started increasing each day. Dawn had been staying late in the evenings, just trying to keep up with the next day's demands. She still wouldn't let Marnie attempt to make the ice cream, because she was convinced Marnie would use a pasteurized, premade base. And she would be right. Spot-on. Attending Ice Cream School at Penn State last year only made Marnie double down on the benefits of using a premade base, like nearly every high-end ice cream shop did. But there was no changing Dawn's mind. She was a small-batch, artisanal ice cream maker. Every scoop that came out of the Creamery's kitchen was handmade from organic products.

As one large group of customers went out the door, a man stepped around them to come in. Marnie felt herself tighten up the second she realized that customer was Bear, Lincoln's son.

Her mind started racing. She thought about getting Dawn to cover for her, but no sooner did she think it than the ice cream machine started up. Dawn wouldn't budge from the barrel for the next seven minutes. Then she wondered if Bear would think it weird if she shouted over the machine's noise to ask Brynn to come into the main room to serve a customer. Yes. That would seem weird. The ice cream machine's sound didn't carry strongly into the main room, but it was loud in the kitchen. She would have to practically scream for Brynn to hear her. Brynn was in the middle of washing a sink full of dirty spoons and scoopers that were needed at the counter ASAP. She was trapped. So she plastered on a fake smile and tried to act completely at ease, though she felt anything but. She sensed a hot flash coming, triggered by her nervousness.

Flustered, Marnie turned her attention to two children whose noses were plastered against the glass case as they tried to decide on an ice cream flavor. Bear stood patiently in line behind them. The girl chose blueberry buckle, the boy chose banana cream. After they left, Bear stepped up to the ice cream case. He gave Marnie a thin smile, the kind that didn't quite reach his eyes.

She lifted a clean scooper in the air. "So you found the Main Street Creamery."

"So I did." He turned to the window as the boy and girl sat on a bench outside, licking their ice cream cones. "Think they're twins?"

"I don't know. They don't look alike."

"Then again, my sister and I don't resemble each other either."

"No," Marnie said. "That's true." Why was he here? He made her very uncomfortable, like there was something on his mind that he wasn't saying. And yet, in a way, he was saying it. "Would you like to try a flavor? We have small taster spoons." It had been Marnie's idea to add the taster spoons this year. Dawn had objected. She said it would only slow down the customer lines, but Marnie insisted it would bring customers back to the shop. They were both right.

Bear took a step closer to peer into the case, and she used his distraction to study him. She had to admit that he made an impressive sight in a navy-blue short-sleeved Polo shirt, tucked into khakis. He was male-model handsome, with dark hair and brown eyes. She wondered if this was how Lincoln had looked when he was Bear's age.

He glanced up at her, as if he knew what she was thinking. "What would you recommend?"

"If in doubt, go for vanilla. It's the most popular flavor in all the world. My daughter Dawn is the ice cream maker at the Creamery. She tested her vanilla recipe fifty-nine times until she got it right. Since then, she's created yet another. This one is called Double-Fold Vanilla."

"Why is it called Double Fold?"

"Something to do with doubling the amount of vanilla extract. Sometime, Dawn can give you the details." Not right now, though. The machine was still churning away in the kitchen.

"I've got to try *that*." His eyebrows waggled at that, and for the briefest of seconds, Marnie saw past the harsh Bear to a slightly more likable one.

"Did you see that the creamery was named Best of the Cape?" She pointed to the frame hung on the wall, then scooped out the ice cream into a paper container and handed it to him, waving her hand when he tried to pay for it. "On the house."

He lifted an eyebrow. "Family discount?"

Ah. There it was. "Your dad and I are friends."

"Good friends, I take it." He pinned her in place with a hard-edged gaze.

"Yes." She held his gaze. "When Dawn and I first moved here, your dad helped us restore the building. It was in terrible condition, just terrible. Your dad came every afternoon to help us get it into shape so that we could open for the summer season. A lot rested on that first summer. Your dad was extremely generous with his time."

"Generous . . . just with his time?"

There was an icy insinuation in Bear's question. Marnie didn't quite know how to answer him, because the truth was that Lincoln *had* been very generous to the entire Dixon family, both time and money. As a wedding gift to Dawn and Kevin, he had the fireplace repaired and converted into gas. He had started a business with Kevin and acted as the silent investor. He had provided the seed money for Callie's cooking school. Marnie felt as if they were dancing around the topic of Linc's generosity like a couple of bears dancing around a beehive. "Bear, is there something on your mind?"

As he considered her question, his gaze swept the shop like a searchlight. As if he knew all the things his father had done, or bought, to help Marnie and Dawn launch the ice cream shop. More than launch—he helped to keep this shop running. It was as if Bear knew how many times Linc had offered interest-free loans to help Marnie out of a pinch. She had adamantly refused those loans, but there were plenty of other ways Linc had provided for the Creamery. He had found plumbers, electricians, and a floor refinisher who was willing to come in nights to help restore the beautiful old floorboards after a leak from the upstairs bathroom ruined a corner of the front room. The bills from those tradesmen never seemed to arrive, despite Marnie's repeated requests for them. And then she would forget about them, until the next house emergency. Dawn called Linc their fairy godfather. It was true that the Main Street Creamery wouldn't be thriving without Lincoln Hayes, although he insisted that he was the one on the receiving end. Yet she felt shaken by Bear's incriminating tone.

Before Bear seemed to have decided what he wanted to say, the chimes of the door rang and more customers came in. He lifted the vanilla ice cream in the air. "Thank you for this." And out the door he went, just as Dawn turned off the ice cream machine and the humming noise in the shop fell oddly quiet.

● ● ●

Tuesday morning, June 28

The Main Street Creamery wasn't close enough to the water to hear the sound of waves churning and rolling, but sleeping with open windows and a sea breeze was more than enough for Brynn. She slept soundly and woke early to birdsong. She dressed in her running clothes for an early morning run with Dawn. They planned to meet up near the lighthouse and end at a coffee shop.

Brynn was waiting for Dawn, warming up, stretching arms and legs, admiring the arch of blue sky over the gleaming ocean, the salty breeze . . . and suddenly a big golden retriever came charging straight toward her. Dogs frightened Brynn, and her instinct was to flee. She took off down the beach as fast as she could, trying to outrun the beast, barely striding ahead of it. She kept looking back at it, hoping it would lose interest in the chase. But it kept chasing her! Somebody let out a loud whistle and the dog reversed its path and spun around, galloping toward the whistler way off in the distance. Brynn slowed down, then bent over, hands on knees, gasping for breath.

Dawn jogged to catch up to her. "Why did you run? You should never run from a dog. It only makes him think you're playing a game with him."

"Couldn't help it," Brynn said between gulps of air. "Sheer instinct. Fight or flight and I chose flight."

"Mayor would never hurt you."

"Mayor? The dog owner is the town mayor?"

"No. The dog. Linc named him Mayor because he knows everyone in town."

She looked up the beach. "That's Lincoln?"

"Yep." Dawn waved to him, but he had bent down to pat the dog, then threw a piece of driftwood in the opposite direction. The big dog went galloping after it. "He must not have seen me."

Brynn watched the man and his dog as they headed toward the road. Something about him struck her as familiar—his gait, the way he held his shoulders back. Argh! She saw TD *everywhere*. In *every* adult male. Her mind couldn't seem to stop from veering off toward memories of him. That heavy feeling came over her—both longing and shame. The combination made her miserable.

"Ready?" Dawn was stretching while Brynn, catching her breath, watched the man and his dog recede into tiny pinpoints on the sand.

Brynn turned back to Dawn, shaking off any more thoughts of TD. "Ready." Totally ready. "Let's get going."

Brynn set the pace, steady and slow, because she wasn't sure how much running Dawn had been doing lately. But maybe she was the one who needed the slow, steady, forward pace. Her equilibrium had shifted out of whack and it was time to get it back.

• • •

Maeve
Have you met Linc's ex-wife yet? Jeannie, right?

Marnie
Haven't met Jeannie yet.

Aren't you curious about her?

HUGELY.

Chapter
SIX

Eating ice cream and not exercising is great. The downside is your health isn't so good.

—actor Jeff Bridges

Marnie was alone at the Creamery and had just finished texting Maeve when Lincoln knocked on the back door. She knew it was him because of his unique tapping, and because only family, including Linc, used the back door. "Hi. I didn't expect to see you this morning." His face was gray, drawn tight. "What's wrong?"

"The caterer for Ashleigh's wedding has come down with Covid. The entire staff has tested positive."

Whoa. "The wedding planner must have a plan B in mind." Marnie knew of this wedding planner's reputation. Deidre Klassen. Surely she had experienced all kinds of unexpected twists.

"You'd think so, but she's in a complete tailspin. She's crying, Ashleigh's crying, Jeannie's crying."

Jeannie. So Linc's ex-wife had arrived. "There's got to be a caterer in Chatham who'd love the work."

"Not in Chatham. Not on the entire Cape on the Fourth of

July weekend. Apparently, that's the reason Ashleigh chose to have the wedding at the cottage. Every place else was completely booked out. The entire Cape. The global pandemic has created a backlog of weddings."

Everything Linc was telling her was slow to sink in. "But," Marnie said, "the wedding is only days away."

"I know." He looked down at his feet. In a meek voice, he said, "Marnie, I told them I would fix this."

Such a dad thing to say. She had to swallow a smile. She could imagine Philip saying the same thing to Dawn. Anything his little girl might need, he would find a way to give to her.

"I want to do this for Ashleigh. Give her the wedding she's always dreamed of."

Sweet. "So what are you going to do?"

He lifted his eyes sheepishly. "I was thinking . . . maybe . . . of asking Callie?"

Marnie's first reaction was to say no, no, no. No way! It wouldn't be fair to ask Callie to step into such high expectations at the very last minute. It could be a recipe for failure, and who knew how far-reaching the impact could travel. Callie's cooking school was just getting off the ground.

No sooner did Marnie think those thoughts than she recognized them as rooted in her own pitiful insecurities about Lincoln's children. Maybe Callie might welcome this opportunity. She was certainly qualified. She'd been an executive chef at a restaurant before she came to Chatham. She thrived under pressure.

The more that she considered it, the more she realized how thoughtful it was of Linc to consider her niece for such an important role. The more appealing it became. Maybe this could be an opportunity to connect the Dixons and the Hayeses. She grabbed her purse. "It can't hurt to ask. Let's go."

"Now?"

"Yes! Shop opens in less than an hour." At the door, she paused.

"Do you think Ashleigh would be flexible about the menu? Or will it have to match the caterer's exactly?"

He scrunched up his face in a question. "I don't know. I wasn't involved in that part of the planning."

Marnie stifled a laugh. He hadn't been involved in *any* part of the planning. "Well, if Callie says yes to catering the dinner, she and Ashleigh can work out the menu."

"Marnie, hold it a minute. There's more than just the dinner."

Hand on the door, she turned around. "What do you mean?"

"The caterer was supposed to do the cake."

This was getting more complicated. "Just how many people are invited to this wedding?"

"Last count, I think I heard one hundred and fifty."

Last count? As in, the number was changing? "Do you know what kind of cake Ashleigh has in mind?"

"A tall one. That's all I know."

That would mean a three-or-four-tiered wedding cake, plus extra sheet cakes. Marnie was back to feeling protective of Callie. How much was too much to ask of her?

"I can bake it."

They spun around to find Brynn, back from her run on the beach, standing by the back door. "I'd love to keep busy."

"Lincoln, this is Brynn. Dawn's friend. I think I told you she's come for a visit."

Lincoln smiled, a little confused. "You're a baker?"

"Well, I'm a civil engineer. I bake a lot, though."

"Same kind of precise skills," Marnie said, though she really had no idea. "Brynn is a terrific baker." Brynn was like Dawn in that way—anything she did, she did well.

"No doubt," Linc said in his diplomatic way. "But this is a wedding cake."

Brynn tucked her hands in the pockets of her yoga pants. "I've done wedding cakes."

Linc cleared his throat. "Professionally?"

"Well, they haven't paid me," Brynn said, "if that's what you mean by professionally. But the cakes have turned out rather well, if I do say so myself."

"That's true," Marnie said. "They looked like they could be in a magazine." Dawn had said so, anyway.

A loud ring from a cell phone interrupted them. Linc grabbed his phone out of his pocket and went outside to answer it.

"So that's Lincoln," Brynn said.

"That's him."

"Dawn was right. She said he looked like a retired astronaut." Marnie smiled. "You know, I think she's right!"

"Right about what?" Linc said as he returned to them.

Before Marnie could answer, another ring from a cell phone made them all stop to listen. "That's mine," Brynn said, pivoting to the stairs. "I'd better get that. There are a few problems at work to deal with. Just let me know if you want my baking help." She trotted up the stairs and closed the door behind her.

"What do you think?"

Linc remained unconvinced. "A wedding cake . . . it's just . . . isn't it a big deal at a wedding?"

"Here's an idea. Brynn can do the baking. Callie can supervise the icing. Together, I feel confident the cake would be up to Ashleigh's standards."

"It's not Ashleigh I'm worried about."

"Then who?"

"Her mother. She has . . . rather strong opinions about this wedding."

Interesting! That might've been one of the first things Linc had ever volunteered about his ex-wife. "Well, let's take things one step at a time. First, we head over to talk to Callie." As sorry as Marnie was that the wedding faced a serious glitch, she thought it might be a blessing in disguise. Maybe it would end up as an opportunity to connect with Ashleigh and her cold brother Bear. A way to show them that the Dixons weren't just receivers of Lincoln's generosity but that they could reciprocate it too.

As they settled into Linc's car, she saw some color had returned to his face. Before pressing the ignition button, he turned to her, his appreciative eyes seeking hers. He was looking at her in that way he had, the one that made her feel so cherished. "Marnie, thank you."

She laughed. She hadn't done anything. "For what?"

He took her hand to kiss it. "For everything."

●　●　●

Kevin had asked Dawn to pick up a few things at the Chatham Paint & Hardware Store, down the street from the Main Street Creamery. As she walked along the busy sidewalk, she thought of how hardware stores had been a mainstay on Main Streets all across America. They were a necessary commodity, like a grocery store or post office. She had always enjoyed going to local hardware stores. They had a certain scent—freshly cut lumber, a whiff of oil, and the tinge of garden chemicals—that sent her down memory lane. She used to tag along with her dad to hardware stores whenever he needed to buy electrical supplies. Her mom, knowing of her unique fondness, had given her a scented candle for Christmas that was called The Hardware Store.

As much as Dawn liked to give business to local retailers, Kevin preferred to buy most of their construction supplies at the Home Depot in Hyannis. They'd forgotten a few things in their last run, and she should have thought to stop there on Sunday when she had picked up Brynn at the airport, but it didn't even occur to her. She'd been distracted with worry about Brynn, and then had driven past the fertility clinic and became distracted by that.

She was still distracted by *that*. Earlier today, she'd confirmed the appointment for tomorrow. Kevin might not be on board yet, but she was pretty sure he'd come around to see things from her

65

point of view. He just didn't understand the hollow, heavy ache in her chest each month when her period arrived.

She wished she could talk this all over with Brynn, but not now. Normally, Brynn offered an objective point of view. Right now, Brynn was a mess. It was still hard for Dawn to believe that Brynn Haywood, of all people, had gotten married on a whim. Brynn was not an impulsive person. She wasn't even a particularly passionate person! To think that she threw caution to the wind and married a guy she'd only known for a day was shocking.

Her thoughts drifted to finding a lawyer who could undo everything for Brynn. She hoped this could be easily untangled. What was the difference between divorce and annulment? She had no idea.

She pulled her phone out of her purse to check her shopping list. Five rolls of blue painter tape. She went to the paint aisle and found the tape. When she looked up, she saw a man down the aisle who looked a lot like Lincoln Hayes, only younger. "You have *got* to be Lincoln's son!"

The man's head lifted, a blank look on his face.

"Wow. You look a lot like your dad." Dawn walked down the aisle to him. "You're Bear, right?"

"I'm sorry. Do I know you?"

She shifted her heavy basket to her left hand and held out her right hand. "I'm Dawn. Marnie Dixon's daughter."

He shook her hand and released it. "You're one of the ice cream people."

Dawn laughed, though he didn't say it in a funny way. More condescending. "Yes, I guess you could call us that. We run the Main Street Creamery." His face didn't register any enthusiasm, which struck her as odd. Most everybody responded with pleasure. "Artisanal ice cream. Small batches. We use high-quality organic ingredients."

"Right. I stopped in yesterday. I tried the vanilla."

Most people would've added "and it was delicious." Not Bear Hayes. He said nothing more. Unfortunately, when Dawn got nervous, she started to talk nonstop to fill the void. It was the only character trait she shared with her mother. "I worked on that vanilla recipe over fifty-nine times until I got it right. Did you know it won the Best of the Cape for ice cream last year?"

"I believe your mother pointed out the award framed on the wall."

She felt as if she were priming a dry water pump and nothing was coming out. "It's nice to finally meet Lincoln's family. We all just love him. Your dad has been wonderful to us."

His eyes narrowed, ever so slightly. "How so?"

"He's helped us in so many ways. The Creamery was in terrible condition when Mom bought it, and your dad kept delivering help in the nick of time." She rocked her hand in the air. "Things were pretty dicey there, for a while. Pretty touch-and-go. Lots of times when I wasn't at all sure the Creamery would survive."

"Must be nice to have a wealthy benefactor for a friend."

A benefactor? Wait. What? "That's not what I meant. He's not a . . ."

"Sugar daddy?"

"No!"

One eyebrow arched. "So he hasn't provided financial help to the Creamery?"

She stood before Bear, her mind sputtering away. She wanted to say that Linc hadn't provided financial help to the Creamery, but . . . he had. Countless times, Linc had bailed them out. Dawn had always tried to pay him back and sometimes she was successful, but he often refused. He said he was the one who was benefiting from the Creamery. His friendship with Mom, Dawn knew he meant. But how to explain all that to this unfriendly man, who clearly thought they were taking advantage of his father.

"I'd better keep shopping. Lots to do for my sister's wedding." He took some paintbrushes off the wall and gave her a thin smile before heading back down the aisle.

Distracted, bothered, she did the same. She counted out five rolls of blue painter tape, found the other items on Kevin's list, and went to the register to check out.

The cashier, whom Dawn knew, asked, "Want me to just add this to Linc's account like usual?"

"Yes. Thanks." Dawn took the large bag from the cashier and spun around and came face-to-face with Bear. From the look on his face, he'd overheard the conversation with the cashier. She froze. "That's not what it sounds like."

"No?"

Before she could explain that his father was a silent investor in a house-flipping business with Kevin, that the whole thing had been Linc's idea, and that she kept careful records so that the finances were well documented, the federal and state taxes were squeaky clean . . . he had moved around her to pay for his paintbrushes and whatever else he'd bought. His back was to her. An icy metaphor.

Dawn kept her mouth shut. She decided that any explanation about the house-flipping business belonged to Lincoln. It was his money, after all. He's the one who'd had the big career.

But as she left the store, she sensed a foreboding for her mother. No wonder Mom sounded vague about Bear Hayes. She probably couldn't think of anything nice to say about him. Bear might look a lot like his father, but he was nothing, *nothing*, like Lincoln Hayes.

● ● ●

Marnie
Can Linc and I swing by the cooking school? He has a question to ask you.

Callie

Class ends in ten minutes. Next one starts at
11.

We'll be quick!

Is something up?

More like . . . something's down. Will explain!
See you soon.

Chapter

SEVEN

No use crying over spilled milk. But I will cry over melted ice cream.

—Unknown

Marnie and Linc arrived at the Intuitive Cooking School kitchen to find seven-year-old Leo, dressed in leather chaps over jeans, a red-plaid flannel shirt, and a cowboy hat, lassoing garden gnomes in the front yard. Class members were leaving out the front door, each one carrying a large bag with the Intuitive Cooking School logo on the side. The school was a weathered-gray Cape Cod–style house that had been painstakingly remodeled by Kevin to preserve its historicity. While the exterior had been modestly updated, the interior had been completely opened up with supporting beams to allow for a large commercial kitchen. Stainless steel islands on rollers filled the room so students could work at their own stations.

Opening the door for Marnie, Linc took in a deep breath. "My mouth is watering." They could smell the rich tomato-onion-garlic aroma wafting out the kitchen door. Something Italian, Marnie guessed. Lasagna, maybe.

Callie had created a wonderfully innovative concept for a cooking school. In advance of the class, she purchased all the needed ingredients for a specific recipe, enough for everyone to make their own. She would walk the class through every step, teaching them skills along the way as they cooked and assembled. Then they would take the meal home, ready for tonight's dinner. Callie had prepared sides to go along with the meal that could be purchased as add-ons—a fresh green salad, a baguette of garlic bread, a tin of homemade almond sugar cookies. It was a brilliant concept for a tourist destination like Chatham. People had time and money and were always hungry.

"Hi, Leo!" Marnie bent down to give him a hug. "Are you helping Callie today?"

The little boy nodded solemnly. "Dad's teaching a summer school class."

Leo's father, Bruno Bianco, was a professor at the 4Cs—Cape Cod Community College. Bruno and Callie were married a few months ago in a small but very elegant ceremony, with Leo as best man.

Marnie and Dawn adored Cowboy Leo. There was just something about him that had a way of stealing your heart. Chubby cheeked, short and stocky, always dressed in cowboy attire—boots, hat, chaps, vest. He even wore a leather gun belt, sans a gun. His dad was firmly against guns. So Leo would find sticks that looked like guns and put them in the pistol holster.

"Don't go in! Callie will make you wash dishes."

Ah, no wonder he was outside. Marnie turned to Linc. "Why don't you talk to Callie about the wedding while Leo and I start scrubbing?"

Leo groaned.

As they went inside, they saw Callie whisking dishes off the counter space and into the sink. She didn't even realize they were there until Marnie said something. "Callie, can you spare a minute?"

Callie whirled around. "Morning! Sorry, I can't stop, but I can talk as I wash dishes. I have an advanced class coming in a few hours. I need to clean up and prep."

"Can we talk if we help?"

"Sure." She pointed to another counter, full of dishes. "The beginner's class this morning was messy. I think they used every pot in the kitchen. Typical of beginners."

Or of messy cooks. When Marnie cooked, she tended to use every pot too.

Lincoln picked up some bowls and carried them to the sink. Marnie had opened one of two dishwashers and started to load. "A problem came up for Lincoln and we thought you might be able to help." She looked to Lincoln to continue, but he had his head down. She coughed and gave him another look. He was avoiding her eyes. Good grief. "Lincoln's daughter is getting married soon and the caterer came down with Covid. The entire staff has it."

Callie had been scrubbing a pot in the sink. Leo had dragged a stool over to the sink and was peering into the soapy water. Still scrubbing, Callie turned her neck so her eyes were on Marnie. "Don't tell me. All the caterers on the Cape are booked."

"Bingo."

Callie stopped scrubbing, lifted her shoulders up, then down, and turned to Linc. "How many covers?"

He set the bowls next to the sink. "Covers?"

"Guests?"

"Oh. One hundred fifty."

"Is there a menu already set?"

"Yes."

"Set in stone?"

"Um, not sure. Ashleigh, my daughter, and her wedding planner would be the ones to ask."

"Who's her wedding planner?"

"Deidre Klassen."

Callie turned to Marnie. "He's kidding, right?"

Marnie shook her head.

"Is this a royal wedding?"

Linc smiled, a little ruefully. "Close but not quite."

"Do you mean to tell me that Deidre Klassen can't call in a few favors and find a caterer?"

"Apparently not," Linc said. "Something about a wedding backlog due to the global pandemic."

Callie squeezed her eyes shut. "When's the wedding?"

"This weekend."

Her eyes popped open. "This weekend?!"

Marnie saw that odd look on Linc's face again, like he'd felt a jab of sharp pain. This wedding meant so much to him. She had to help. "Callie, you can do this. This is what you did before you came to Chatham!"

Callie had turned back to scrubbing the big pot. "This is Deidre Klassen's event. It's really her responsibility."

"Exactly!" Marnie said. "It's an incredible opportunity for you. If this goes as well as I know it will, just think of the publicity. Intuitive Cooking School will be on the map."

"And I'll pay for everything," Linc said. "There's an envelope on the bulletin board at the Creamery for receipts. In fact, Marnie has my ATM card. Feel free to ask her for it if you need it."

Callie looked at Marnie, then back at Lincoln. A long moment passed before she let out a sigh. "If it were anybody but you, Lincoln Hayes, I would say no. But I owe you . . ." Her gaze went around the entire downstairs—Linc and Kevin had renovated it to Callie's exact requirements. "Well, I owe you so much. This entire building. Intuitive Cooking School wouldn't be here if it weren't for you."

A male's deep voice came out of nowhere. "Is that so?"

They spun around to find Bear Hayes standing at the open

73

door. "I was driving past and saw you and your friend"—his eyes shifted to Marnie—"in the parking lot. So I turned around and came to bring you these things from the hardware store for that wedding planner lady." He lifted a bag from the hardware store. "I have to head over to Hyannis for a meeting."

Linc smiled. "Bear, I'm glad you're here. The caterer canceled for Ashleigh's wedding. Marnie and I are talking to Callie about stepping in to take on the job. Callie's a professional chef."

"I don't believe you've met my niece Callie," Marnie said. "She runs this cooking school. Callie, this is Linc's son."

"I can see the resemblance," Callie said.

"You're related to the Dixons too?" Bear said. "Seems like my father and the Dixon family are thick as thieves."

Marnie ignored that remark. "And this is Leo. He's the resident cowboy of Chatham."

For just a split second, as Bear looked at Leo, his face transformed. Softened. His dark eyes crinkled at the corners. "Howdy, pardner." There it was—the tender Lincoln look. Here and then gone. His face grew hard again as Linc crossed the room to take the bag from him.

"What kind of meeting do you have in Hyannis?"

Bear looked away from his father. "Just a small issue that needs handling. I'll be back this afternoon." He gave a nod to Callie and Marnie, looked straight at Leo and lifted his hand in the air like a gun, then placed it in an imaginary holster, before he turned and left.

Leo was charmed. He turned to Linc. "He looks a lot like you."

"He's my son."

"I like him," Leo said. "I like him a lot."

If only, Marnie thought. If only she could see what Leo saw in him.

Leo slipped outside to practice his rope lassoing on the garden gnomes.

Callie was back to scrubbing pots with vigor. "One hundred fifty covers will require a lot of prep. I might see if a few in my advanced class would be willing to help."

"I'll pay anything," Linc said. "Money is no object."

"To be honest, Linc," Callie said, "it's not about money. It's about getting enough kitchen help."

"We can help."

"I appreciate that, but I need sous-chefs. Trained people." She turned around in a panic. "What about the cake? That's coming from a separate vendor, right?"

Marnie and Linc exchanged a look. "No, but I did think of a solution," she said quickly. "Brynn is visiting us."

"Dawn told me she'd come to Chatham." She turned back to the sink.

"She loves to bake."

Shrugging her shoulders, Callie said, "She's a hobby baker."

Callie made *hobby* sound like a distasteful word. "Yes," Marnie said, "but she has done wedding cakes for friends."

Callie didn't say a word, but Marnie had a feeling she was rolling her eyes.

"I've seen them! They're beautiful. Really!" But Marnie could tell that Callie wasn't buying it. Her standards were off the chart. Added to that, Callie had always been a tiny bit jealous of the close relationship that Dawn and Brynn had. Callie and Dawn were cousins, but Brynn held the coveted best-friend status. "Here's an idea. What if Brynn baked the cakes and you did the decorating? Or maybe you could just supervise the decorating. Add the finishing touches."

"I'd have to supervise the baking too. The humidity is high this week. Amateurs don't understand how weather can affect baking." Okay, now Callie was starting to bend.

"Anything," Marnie said. "Whatever you want."

Callie turned back to the sink and started scrubbing again. "I'll do it. But like I said, only because Lincoln is Lincoln." She tilted her head to grin at them. "And I have to admit that I'd love an 'in' with Deidre Klassen."

"You will be *so* in with Deidre after this. She's quite distraught. She said her entire reputation is on the line." Lincoln had been bringing dishes over to the counter to create an assembly line of dishwashing. "She seems to be a bit dramatic." He set the dishes down and gave Callie a kiss on her cheek. "Bless you."

"I'll take that blessing," she said as she rinsed off a glass bowl. "I'm going to need it. Shoppers, too, who are willing to find all kinds of ingredients. No swap-outs allowed."

"You can count on me," Linc said.

Marnie and Linc stayed until every last dish had been washed, dried, and put away. A record time for cleanup, Callie said, but Marnie and Linc were highly motivated to impress her. As they got ready to go, Callie said Linc should have Deidre Klassen connect with her, to get the menu to her ASAP so she could start planning. Start delegating the shopping list. Start delivery orders. She did look pleased whenever she said the name Deidre Klassen. Her eyes shone with delight.

Back in the car, Lincoln reached to pull his seat belt and gasped, freezing in place.

"What is it?"

Slowly, he clicked his seat belt. "Just a stitch in my side."

"Linc, are you feeling okay?"

"I'm fine." He glanced at her, backing out of the parking spot. "A lot of moving parts lately."

True, but she wondered if it was more than wedding stress. He just hadn't seemed himself lately. Quiet, subdued. Not typical of Linc. "Have you thought about seeing a doctor?"

"Marnie, trust me, I'm fine." His face set stubbornly, and there was a tone in his voice that clearly communicated this conversation was over.

That, too, wasn't typical of Linc. "Just answer one question for me. I want an honest answer. Are you in any pain?" When he didn't respond, she added, "Let me rephrase that. If you do feel consistent, unexplained pain, will you please go see your doctor?"

He gave her a look. "I *am* a grown man."

Marnie rolled her eyes. Men. *Such* big babies.

• • •

Wednesday, June 29

Dawn sat in the fertility clinic in Hyannis, waiting to be called in. She hadn't told Kevin that she was going to the consultation appointment. She hadn't lied to him, not exactly. She didn't need to. Callie had given her a reason to head down the Cape with a huge shopping list for BJ's in Hyannis.

A lengthy yawn escaped. She'd been getting up extra early to rush to the Creamery to make the day's ice cream. She was going to need to fill the freezers, plus more. Somehow, Ashleigh Hayes had picked *this* weekend for her wedding, and it was consuming the entire Dixon family.

How crazy! To think a caterer's entire staff had gone under with Covid. Amazing that there was no other caterer on the Cape who could step in at the last minute. Poor Callie. What a huge undertaking! She wished Mom had talked to her before asking Callie to act as caterer. Callie had the chops, but to put on a wedding meal of this magnitude—one hundred fifty guests—was overwhelming! All while trying to impress Deidre Klassen. The very thought of it exhausted Dawn. Last night, as Callie gave Dawn today's shopping list, she said that Deidre had hinted the mother of the bride seemed to enjoy making this wedding a challenge. As if there weren't enough challenges with this wedding!

Poor Lincoln.

Dawn was so glad that Lincoln had the Dixon family to support him. Each member of the family, even Brynn, was doing all they could to help Callie deliver on that promised wedding meal. Callie had given Dawn and Mom shopping duties for all nonperishables. Callie insisted on purchasing the perishables herself on the day before the wedding. She trusted no one else with that task, but she did let the entire Dixon clan know (including Kevin and Bruno) that they would be needed in the kitchen to chop and prep. Brynn said she'd get to work on baking test wedding cakes today.

Brynn. Poor Brynn. She needed a good lawyer.

Dawn was sure that Lincoln would have one to recommend. Knowing Linc, he would drop everything to help Brynn. Dawn didn't want to bother him, not now, not during the high-stress wedding week for his daughter, which was turning more high stress with each passing day.

Still waiting to be called in for the consultation, she googled the difference between an annulment and a divorce. Each state, she read, had different definitions for them, so she clicked over to Nevada and was floored by how many divorce attorney–sponsored ads showed up at the top of the search. Clearly, Brynn wasn't alone in her spur-of-the-moment wedding that came with morning-after regret.

"Dawn Collins?"

Dawn looked up to see the nurse at the door.

"Ready?"

"So ready," Dawn said, as she clicked off her phone and tucked it in her purse.

● ● ●

Maeve

Just checking in before the 4th of July weekend gets underway. Camp Kicking Moose is already full! The Grayson clan is busier than one-armed paper hangers.

Marnie
Same here! Chatham is packed with tourists.
And Ashleigh Hayes's wedding is . . . well, that
update will have to wait for a phone call. Too
much to text.

Just know that I'm sending prayers your way.

Thank you! I have a feeling we're going to need
them.

Chapter
EIGHT

Ice cream cravings are not to be taken lightly.
—intuitive creativity coach Betsy Cañas Garmon

Marnie should've known. Not two minutes after Brynn had left in her car to take the test wedding cakes to Callie's for approval, the customer line at the Creamery grew until it was snaking out the door. She scooped as fast as she could, hardly interacting with people. And suddenly, Ashleigh Hayes and fiancé Ryan stood at the front of the line.

"Oh, hi!" Marnie pushed her hair back off her face. "I'm so glad you came in." Just like with Bear's visit, she wished she'd had some warning. She felt flustered, sensed her face was turning red with an annoying hot flash. But Ashleigh and Ryan seemed hardly aware of anyone around them. They were holding hands as they peered in the case, oohing and aahing over the unique flavors.

"My brother said to be sure to stop by," Ashleigh said. "Last night he was raving about your ice cream."

Really? Marnie's feelings toward Bear softened a tad.

"Mom said she was going to stop by too. Or maybe she already has?"

What?! Had she? Marnie had no idea what Jeannie looked like.

80

She tried to think of any customer today who might have been Lincoln's ex-wife, but their faces all blurred together.

Ashleigh was texting on her phone, then waiting for a response. "Yep. She said she stopped in. She tried the Double-Fold Vanilla."

Seriously? Marnie had been so busy, she'd hardly noticed individuals. Could Jeannie have come when the shop was at its busiest and Marnie was at her worst? Hot and sweaty, scooping up ice cream just as fast as she could. Not the way she had wanted to meet Lincoln's former wife. She tried to think back to any customers ordering Double-Fold Vanilla, but it was their most popular flavor. Nearly one out of every three customers ordered it. Good grief. She gave up thinking about it. "How's the wedding week coming along?"

Ashleigh and Ryan exchanged a look. "You'll have to ask my mom," Ashleigh said. "This is really her show. We left everything in her hands."

Ryan put his arm around Ashleigh. "We'd be happy with a simple ceremony on the beach."

Ashleigh gazed up at him as if he hung the moon. "We really would," she said with a sigh.

Marnie's jaw dropped. The amount of work that Callie (and, by extension, all the Dixons) would have to do to cater this wedding reception was staggering. So was its cost. "Then why don't you?" Marnie said, knowing that if Dawn were here, she would give her a frown to discourage her from voicing her thoughts out loud. "Why don't you tell your mother that you'd rather, um, dial things down?" Like, go to the beach for the ceremony and have pizza delivered? Maybe some ice cream from the Creamery to finish the night? Dawn had once experimented with a wedding cake–flavored ice cream. Too sweet for most palates, so she nixed it. But maybe she could be persuaded to dust off the recipe and try again.

"Well, it's complicated," Ashleigh said, in a conciliatory tone that Marnie thought might reveal a lot about her. "You see, Mom never had a big wedding. She and Dad sort of eloped."

They *what*? This was news to Marnie. "They eloped?"

"Sort of eloped. Their parents knew."

"They didn't mind?" Philip would've been outraged if Dawn and Kevin had eloped.

"They encouraged it. I think my grandparents even went to city hall with them for the ceremony. They were all as poor as church mice and couldn't afford a wedding. So," she said, sharing an insider look with Ryan, "since I'm the only girl and Bear will probably never get married, Ryan and I just decided that it would be best to give Mom this wedding, to let her do whatever she wanted to do."

Marnie had to ask. "Why do you think your brother will never get married?"

Ashleigh looked up in surprise. "Maybe 'never' is too strong a word."

"My theory," Ryan said, "is that now that Ashleigh is getting married, Bear will be more open to a commitment. He's been very protective of his sister and mother."

"My parents' divorce hit Bear hard." Ashleigh lifted her palms. "But, of course, I'm sure you've heard all that."

No, Marnie wanted to say. *No, I haven't heard all that. Tell me more. Tell me everything.* But she did her absolute best to keep an unaffected expression on her face.

"I do hope Bear gets married one day," Ashleigh said. "But I think he considers love as a liability."

Marnie took that in as they tried to decide on flavors. She wished she could pepper them with more questions. She was acutely interested in Ashleigh and Bear. She wanted to know everything about them. For the first time *ever*, she wished the shop was empty so she could spend more time with Ashleigh, but customers behind them were growing impatient. Unlike Bear's immediate choice of vanilla, Ashleigh and Ryan hemmed and hawed, deciding and changing their minds. Sampling different flavors. Finally, they chose three scoops each of unusual flavors, six flavors in all, planning to try each other's choices.

Ashleigh took the cup of ice cream from Marnie and said, "This is another reason it's best to let my mom handle the wedding. We can't decide on anything!"

"True. Except about each other. That was easy." Ryan looked adoringly at Ashleigh and she blushed back.

They made Marnie smile. They were a joined-at-the-hip kind of couple. Ryan reached into his pocket and pulled out a handful of severely crumpled dollar bills. She waved him off. "On the house. A wedding present from me."

They thanked her and moved out of line, spending some time looking around the shop—at the dry sink filled with ice cream–related tchotchke for sale. The freezer case that held to-go cartons of Dawn's ice cream. And then the fireplace that served as a dramatic focal point in the room, especially during the winter. Marnie would've loved to tell Ashleigh about Dawn and Kevin's wedding, how the gas insert was a gift from Lincoln. She wanted to describe how simple yet elegant the wedding had been, and that it had been held right here, right in the ice cream shop. That an ice storm had blasted New England and kept out-of-town guests from attending. She wanted Ashleigh to know what a huge help her dad had been to the Dixon family, to make sure Dawn and Kevin's wedding happened. And that it was the best wedding Marnie had ever been to.

But those few unpleasant interactions with Bear had taught Marnie to remain silent. As Ashleigh and Ryan left the shop, they turned and waved to Marnie. Ashleigh even blew her a kiss.

Amazing, just amazing, how different two siblings could be. Twins, no less.

* * *

Brynn thought she might have heard from TD by now. He would've had to dig to find more info about her, just like she would have had to go looking for info about him. So far, she'd done nothing to find him. Not a thing, not yet. Next week, she thought she'd be in a better mental state to start digging. This week, she was absorbed with scooping ice cream and baking cakes.

Since Monday, Brynn had scooped more ice cream than she thought existed on this planet. How did Dawn keep up with the demand? The customer lines never ended. Today, whenever Marnie didn't need her behind the counter, Brynn scooted into the Creamery's kitchen to bake test wedding cakes.

On the upside, all this baking and scooping up ice cream kept her mind busy and off TD.

This wedding cake was taking quite a bit of Brynn's time. Callie didn't trust Brynn's baking and decorating abilities. Not at all. Brynn had drawn up several plans of wedding cake decorations to present to Callie for approval. So far, nothing had satisfied her. Marnie apologized profusely for Callie's patronizing attitude, but it really didn't bother Brynn. Callie was fascinating to her—very bold, very upbeat, very creative, very knowledgeable about baking. She was eager to learn as much as she could from her while she was in Chatham.

Some might be offended by such intense supervision, but it was no problem at all for Brynn. After all, she was an engineer. She was used to feedback. In fact, she appreciated it. It helped make the end result as faultless as humanly possible.

Late last night, Brynn baked a test cake, just to make sure the batter was right for this hot and steamy weather. As she feared, it was sluggish and would need adjustments. Humidity lessened the absorption capacity of flour, so the batter required a little more flour. She thought the oven ran a little too hot.

This morning, Brynn woke extra early and baked another test cake. And another and another, tweaking the recipe just so. Then one more. And that one turned out flawless. Absolutely perfect. As soon as the cake came out of the oven, a critical cooling period had to be carefully observed. After reaching room temperature, the cake had to be wrapped up in cling wrap so it wouldn't dry out. Around noon, there was a lull in the shop's customers, so Brynn asked Marnie if she could borrow her car to take test cake #5 over to the cooking school to see if it met with Callie's approval, and of course she said yes.

As Brynn pulled into the Intuitive Cooking School parking lot, she reached over and picked up the cooled, wrapped cake in her hands, and smiled. She loved to bake—something about it was very calming and soothing and soul-satisfying.

There was even a time in her life when she had seriously considered being a full-time baker. Her interest had started in college when she began to bake thick, chunky chocolate chip cookies, just for fun. As she improved her skills, she expanded her recipes. She taught herself to decorate with delicate piping. Friends started ordering cookies for special moments—birthdays, final exams, sorority events. She branched out into cakes, expanding her decorating skills. She even entered a Christmas gingerbread house contest and won second place. As an engineering major, she had noticed similarities with baking. Precision, construction, execution, repeatability. But baking provided a spark of creativity that was much more exciting than engineering. That was the point when she had considered making a switch from engineering to attend a culinary school.

But when she shared her idea with Dawn, she talked her out of it. Relentlessly. With Dawn's CPA-in-training logic, she started to list what was wrong with Brynn's "whimsical idea," and she brought up several good points about a career in baking that were hard to dispute:

Long, terrible hours, little pay.

High risk, low reward.

Poor job security.

Primarily blue-collar labor.

Workday done when the rest of the world was just waking up.

Weekend and holiday work.

Dawn reminded Brynn of the recognition she'd been receiving for her engineering projects. She'd won some student awards, and that summer she'd been offered a highly sought-after internship which would probably lead to a great job right out of college. Which would lead to a solid, rewarding career. All good points.

But this was the one point that was hardest to dismiss: You can "hobby" baking. You can't "hobby" civil engineering.

Dawn hammered away on those points until Brynn felt her full-time bakery idea had been a spark doused by water. Career-wise, that was. Not hobby-wise. She kept on baking whenever she could. She'd made several wedding cakes for friends . . . and now she was making a cake for the extraordinary, renowned wedding planner Deidre Klassen. *Amazing.* Because of Callie.

All Brynn had ever thought about Callie was that she was the opposite of Dawn in every way. Dawn was reserved, Callie was effervescent. Dawn resisted change, Callie embraced it. Dawn was slow to decide, Callie was decisive. Even their looks were so different—Dawn had casual good looks with long, strawberry blond hair that she wore mostly in a no-nonsense ponytail. She radiated *stability*. Callie was striking, tall, and lithe, with big brown eyes. She wore her thick blond hair in unique styles to keep it out of her face. Callie radiated *presence*.

Brynn knew there'd been some kind of childhood rivalry between the two girls. Dawn had always seemed mildly annoyed with Callie. But some kind of relational change had occurred between them after Callie had moved to Chatham. Dawn and Callie seemed more like family than they used to. More like sisters who occasionally rubbed each other wrong than cousins who regularly bugged each other.

Brynn found herself intrigued by Callie. She'd picked up on this much: Callie stayed on task, all business. As for kitchen skills, she was very hard to impress. Her expectations were sky-high.

That didn't bother Brynn at all. She was going to wow Callie Dixon *and* Deidre Klassen with this phenomenal wedding cake. And test cake #5 really was exceptional. With that boost in confidence, she headed into the cooking school with her cake.

Callie stood behind the counter, surrounded by cooked lobsters. She was shelling the meat as she glanced up at Brynn. "Ashleigh's mother changed her mind because of the heat wave. Now she wants chilled lobster salad served in martini glasses for the first course."

"Can a client keep changing her mind like this?"

"There's usually a cutoff date, but this isn't my first rodeo. I've learned to never buy perishables until twenty-four hours before the event." She held up a lobster claw. "Except for this. It needs time to marinate in the dressing."

"In the construction world, every change order means a steep fine."

Callie shrugged. "Lincoln said to do whatever Ashleigh wants. Which translates to whatever Ashleigh's mother wants." She grinned. "All of these changes are actually bonding Deidre and me. She told me that she thought the caterer might have canceled because Ashleigh's mother drove them crazy."

Brynn lifted the wrapped cake. "I made some adjustments to the batter and wanted you to try it." She tilted her head. "Unless there's been a change to the wedding cake? Does the bride's mother still want lemon with a lemon curd filling?"

"No changes with that so far, thank goodness." Callie pulled off her gloves and washed her hands. She took out a plate, a cake knife, and a fork as Brynn unwrapped the test cake. Studying it critically, Callie took a sniff. "Good fragrance." She turned the cake over to examine both sides. "Slightly domed. Lightly browned. Sometimes the Creamery oven runs hot. You'll have to be careful about that."

Yep. Brynn had already figured that out with test cakes #1 and #2.

Callie sliced a piece and examined the interior like a judge at a county fair. "Ingredients seem to be well mixed. And I don't see any tunnels."

"Tunnels?"

"Air pockets." Callie pressed one finger against the slice. "Not gummy." Using her fork, she clawed at the slice. "Not crumbly. Fluffy and moist." Then she took a bite. She took her time before swallowing. She took another bite. Her eyes lifted as she smiled. "It'll do."

Brynn practically did a little jig. *It'll do, she said!* From Callie, that was high praise.

"Next, I want to sample the lemon curd filling."

"On it."

"And after that, the buttercream frosting."

"You bet." Brynn felt elated. She had assumed Callie wouldn't let her make the frosting at all.

As she started Marnie's car, she cranked up the air conditioner and let out a loud "Woohoo!" Baking always had that effect on her. The feeling trailed her, all the way through the beautiful streets of the historical district of Chatham, until she stopped at a red light. Something in her spine caught a small jolt of current. The car in front of her made a left turn, and for a split second, the driver's profile made her heart skip a beat. She could have sworn the driver was TD.

She squeezed her eyes shut. She saw him everywhere, even with her eyes closed. She remembered him laughing at something she had said. She thought of how he had looked at her as if he felt like the luckiest man in the world to be with her. She relived their first tender kiss on a busy, crowded boulevard in Las Vegas—of all places—and it felt as if they were the only two people on the planet.

The light must have turned green because the car behind her honked twice, loud. She opened her eyes and stepped on the gas pedal, lurching the car forward. She could hardly see clearly because tears were clouding her vision, streaming down her cheeks. She sniffed, wiping them away with the back of her hand.

She had left Callie in a mood of utter happiness and had fallen into deep despair in less than two minutes. A roller coaster of emotions. Brynn Haywood! A woman known for her even-keeled disposition.

No longer. She had lost her even keel.

• • •

Dawn left the fertility clinic filled with new knowledge and emptied of peace of mind. Today's appointment was just a consultation, a chance to ask questions, learn about the options, figure out how much insurance would pay. Or more likely, how much insurance would refuse to pay. A full physical exam would come next, and the doctor highly recommended that Kevin should also have an exam. According to the doctor, one-third of reproductive issues are because of the male. One-third are because of the female. And one-third are because of both male and female. The doctor said it would be best to start the process together, united.

Dawn could just imagine how Kevin would react to news that he would need to undergo some rather privacy-invading tests to rule out being the source of their infertility. In her heart, because her mom had trouble conceiving, she knew the problem, most likely, was with her. Without saying so, the doctor seemed to agree. When Dawn mentioned that fact about her mom, the doctor immediately started pecking away at the computer. She asked all kinds of questions about Marnie—leading Dawn to think there might be something genetic going on.

Until now, Dawn had never thought about why her mom had trouble conceiving, or how that might have felt for her as a young wife, especially as nieces and nephews started arriving. Had it been a lonely time for Mom? Had Dad been supportive? Probably not, Dawn thought. Dad would've acted like Kevin. The two men shared that "if it's meant to be, it'll happen" attitude.

She opened the brochure and read another page. The top treatment, as in the most successful one, was in vitro fertilization. IVF. It was also the most expensive one. Ridiculously expensive. Dawn and Kevin were both self-employed so, most likely, their insurance wouldn't cover the procedure. There was another less costly option to consider: intrauterine insemination. Dawn had a colleague in Boston who had success with IUI. She called it the turkey baster method.

After that, there were options that she knew Kevin would shoot down because they were going outside of what he called God's family planning. Donor eggs or donor sperm, in particular. Kevin's father was a pastor and held very strong views about such matters, ones that he wasn't shy to express. Or maybe Kevin just seemed to be embracing those views as his own faith deepened.

Dawn wished she had Kevin's rock-solid faith. His belief in God's sovereignty in all things was why he felt no angst about getting pregnant. Eager to become a father, he hoped for at least two or three children. In some ways, he was more excited about parenthood than Dawn was. He talked about being a father a lot—the kinds of things he wanted to do with his kids. Camping, for example. Annual trips to Disney World. He couldn't wait to be a dad, but he had put the whole matter in God's hands, and unlike Dawn, he left it there.

Dawn would try to put the whole matter in God's hands only to snatch it back. Like now. She tucked the brochure into her purse. "Okay, Lord. I'm giving it back to you."

She meant it, or at least she wanted to mean it. But one last remark from the doctor was hard to ignore. "I can't tell you how many couples come in here in their late thirties, early forties, desperate to conceive. We do the best we can to help each patient realize their dream, but the older a woman gets, the more her chances to become pregnant decrease. I applaud you for not letting time pass before taking action."

The passing of time, Dawn realized, something no one could control, had become her trigger of panic.

● ● ●

Callie
Wedding cake alert! Bride's mother wants to sample chocolate.

Brynn
So scratch the lemon curd?

Bride's mother liked the lemon cake. Better make the curd.

So make a chocolate cake and a lemon curd.

Have you ever made a red velvet cake?

A few times.

Good! Make a sample.

Okay. Will work on a chocolate cake, a red velvet cake, and a lemon curd.

And . . . a carrot cake. Bride's mother wants choices.

The wedding! 3 days away! 😧

I know! 😔

Chapter
NINE

Age does not diminish the extreme disappointment of having a scoop of ice cream fall from the cone.

—gemstone expert and jeweler Jim Fiebig

It occurred to Marnie that Callie and Brynn, both, might be a little obsessive. Both of them were singularly focused on preparing the food for Ashleigh Hayes's wedding reception, acting as if their entire life depended on the outcome of this meal.

Callie, Marnie could understand. This was an incredible name-recognition opportunity for her cooking school. She was a hard worker and deserved this chance. It sounded as if she and Deidre Klassen had really hit it off—another bonus.

But Brynn's intensity about this wedding cake took Marnie by surprise. All Wednesday morning, she baked and baked and baked, tossing cakes into the bin if they weren't exactly perfect. The slightest brown edges or a dome that didn't *dome* quite enough. Marnie had this odd flashback to the time when Dawn was making vanilla ice cream and redid her recipe fifty-nine times. Were Brynn and Dawn *that* much alike?

Or worse . . . had Dawn imposed her perfectionism streak onto Brynn? The two girls met as roommates when they were only eighteen, so young, so impressionable. Brynn's home life had been one of benign neglect. She had latched onto the Dixons like a life raft. To her, they had the family life that she'd always wanted. Yet as independent as Brynn seemed to be, Marnie had always noticed how she would defer to Dawn. Her daughter had strong opinions about most everything, and Brynn would accommodate her.

A worry kept flitting through Marnie's mind. Was Dawn trying to "fix" Brynn's impetuous marriage? This was Brynn's problem to solve, if it was indeed a problem. Marnie wasn't convinced it was. Not yet, anyway. The only thing she felt convinced about was that Brynn needed to have a long talk with her groom. First, she needed to find him.

Brynn had left to take lemon curd over to Callie to sample when Dawn arrived at the shop with cartons of cream and milk to make ice cream. As soon as there was a lull in customers, Marnie hurried to the kitchen. "I tried to catch you before you left the store. Brynn's used up all the sugar."

"I know. She called. Callie texted. Those two are running me ragged. I have bags of sugar and flour in the car. Lemons too. And they're not cheap." Dawn set the milk cartons on the counter. "Linc is going to reimburse us for this monster cake, isn't he?"

"Yes. In fact, he tacked up an envelope on the bulletin board for receipts. And he even left his ATM card with me in case Brynn or Callie needed more supplies."

Dawn stuffed the receipt in the envelope. "Whoa. Linc gave you his ATM passcode." She waggled her eyebrows. "Things must be pretty serious between you two."

"More like . . . he wants his daughter's wedding reception to be the stuff of dreams."

"Crazy, isn't it? I can't imagine what Deidre Klassen would

have thought about my tiny wedding that took place during an ice storm."

"Your wedding was just what you and Kevin wanted. That's what a wedding should be. So Ashleigh and Ryan's wedding might be a little bit more deluxe." She grinned. "But you both have the same caterer in Callie."

"True! Callie's going to get a reputation for the caterer to call when you're in a terrible bind."

Marnie thought Dawn's mood seemed light enough that she could broach the subject of Brynn's marriage. "Dawn, I think Brynn needs to find her young man and have a conversation with him."

"I agree."

"Before any lawyers get involved."

Dawn paused but didn't respond. She went out to the car to get the last of the groceries.

Oh well, Marnie thought. *At least I said it.*

Dawn came back inside and set the bags of groceries on the counter with an *oomph*. "I completely forgot to tell you that I bumped into Linc's son at the hardware store the other day."

Marnie had been putting milk and cream cartons in the fridge. She turned back to Dawn. "And?"

"Well, to start with, he's very good looking."

"He is that."

She tilted her head and scrunched up her face. "But I got a vibe."

"What kind of vibe?"

"I got this weird feeling that he thinks the Dixons are after Linc's money. It wasn't like he came out with it . . . he was just sending off a suspicious kind of vibe."

Yep, that was the same vibe Marnie had gotten from him too.

"Lincoln doesn't think that we care about his money, does he?"

"No. No, of course not."

"Because . . . it did occur to me that he has been awfully generous to us."

Marnie closed the refrigerator with a sigh. "I've had the same thoughts." She went to the end of the kitchen and looked into the shop. Still no customers. "We wouldn't have survived without him."

"I tease about Linc being our fairy godfather . . . but maybe I should retire that phrase."

Marnie smiled. "Well, maybe just while his son is in town."

"That won't be long, right? Like, he'll probably leave right after the wedding, don't you think?"

"I would think so," Marnie said. She wondered how things were going over at Lincoln's house. She wondered about his ex-wife. She had hoped to meet her before the wedding. Chatham was a small town, but it was a crowded one this week.

Holding the back door open by the handle, Dawn said, "Bear. Such a silly name for a grown man."

"There are worse nicknames. I once knew an old man named Skippy."

"It's hard to believe that Bear is related to Lincoln." Dawn went out the door to get more groceries from the car.

What Marnie found harder to grasp was that Lincoln was once the kind of father who produced a son like Bear.

• • •

When Brynn arrived at the cooking school with the sample of lemon curd in hand, Callie had a funny look on her face. "The bride's mother has changed her mind," Callie said. "Deidre said that now she wants individual cakes."

"You mean, cupcakes?" Nice. That would be easy.

Callie coughed a laugh. "I mean . . . mini–wedding cakes. Different flavors, different decorations. It's the latest trend, apparently."

Brynn knew about floral cakes, chocolate spheres on top of

cakes, separated tiers, black-colored cakes, naked cakes—but she had missed the mini–wedding cake trend.

"I'll send you some pictures of what Deidre has in mind." Callie whipped her phone out of her chef jacket's pocket and started sending pictures.

Brynn was still trying to absorb this news as the pictures came through via text message. When she saw the first one, her heart sank. It was tiered, with intricate decorations. "Callie, do you mean to say that we will need to make one hundred and fifty mini–wedding cakes?"

"Two hundred," Callie said in a weak voice, like it hurt to say it aloud. "The bride's mother has added guests to the list. I'm hoping your piping skills are as good as Marnie said they were."

Well, they were. But still! Two hundred miniature wedding cakes. Brynn blew out a puff of air. "You sound pretty calm. Aren't you freaking out?"

"Not since I decided to leave the wedding cakes entirely to you."

"Really?" Exciting! She thought Callie wanted to be responsible to decorate the cake. Correction. *Cakes.*

"I've got to manage all the last-minute changes the mother of the bride has made to the menu."

"Why isn't Deidre telling the bride's mother there can't be any changes? I thought wedding planners had a reputation for running the show. Their way or no way."

"Four reasons. One, the bride's mother doesn't give her an option to say no. Two"—Callie ticked each one off with her fingers—"the bride's mother doesn't care about paying exorbitant change fees. Three . . . Deidre loves the drama. Four is the best reason of all. Deidre is thrilled to enhance this wedding in every possible way because . . ." Her eyes twinkled with delight. They literally twinkled. "Because Deidre just found out that this wedding might be featured on *The Knot.*"

Brynn gasped. *The Knot* was one of the biggest go-to social media sites for wedding planning. "How? Who?"

"Connections. All Deidre." An oven timer went off. "A lot is riding on this, Brynn. We have to knock this out of the park. Plan on doing all the baking at the cooking school. The Creamery's ancient oven can't be held responsible for churning out hundreds of perfect cakes."

Brynn's first thought was of the ice cream shop. Poor Marnie. She was going to have to man the counter alone for the next few days. "Text me some times when you're not teaching, and I'll be there."

"You're going to need more time than that. Go ahead and take a corner of the kitchen. Make it your own. Brynn, I'm counting on you to come through with those cakes."

Without realizing it, Callie had just given Brynn exactly what she needed right now. She loved to bake, and Callie was counting on her. Deidre Klassen was counting on her. This impossible mother of the bride was counting on her. There was no free space left in Brynn's mind to marinate in her abandoned-marriage misery.

● ● ●

Later in the afternoon, Nanette burst into the Creamery like she was about to explode with fresh gossip. This was not unusual behavior for Nanette, who lived across from the Creamery and ran a T-shirt shop, so Marnie didn't pay much attention to her. She was busy with a line of customers, but Nanette just pushed her way right to the front—"Don't mind me, hon"—and slammed her palms on top of the glass case. "Marnie, you won't believe what just happened at the Cape Cod 5!"

"The bank?" That was where most of the locals kept their money, Marnie included.

"I took in all Michael's pennies that he'd been saving for the last umpteen years. I sat in that bank for over an hour while a little machine weighed all those pennies. I counted right alongside it, just to be sure I wasn't getting shortchanged. You know how banks can be. All kinds of hidden fees."

Marnie half listened to Nanette's story as she scooped ice cream for customers. "Well, sounds like your time was well spent."

"It was! But not because of Michael's pennies. Marnie, are you listening to me?"

Marnie handed a customer a cone and paused for a brief moment to give Nanette her full attention. "I'm all ears."

"Good. Because this is the part you're going to want to hear. Into the bank came a fellow. Handsome boy. In his thirties, I'm guessing. Very well spoken. Well dressed. Nice head of jet-black hair. Guess who he was?"

Marnie stiffened. "Lincoln's son."

"Lincoln's son!" Nanette said. "Isn't he a handsome one?"

Marnie turned her attention to the next customer and took his order. Nanette was famous for her rambling verbal bunny trails. She wasn't about to get drawn in.

But that didn't stop Nanette from trying. "So Lincoln's handsome son sat down with one of those bank vice presidents. They happened to be right next to where I was counting up Michael's pennies. I didn't mean to eavesdrop, but I just couldn't help myself."

I'll bet, Marnie thought.

"And you won't believe what that boy is up to."

Marnie closed the ice cream case to keep the cold in. "Wouldn't I?" She wasn't particularly interested in the answer. Nanette's nickname was Nosy Nanette. She acted as Chatham's town crier. A different role than Mrs. Nickerson-Eldredge, who appointed herself as the guardian of Chatham. Both women had a tendency to believe that nothing should happen in Chatham without their knowledge and permission.

Eyes bright, Nanette leaned against the ice cream case. "He said he's concerned that his father is being financially exploited."

Marnie's head snapped up. "Lincoln? Someone's trying to exploit him?"

"He says that he thinks his father might be a victim of an opportunist."

"So he thinks someone might be scamming Lincoln?" That was hard for Marnie to believe. Linc was very astute, very on top of things.

"There was a phrase the boy kept repeating. Putting undue influence on his father." Nanette put her hands on top of the counter and leaned over it, staring right into Marnie's eyes. "And he thinks *you* are the one who is putting undue influence on Lincoln. He said that very thing! He named you and Dawn and Callie, but mostly you. He said that he has evidence that you help yourself to Linc's ATM card, and that there's undocumented loans with members of the Dixon family." Nanette took another deep breath. "And then he said that undocumented loans will tip off the IRS to sniff around, looking for signs of tax evasion."

Marnie felt as if she was going to be sick. Everything Nanette said was true. It was all true. But she hadn't put undue influence on Lincoln! She hadn't exploited him. Linc had practically foisted his money on them. He'd given Callie an interest-free loan to purchase her property after the bank had declined her loan. The historical preservation construction company that Linc had set up with Kevin had yet to turn a profit, yet Linc kept sending cash into it, providing a salary for Kevin and Dawn so the work could continue unabated. And don't even get Marnie started on the amount of money he had infused into the Creamery to keep it afloat.

And then came another Nanette bombshell. "The boy said he's concerned his father might be starting to show signs of dementia."

How dare Bear make such an accusation? How dare he! Lincoln's mind was just fine. He had a better memory than anyone Marnie knew.

Nanette was staring at Marnie, waiting for a reaction. The little woman looked like she might jump right over the counter.

Marnie cleared her throat. "What did Bear seem to want out of this meeting?"

"Apparently, he's a lawyer. Did you know that?"

Vaguely.

"He wants safeguards to be put into place to protect his father."

"Safeguards?"

"A trust for assets. Power of attorney. Two signatures for each check. He said he wanted to avoid inheritance theft or financial abuse."

"What did the bank vice president have to say?"

"She said that there's nothing wrong with good estate planning."

No. Unless the one who held the estate—the one who earned the estate in the first place—had no say-so in the matter. "And I suppose that Lincoln knows nothing about his son's conversation at the bank?"

"Didn't seem like it." Nanette leaned closer to the counter. "You know I never give out advice unless I'm asked—"

Marnie nearly choked back a laugh.

"—but honey, I know you and Linc are good friends. I've seen a lot of family drama in my years. Money brings out the worst in people. Things can get ugly. Be careful! This boy, he's got a thorn in his paw." The door chimed as more customers came in. "I'd better scoot. Remember . . . you didn't hear any of this from me." She gave Marnie her little five-finger wave. "Toodles!"

A thorn in his paw. Marnie squeezed her eyes shut. She knew that a wounded animal was a dangerous one.

● ● ●

Brynn
Lots going on! I can't help your mom at the
Creamery. Will you tell her for me?

Dawn

What's going on? Did you hear from TD?!

> Haven't heard from TD. It's the wedding. Big
> changes. Callie wants me to bake at the cooking
> school.

You don't have to bake this wedding cake,
Brynn. You can say no to Callie.

> But I don't want to say no.

Chapter
TEN

I always say whoever can figure out how to make ice cream healthy will be a gazillionaire.

—actor Justin Deeley

Marnie needed a minute to herself to absorb what Nanette had overheard at the bank. She wanted to call her friend Maeve and vent, run everything by her to get her opinion about what she should do about Linc and Bear. Plus, she had to go to the bathroom.

As soon as there was a dinnertime lull in customers, Marnie left the front room to ask Brynn or Dawn to take a turn at the counter. There was no Brynn or Dawn to be found! Instead, there was a note on the counter, in Dawn's handwriting:

Mom—big changes with Ashleigh's wedding. Brynn's baking at the cooking school for the next few days. I'll be back early in the morning to make ice cream.

Dawn XO

Good grief. What had happened to her helpers at the ice cream shop? This grandiose wedding, that's what happened. Marnie couldn't wait for it to be done with. She peeked around the doorjamb that led from the kitchen to the shop—the main room was still empty of customers and she knew it wouldn't last long. She grabbed her phone and dashed upstairs. First to go to the bathroom, and then to call her friend Maeve.

Happily, Maeve picked up on the first ring. "Hey there! I'm surprised to hear from you during the day. Isn't the shop pretty busy?"

"Yes, and I only have a minute." Quickly, she gave Maeve the highlights of the week. When she finished, there was silence. "Are you still there?"

"Wow. This is like a bad soap opera."

"Right?" She knew Maeve would understand. "So what should I do?"

"Nothing."

Marnie's eyes went wide. "What do you mean, nothing? Shouldn't I let Linc know what Bear is up to?"

"I think you know the answer to that, Marnie. You know, and Linc knows, what the real story is between you."

"Yes, but Lincoln—"

"This week is all about Lincoln reconnecting with his children. Marnie, you really shouldn't interfere with that. If you do, it'll come back and bite you."

"Yes, but shouldn't Lincoln be told the—"

"The whole story?" Maeve had a habit of finishing her sentences but sometimes she did a better job of it than Marnie would have, anyway.

"Yes! Linc deserves to know the whole story."

"Marnie, that could be true of you too. You don't have Bear's whole story. Have a little restraint here. You should be concentrating on what's best for Lincoln."

"I thought I was. A crafty, shrewd lawyer can create all kinds of problems. At the very least, Bear could tie Linc's freedom in knots. Or worse, what if he tries to have his father declared as unfit?"

"Marnie. Let's get real. You're insulted by Bear and trying to defend yourself. And at the core of this is probably an insecurity you're feeling about Lincoln."

Ouch. Ouch, ouch, ouch. Why did she think calling Maeve would be a good idea?

"Do you truly have any reason to feel insecure about Lincoln?"

"No, I suppose not. I guess . . . I'm just worried that—"

"You're worried that Lincoln's son will influence how he feels about you."

Bull's-eye. Marnie didn't even know that was what she'd been worried about until Maeve said it aloud. She did feel a spiral of anxiety about Lincoln.

Good grief. She was acting like a teenager. Shouldn't romance be easier at her age? More mature?

"Look, my friend, let me offer a better solution. Pray about this and leave it to God to untangle."

Well, yes. There was that option. She sighed. The best option.

The door chimes rang downstairs and Marnie heard voices. "I'd better go."

"I'll pray too, Marnie. Keep me posted."

They hung up and Marnie hurried down the stairs to wait on the customers. She stopped abruptly at the doorjamb, not quite trusting her eyes.

There stood Bear Hayes with a baseball cap on his head. He was wearing a well-worn sweatshirt with the Boston University logo emblazoned on its chest. And he was wearing jeans like a normal guy. Beside him was Leo the Cowboy, peering into the glass case.

Flustered, Marnie wished Brynn were here, baking a wedding test cake, so she could send her in to wait on Bear Hayes. She wanted to avoid him at all costs and Brynn wouldn't care. She had no history with the man. But her shop helpers had deserted her. The cavalry wasn't coming.

Slowly, Marnie entered the front room and slipped behind the counter. She tried to smile, but it came out all wrong, tight and forced. To recover, she focused on Leo. "How did you two end up together?"

Bear answered for him. "Leo was walking down Main Street, trying to lasso hydrangeas. I asked him where he was going, and he said he was sent to the Creamery."

Leo nodded. "Callie thought you might need some help."

Marnie had to smile at that. "Callie's pretty busy right now." She cast a glance at Bear. "The Dixon clan is working hard to pull off your sister's wedding."

"It must feel good to have an opportunity to reciprocate the Hayeses' kindness." Bear's cold tone matched his blunt statement.

Hayeses' kindness, like it was a family trait. Marnie wanted to smack him.

Leo was pointing at the case. "Can I try a scoop of that yellow one?"

"Sure. That one is Coconut Banana Pancakes." She scooped it out in a cone for Leo and handed it to him. "How about for you?" She was noticing Bear's eyes, the same shape and color as Lincoln's. So similar to his father's, yet lacking depth, warmth. Were eyes a window into the soul? If so, what did she see in Bear's soul? A cold dark pit. She nearly shivered. She shouldn't think such thoughts about Lincoln's son. Maeve was right. She didn't know Bear's whole story.

"I'll just try that vanilla you gave me the other day."

Marnie tipped her head. "You don't want to try another flavor? This morning Dawn made a batch of Chocolate Gooey Brownie. That's been a favorite for locals."

"No need. Vanilla suits me. It was excellent. I'm a man of commitment."

Marnie handed him the Double-Fold Vanilla ice cream. "Is that just with ice cream? Or all things?"

"All things, I would say. When I set my mind on something, I don't budge."

He took out a ten-dollar bill and set it on the counter.

Marnie shook her head. "These are on the house. Leo's part of our family. And you're Lincoln's son."

There was a beat of silence as Bear didn't reach out to take his money back. "I prefer to pay my own way in this world. It's not a comfortable feeling to be beholden to anyone." He kept his eyes on Marnie—those dark eyes—and she knew exactly what was running through his mind, accusations that went unsaid. *You are beholden to my father and that is going to stop.* The air in the shop grew thick and heavy, as before a storm.

Marnie realized that her hands had curled into fists. Finger by finger, she relaxed them.

He broke eye contact and gave Leo a pat on the shoulder. "See you around, pardner."

After Bear left the store, Marnie had to take a moment to collect herself. She wanted to find Lincoln and tell him everything Bear was doing behind his back, all the silent accusations leveled at Marnie. At Dawn, at Callie! She wanted Linc's reassurance that he didn't feel taken advantage of by them. That he never had, and never would. But Maeve's advice struck her heart. She shouldn't talk to Linc of doubts about his son—their relationship was so fragile, so tentative. This was Bear's first visit to the Cape in years. And this was Ashleigh's wedding week. The last thing Marnie wanted to do was set things back for Linc and his children.

She turned to see that Leo was watching her carefully. "Leo, you let Callie know that you were with Bear, didn't you?"

"Yep. He called her and she said it was okay to get in his car."

"Good."

"He's really, really nice."

"Is he?" Marnie's voice sounded flat, even to her own ears.

"He took me around to some of the places he used to go when he was a little boy here."

"Like where?"

"There's a fishing spot on a pond that no one knows about. And he showed me the climbing tree."

"The climbing tree?"

"Yep. You can climb up and see all the way to the Chatham Lighthouse."

"Did you do that?"

"Yep. We both did."

It was hard to imagine Bear Hayes climbing a tree. Even harder to imagine him as a carefree boy.

"And then he took me out to the Chatham Anglers' baseball field where he used to play."

"Bear played baseball?"

"Yeah. Did you know that the lights go on at night?"

"Bear played baseball for the Chatham Anglers?" she repeated.

"Yeah. He was a pitcher until he hurt his shoulder."

He must have been quite a good pitcher. Linc had never told her that Bear played baseball. He'd never said anything about Little League, or high school baseball. Not college baseball, and definitely not for the Chatham Anglers. Yet that must have been Bear's path. She knew enough about boys from her friend Maeve to know how baseball progressed. She wondered why Linc had never said anything about it. She was pretty sure she had told him everything Dawn had ever done—space camp, coding camp, plus all kinds of lessons. Piano, gymnastics, ballet, tennis, golf, ice skating. And then, of course, attending Ice Cream School at Penn State with her dad when she was a senior in high school. Why had Linc never said anything about Bear and baseball? Or, for that matter, anything Ashleigh had ever done. "Sounds like you had a good time together."

"Yep. He says being here brings back a lot of memories."

It was good, Marnie thought, to try to not think of Bear as a villain. She smiled at Leo, feeling more settled. "Want another scoop?"

He grinned and held out his melting cone. "Two, please. I'd like to try the vanilla."

"Just like Bear."

Leo nodded. Slowly, he took off his cowboy hat and ruffled his hair. "I need to go see Nanette."

Marnie handed him the ice cream cone. A new one. "How come?"

"I want to get a baseball cap."

No! Marnie squeezed her eyes shut, cringing. It would break her heart to see Leo retire his cowboy-ness.

●　●　●

Wednesday evening, Brynn whipped up cake batter to make little cakes. Chocolate, vanilla, lemon, coconut, carrot, red velvet, over and over and over. Callie had only twelve small cake tins, so the baking was slow going, but that allowed Brynn time to be cautious in mixing and folding ingredients. With each small batch she made, the easier it became. "Repetition," Callie said, "is the secret of the restaurant industry. You do something often enough and it becomes second nature. You become an expert at it."

Brynn enjoyed being in the kitchen with Callie, watching her, learning from her. Callie was in constant motion, yet with a remarkable economy of movement in a small space. She reminded Brynn of an athlete, so well trained and experienced that she could anticipate each step. Graceful, no flailing about the kitchen hunting for ingredients the way Brynn was doing. It was humbling and inspiring, both.

Brynn had always been a bit smug over her own top-notch natural organization skills. Even Dawn, who was hard to impress, had been wowed by Brynn's ability to maximize space in a tiny dorm room. Organizing came naturally to Brynn; it was how her mind made order out of things. Later, her apartment was just as well organized. Spices in alphabetical order. Clothes lined up in the closet by color, from dark to light.

But she had met her match in Callie.

Callie's mental organization surpassed Brynn's. The careful way she prepped and lined up ingredients before starting something, the deliberate way she moved ingredients from left to right so she knew they'd been used, the steady cleanup as she went. Deliveries were starting to arrive for the wedding, some members from an advanced cooking class came to help prep, and she was able to both delegate and supervise, keeping the kitchen humming along.

Brynn had been allotted the use of one corner of the large kitchen, over near the ovens and away from the prepping. Callie called it a workstation. Brynn could work undistracted by whatever was going on in the kitchen. The only problem was that the better the cakes got, the less she needed to concentrate so intently on every step as she made them. And that meant that her mind was free to keep floating to thoughts of TD.

Dawn had wanted her to call the Safety in the Workplace Conference manager today—she was emphatic about the urgency—and ask for TD's contact info. Brynn should've. She could've. But she didn't.

Dawn would want to know why she couldn't have found two minutes to make one phone call. Brynn could lie and tell her that the cake making thoroughly consumed her and remind her that she was doing a big favor for Lincoln's daughter.

But the truth was that the moment she contacted TD, it would mean the dissolution of their impulsive marriage would begin. It needed to be dissolved. It was a terrible mistake.

No. It wasn't a *terrible* mistake. But it was a mistake. No one in their right mind should marry on a whim.

So why didn't she make that call to the conference manager? Why was she stalling?

She supposed it was the conversation she'd had with Marnie.

She made it sound as if Brynn might have had another reason for making such a rash decision. She asked if Brynn had felt she'd been needing a change, and she'd had no answer for her.

It was true that Brynn had a vague feeling of emptiness this last year. It came right after she received a big promotion—the one she'd been aiming for since she started at the firm out of college. She'd hit her target, a few years ahead of schedule. Nipping at her heels were these thoughts: *Is this all there is? What do I do with the rest of my life?*

The oven timer went off, jolting Brynn back to the present. She put on mitts and took out the chocolate cakes. No cracks. Pulling slightly away from the edges. The darkness of chocolate made it tricky to judge when the cake was properly baked. She pressed a finger lightly and was pleased by how each cake held its shape. She set them on the counter to cool, and as she pulled off her oven mitts, she realized Callie was standing nearby, a cell phone in her hand, a stricken look on her face. "Deidre Klassen just called."

"Let me guess. Another change order?"

"Yes."

Brynn almost laughed. Almost. Callie's somber tone stifled it.

"Apparently, the bride's brother has been raving about the vanilla ice cream at the Main Street Creamery. They'd like it served at the wedding."

Brynn felt her shoulders relax. That request belonged squarely in Dawn's department.

Callie's gaze swept the counter of cooling mini-wedding cakes. Over one hundred of them, baked to perfection.

Brynn's shoulders tensed up. "Something else?"

"The bride's mother added her own twist. She wants the ice cream served inside the mini-wedding cakes."

Brynn swallowed. "Ice cream cake."

Slowly, Callie nodded.

"During a heat wave."

Callie nearly buckled. Brynn saw hesitation flit through her eyes. But then she recovered and a firm resolve returned. "We can do this, Brynn. It'll be an incredible challenge, but we can do it!" She lifted two fists in the air.

Could we? Brynn wasn't so sure.

● ● ●

Callie
Good news! Big, big order for your Double-Fold Vanilla!

Dawn
???

Bear Hayes tried it and liked it so much that he talked it up to his mother. She tried it too! And now she wants it served at Ashleigh's wedding.

But . . . that means . . .

Yep. I need 30 quarts by Friday noon.

Chapter
ELEVEN

Sometimes if you've got a story that's interesting enough, you don't need to pour sugar on ice cream. The ice cream is great.

—actor Paul Schneider

Dawn had planned for a quiet evening alone with Kevin to talk over the options of fertility treatment with him, hoping she could convince him to join her at the next appointment. That was the plan. She'd even texted him and told him to come home early, that she'd be making his favorite dinner of sloppy joes—her code word to hint at a night of romance.

A month ago, Dawn had surprised Kevin with sloppy joes for dinner, and he had been so touched by her effort that it led to a very amorous night together. Start-up businesses were exciting and satisfying, but the demands took a toll on a marriage. Kevin worked late and Dawn got up early. If one wasn't exhausted, the other one was. Opportunities for romance were all too rare. They took some strategizing, some planning. And then plans were often waylaid because of a work crisis.

This time, the crisis belonged to her.

Not only would she be unable to enjoy a quiet evening with Kevin, but she would hardly see him over the next few days. Instead, she'd be spending every spare minute at the Creamery making batch after batch of Double-Fold Vanilla ice cream . . . for a bride she'd never even met. For a mother of the bride who enjoyed making this wedding as difficult as it could possibly be.

A few hours ago, Dawn had walked into the cooking school to take some requested groceries to Brynn and was immediately informed by Callie that the bride's mother now wanted the mini-wedding cakes to be mini–ice cream wedding cakes. Dawn's jaw dropped. "Ice cream inside the cake. Does this woman not realize that Chatham is having a heat wave?"

Without missing a beat as she put groceries away, Callie answered. "Yes, she does realize that. Yes, it is going to be a major accomplishment to keep those ice cream cakes frozen until dessert is served."

"How? Ice cream is all about staying frozen! I feel panicky even as I take the ice cream out of the machine, get it into a container, and walk it three steps to the freezer. Crystals start forming. Iciness threatens. The taste of the ice cream will be ruined."

"DiDi is checking into bringing in additional freezers. Warming ovens, too, for the entrées."

So now, Dawn noted, it was Didi, not Deidre Klassen. Buddy-buddy. Chummy.

"We'll figure something out," Callie said. "If nothing else, I told her to bring in nitrous oxide to keep the ice cream cold."

Dawn gasped. "You wouldn't dare! Not my ice cream!"

Callie stopped putting onions in a bowl to look at Dawn. "I would dare. Nitrous oxide is an industry trick. In a pinch, it'll do the job."

Dawn had to sit down. This whole thing made her queasy. At least the cooking school was empty of students and she could speak her mind. "Why can't Deidre Klassen just tell this mother no?"

"I asked the same question. This is one of those high-end, no-expense-spared kinds of weddings. Didi was told there was no budget. None. So without a budget to worry about, this mother is going to do whatever strikes her fancy. And, apparently, no one says no to the bride's mother." She went back to her onions. "Ashleigh Hayes keeps sending me apology texts for all her mother's changes."

"So Ashleigh's not on board with her mother's wish list?"

"I think she just wants to get married and has left the details of the wedding to her mother to take care of. I have a hunch there's a lot more going on than the wedding."

"What do you mean?"

"Well, speaking from my experience in the restaurant world, this is the ex-wife's chance to stick it to Lincoln."

"Poor Lincoln." Dawn leaned back in the chair. "I thought Linc's ex-wife married a librarian. In my head, I had her pictured as the kind of woman who rescued stray cats."

"That," Callie said, "is an incorrect stereotype about librarians. They don't all like cats. And from what Didi has hinted about the bride's mother, she's living easy from the divorce settlement."

Dawn shook her head. "Poor, poor Lincoln."

"Look at it this way," Callie said. "Your ice cream is going to be enjoyed by hundreds of well-connected people with refined tastes. This wedding is good for the Main Street Creamery."

Dawn gave her a look. "You're using Mom's sales pitch on me. This wedding is going to be good for the Intuitive Cooking School."

"Well, she's right." Brynn, standing guard by the ovens, hadn't said a word until now. "And that was before Didi told us that the wedding might be on *The Knot*."

"No promises." But Callie had an ear-to-ear grin on her face. "But Didi thinks there's a better-than-not chance it'll be featured."

Callie and Brynn exchanged a high five. Their eyes were shining. More buddy-buddy stuff had been going on while Dawn was in Hyannis today. *Annoying.* She didn't like feeling left out. It was junior high all over again.

A cell phone chirped. Callie spun around, grabbed her phone off the counter, held it up with an "It's Didi," and went outside to take the call.

Brynn opened the fridge to grab two water bottles. She crossed the room and handed one to Dawn. "You look like you could use some cold water."

"Thank you." Dawn opened the lid, took a swig of water, and swallowed it down. "It is so hot out there. So humid it's hard to breathe." She tipped her head. "Is Callie wearing you out?" She stopped herself from adding "yet."

"Just the opposite. She is a master at time management. She works backward from the clock."

Midsip, Dawn stopped. "Backward?"

"Before she starts something, she figures out how much time she has to give it and then allots incremental time from the end point to the start point. I've never thought to go backward like that. It's an incredibly efficient use of time. She even sets timers when she's mixing. Not just for when she's cooking or baking, but timers to keep her on track. She has timers all over this kitchen." As Callie came back in, Brynn smiled. "Were your ears burning? I was singing your praises to Dawn."

A big smile spread over Callie's face. "Right back atcha. I was just telling Didi that you are a dream to work with and that we can handle any changes the mother of the bride throws at us."

Brynn coughed a laugh. "Don't tell me that Didi called with more changes."

"Just a few. I'll go over the details with you right after . . ." She cast a glance at Dawn.

After Dawn leaves to go make ice cream, was what Callie meant. Dawn finished off the bottle of water, trying not to seem miffed. But she was. She wasn't needed here.

Callie had once confessed that she'd always felt superfluous around Dawn and Brynn. Now Dawn was the one looking in from the outside and it wasn't a very comfortable place to be. She was a little jealous of their obvious affection for each other. "Sounds like you two have got a lot of work to do." She tried very hard to mask the pettiness that was swirling around in her stomach like she'd eaten an underripe apple.

Callie seemed to sense what Dawn was feeling. She came from around the kitchen island and knelt in front of her, grabbing her hands. "We are going to pull off this wedding, Dawn. It's going to be a triumph for us. For all of us." Callie turned to Brynn. "Something wonderful is just around the corner."

The look on Brynn's face! So hopeful. Dawn cringed.

● ● ●

Dawn
I'm so sorry but our sloppy joe dinner is canceled. The bride's mother now wants ice cream at the wedding. Served inside mini–wedding cakes. During a heat wave. Don't even ask me how I feel about this.

Kevin
I have to work late, anyway.

Uh . . . did I mention I was serving sloppy joes?

No worries. I had a big lunch today. I bumped into Lincoln's son at city hall when I was pulling permits. He invited me to go to lunch at Lily's.

Really? So what did you think of Bear?

Smart guy! Really interested in the house restoration company. Wanted to hear all about it. He didn't know that his dad had gotten involved in the construction company.

As bright a guy as Kevin was in some areas, he could be a little naive with people. He trusted them until there was a reason not to. Dawn felt the opposite. She wondered what Kevin might have let slip out that shouldn't have been said. Just as she was about to text him, she saw bubbles forming that meant a text would soon arrive.

> Lily's had a special today. Sloppy joes! Biggest, best one I've ever had. I don't think I'll be able to eat one again for months.

Great. That's just great.

• • •

Marnie hadn't heard from Lincoln all day, though she hardly had a minute to catch her breath. Dawn couldn't help with customers because she had to make Double-Fold Vanilla ice cream.

"We need more than vanilla ice cream," Marnie said. "We're running low on everything."

Distracted, Dawn unpacked boxes of milk and cream cartons, sugar, and vanilla beans. "Mom, I will stay here all night if I have to. I need to get thirty quarts of Double-Fold Vanilla ice cream made for Ashleigh Dixon's wedding as quickly as I can. Otherwise, Callie will be breathing down my neck. She's all fired up about this wedding and Didi Klassen and *The Knot*."

"*The Knot*?"

Dawn's head was in the refrigerator as she moved things around. "It's a wedding website. Big one. Apparently, there's a good chance Ashleigh's wedding will be featured." She closed the refrigerator door and pulled pots out of the cupboard, setting them on the stove. "Callie seems to think that this will be a boon for the Intuitive Cooking School." She gave Marnie a look. "Someone put that notion in her head."

Me, she realized.

Dawn glanced at her. "Yep. You."

"It really should help Callie's business."

"And Callie is convinced that the Main Street Creamery will get a nod if my Double-Fold Vanilla ice cream is as good as Bear Hayes says it is."

"Bear Hayes?" Marnie tried not to make her voice sound flat, but it did. She let out a dispirited sigh. "Maybe it would help to remember that we are doing this for Lincoln."

Dawn was down on her knees, searching through a cupboard. "It does help." She found the bowl she was looking for and straightened up. "But I can't wait until this weekend is over and life can get back to normal for everyone."

A thought occurred to Marnie. "What will be normal for Brynn?"

With a shrug, Dawn lifted her palms in the air. "I haven't even had time to solve Brynn's problem."

"How so?"

"Finding her a lawyer to dissolve their . . . marriage."

Marnie gave that some serious consideration while Dawn started to crack eggs into a bowl. The silence went on so long that Dawn finally paused and gave her a look. "What? I know you're thinking something. Just say it."

"I just don't think this is your problem to solve. It's Brynn's."

"I'm only helping her find a good lawyer. She's not in a good state of mind to make decisions. This cake baking is actually a blessing in disguise for her. The way Callie is depending on her has been good for her. She seems more like herself than when she first got here."

"I've wondered if—"

"Mom." Dawn picked up an egg and went back to cracking, a little harder than before. "I've got it handled. Brynn made a mistake. That's all. It can be fixed, as soon as I find a lawyer and she tracks down the contact info for her . . . twenty-four-hour husband."

"It's just that—"

"That's all there is to it. These things happen, especially in Las Vegas."

"I was going to say," Marnie said a little more forcefully, "that maybe she didn't make a mistake."

Dawn stopped cracking eggs to stare at her. "You've got to be kidding me."

"I'm not. This whole situation is so unlike Brynn."

"Exactly!"

"Which makes me wonder if she did know what she was doing." Marnie patted her heart. "Deep down. Bone-deep. Something instinctive. Intuitive."

Dawn had a look on her face like she thought her mother had lost her marbles. "Mom, this is Brynn. She puts no stock in your hippy-dippy stuff."

Fine. Never mind.

Marnie turned and got down two cups from the cabinet beside the sink. She might as well get a pot of coffee going. She was going to need it to stay awake until the Creamery closed tonight at ten o'clock. Whose big idea was it to keep the shop open so late on summer nights, anyway?

Mine.

● ● ●

Late that night, Lincoln finally texted Marnie back.

> **Linc**
> Sorry to be MIA! Busy day getting the cottage ready for the wedding. Furniture moved out. Rental furniture moved in.

> **Marnie**
> How are you doing?

> Good. Fine. Well, pretty good.

Pause. She waited to see if he would elaborate. He didn't.

119

Everything OK?

> Yes, a little . . . disappointed. Ashleigh asked her brother to walk her down the aisle.

But I thought she asked you to walk her down the aisle!

> She did, but there was a change of plans. Not to worry. All good.

Marnie didn't need to ask anything more.

Chapter
TWELVE

My brain said salad but my stomach autocorrected it to
ice cream.

—Unknown

It was after midnight. Dawn was cleaning up the Creamery
kitchen after making six quarts of Double-Fold Vanilla ice cream.
Each batch took her two hours to prepare and make. She was
pouring water through the ice cream machine to clean it when
the back door opened and Brynn walked in, looking tired but
happy. "Have you finished?"

"Not even close." Brynn set her purse down on a small bench
by the door.

"But you've been baking all day!"

"Callie only accepts cakes that are absolutely flawless."

Dawn rolled her eyes. "And here I thought you and I were the
world's biggest perfectionists."

"Right?" Brynn leaned against the counter. "We have been
trumped by your cousin."

"I'm sorry." She handed Brynn a spoon of vanilla ice cream.

"Don't be. I'm thoroughly enjoying it." She swallowed the ice cream and gave a thumbs-up. "There is so much to learn from Callie."

"So you said." Dawn was at the sink, emptying the container of milky water that had shot out the barrel of the ice cream machine. "Her time management skills."

"More than that, though time management is critical. I'd never thought much about it before, but I've seen the difference it makes in her classes. She sets her students up for success."

"What else?" As much as Dawn admired her cousin's skills, she didn't think she had anything to learn from Callie. Maybe a little, but not much. "What else are you learning from her?"

"Callie says there are three critical steps to improving one's kitchen skills."

"Like what?"

"Repetition, she says, is key. Do something often enough and you will nail it."

Dawn let the last bit of water run down the barrel of the ice cream machine before she closed the latch. "Like . . . Double-Fold Vanilla ice cream."

"Exactly." Brynn let out a laugh. "And another one is to learn the art of mise en place."

"Everything in its place."

"Yes, especially when it comes to the prep. Get everything for the recipe all set up, completely organized, and you'll not only enjoy yourself more, but you'll increase chances for success."

"I do that."

"Really?"

Dawn looked around the kitchen, frowning. Ingredients covered the counter. Maybe she had a little room for improvement.

"Callie has the kitchen organized so everyone knows where everything is. She has labels on practically everything. You open up that freezer and instantly know what something is and when it was made. Same thing in the fridge. Cupboards, shelves. Labels everywhere." Brynn glanced at the row of glass containers that lined the back of the counter, holding ice cream scoopers, flour, white and brown sugar, oatmeal. "I wondered if . . . you had ever thought of organizing the Creamery's kitchen with some of Callie's methods."

A knot of annoyance started creeping into Dawn's stomach. Eighteen months ago, Callie had first come to the Creamery during the winter, the season Dawn and her mom relied heavily on baked goods and coffee sales to supplement the shop's income. For obvious reasons, winter was the toughest season to weather in a beach town: ice cream wasn't the first thing people craved on a bitter cold day. And Chatham's many local snowbirds flew off to Florida or Arizona or somewhere warm and sunny right after Christmas, not returning until April.

Apparently, Callie hadn't felt Dawn's baked goods were up to her standards. But she didn't say so. Instead, she crept down in the night to bake and replace. Dawn realized the nightly swap-outs only after the shop began buzzing with activity. Customers clamored for the Creamery's muffins and pastries. Callie's, *not* Dawn's.

Also, Callie had determined that Dawn's organization system was logical only to Dawn and no one else. So she began another middle-of-the-night secret hobby: reorganizing the kitchen. *Dawn's* kitchen.

But Brynn had no idea that she was hitting Dawn's sore spots. She carried on, oblivious to Dawn's growing discomfort. "Callie said something so interesting. She said that whenever she's in other people's kitchens, she realizes why they feel so stressed when they cook."

Eyes down, Dawn remembered a time when Callie had come for dinner in her Boston apartment. She had watched Dawn cut an onion and then pushed her right out of the kitchen. Literally. Callie took over the meal preparation and cooking.

"Another thing," Brynn said. "Clean as you go."

Thinking back to that onion-cutting moment in her apartment, Dawn remembered watching Callie tidy up as she worked. By the time the meal was prepared, the kitchen was spotless.

Dawn cast a glance at a stack of used bowls. The sink was overflowing with so many dirty dishes that she had set more on the floor.

"And another tip of Callie's is to invest in really, really good knives."

Okay. Time to change the subject. The knives at the Creamery were terrible. It was like cutting with a stick. "I was expecting you would have brought back a cake so we could see how much ice cream would be needed for each one."

Brynn clapped a palm to her forehead. "I should've thought to bring one. There were plenty of not-quite-good-enough-to-pass-Callie's-high-standards ones to spare." She dropped her hand. "Tomorrow. I'll bring a few back to the Creamery tomorrow."

"I know it was a busy day, but I hope you made time to track down TD's contact info. At least to get the ball rolling."

Brynn winced, as if she'd just been stung by an insect. "Um, I didn't. Callie kept me so busy that I didn't have a minute to spare."

"I made a start. I did some digging. I found out the difference between an annulment and a divorce." Dawn rinsed the pitcher of water and set it in the rack to air-dry. "An annulment acts as if the marriage never happened. A divorce ends a valid marriage. Obviously, an annulment is what we want to get for you." When Brynn didn't say anything, she turned to see if she was listening. There was a look on her face that she couldn't quite read. "You okay?"

"Yeah, yeah. Obviously. An annulment sounds like the right path." Her voice sounded a little vague.

"But there's a glitch. There are very few reasons to get an annulment in the state of Massachusetts. Apparently, trying to prove grounds for annulment is much harder than proving grounds for divorce."

"How so?"

Dawn shrugged. "Divorces can be no-fault. With an annulment, you have to prove why the marriage was invalid. Fraud, for example."

"Fraud?"

"For example, could he have used a fake name?"

Brynn's eyes went wide. "You think he was an imposter? No. Absolutely not. No way. Not a chance."

"How well could you have known this guy? I mean, I realize you were swept away by passion, but think of all the things you *didn't* talk about. The concrete details you have about him are so skimpy."

"Concrete details? So you think if I knew his Social Security number, then there'd be less to doubt about his character?"

"It just sounds to me like he could be hiding something."

"Like what?"

"Oh Brynn." Dawn shook her head woefully. "I hate to say this, but it occurred to me that he might already be married. To someone else."

Brynn opened her mouth, closed it. Her brow furrowed. "I hadn't thought of that." She covered her face with her hands.

That's exactly what bothered Dawn! Brynn hadn't thought about a lot of things. Dawn was trying her best to be diplomatic about the situation. "This is why the data says that you should never rush into a relationship. The data on dating says to take plenty of time."

Brynn dropped her hands to look at Dawn. "Data . . . on dating?"

"Yes. Exactly." *People* magazine data. Earlier today, Dawn had read through an issue while she was waiting at the fertility clinic. "Couples should have at least fifteen to twenty dates before becoming exclusive with each other. And the data recommends at least three to four months of dating before anything serious happens."

"Dating data." Brynn frowned. Her voice held a tone of skepticism.

"Yes. Enough time has to pass because someone can't hide 'crazy' for long."

"You can't hide crazy?"

"Well, according to the data, you can't hide crazy for more than ten minutes. But frankly, I think you can. I don't mean to add salt to a wound, but TD sounds like a sketchy dude."

"Sketchy . . . as in you think he's crazy?"

"Sketchy as in . . . not the guy he pretended to be. If he is already married, that could actually be good news."

"How so?"

Dawn couldn't quite parse Brynn's matter-of-fact tone. "Well, that would mean your Las Vegas wedding would be automatically null and void. No annulment needed, no divorce." She snapped her fingers. "Over and done with, like it never happened." Watching Brynn, she tried to read her reaction, but her face was turned to the open window. The faint sound of a dog barking somewhere down the road pierced the quiet night. "That would make life easy, right?"

Brynn lifted her head. "TD just didn't seem like the kind of person who would lie about being married."

"No? Well, by now he should've been able to figure out how to get in touch with you and he hasn't, right?"

Brynn shrugged, but her eyes were shiny.

"You've got to be logical. You just can't be naive about this guy. There's a good chance that he's a complete fraud."

Crushed. That's how Brynn looked.

Squaring her shoulders, Brynn went to the bottom of the stairs and turned. "I'm too tired for this discussion right now. I need to get some sleep. Callie wants me back at the cooking school at the crack of dawn. See you in the morning."

Dawn listened to Brynn's footsteps climb the stairs and hit the squeaky step, and then she heard the bedroom door gently close.

She could hear Brynn moving about upstairs. A wave of fatigue rolled over Dawn as she gazed at the mess on the countertops, the pile of dishes in the sink, the batches of Double-Fold Vanilla still to be made tonight. She thought of Callie's systems and wondered what the day and night would've been like if she'd employed some of her time management ideas. Maybe she could learn something from her cousin.

And maybe she shouldn't have been quite so direct with Brynn. Everything Dawn told her was true, but it could've waited until after a good night's sleep. They were both exhausted, plus facing more hard days of work to prepare for Ashleigh Hayes's grandiose wedding. All the brilliant insights Dawn had explained to Brynn tonight could've waited for a better time. Should've waited. Timing was everything, Kevin often reminded her.

She turned her attention back to the mountain of soapy dishes, feeling discouraged. About Brynn's predicament with her twenty-four-hour marriage, about her own predicament with infertility. This day had started out with such promise. It had ended with a thud.

●　●　●

Brynn brushed her teeth after changing into her pajamas, furious. Why did Dawn have to go and ruin a perfectly good day? Why did she have to remind her that TD hadn't made any effort to contact her? He hadn't. Brynn didn't think he would . . . after all, she was the one who left him sleeping in the hotel room. No note. No explanation. No nothing.

She did a terrible thing by leaving. She could see that clearly now.

As she put her toothbrush back in her makeup bag, she noticed the little paper ring TD had made for her, the one they had used during their wedding ceremony.

Dawn had asked her what they talked about during their brief courtship. Everything! Well, nearly everything. It was like they'd skipped over the first part of getting to know someone and started in the middle. Like they already knew each other, understood each other.

She slipped the paper ring on her finger, remembering.

They'd left the conference to drive out to the Hoover Dam, only about forty minutes away. There, they walked around it, getting a picture of themselves in front of the Memorial Bridge. It was an engineering feat that spanned the Colorado River. On one side was Nevada, the other side was Colorado. They hiked until the heat was too much to handle. It was a dry heat, easier to endure than Boston's high humidity, but oppressive in its own way. They took a guided tour of the dam, and it was just like he'd said—they both geeked out on the engineering aspects. Finally, hungry after missing lunch, they headed back into Las Vegas to get dinner. Brynn had never enjoyed a first date more. The time flew by, and yet it felt like they were just getting started. There were no pauses, no awkward moments. Like they were in sync.

At the restaurant, they'd talked so long after dinner that the waiter finally brought them dessert in a to-go box. "On the house," he said.

TD cast a sideways glance at Brynn. "I think we've overstayed," he whispered. As he paid the bill, she noticed he doubled the tip, and she found such quiet generosity to be touching. Frankly, by this point of the evening, everything about him was impressive to her. He asked her so many questions and listened so carefully, and he talked too. About his emotions! When had she ever, ever known a guy who could talk about feelings? Never. Not her dad, not her many stepfathers. Before the waiter had interrupted them with dessert, TD had been telling her how hurt he had felt when his parents divorced. He blamed his father for it. He said he knew he needed to work it through, but something inside him felt hardened toward his father.

"Is your dad in your life now?"

"It's way too late for that."

"Is it? One thing I've learned from being on a lot of construction sites—things can always get fixed. Made right. Even situations you'd assume were irrevocably broken or unsolvable. There's always a way to fix it. In fact, that's my job. Fixing the unfixable."

"But you're talking about inanimate objects."

"I meant the same for animate objects. Things can get good again."

"Think so? Even with people?"

She smiled. "Especially with people."

"It's a nice thought."

"More than a thought. I've seen forgiveness produce miracles. My best friend was engaged to be married and the groom called everything off just weeks before the wedding. Everyone in our friend circle thought those two were done. Over. I sure did. But little by little, they started to connect, then talk, then address the problems between them that had been getting ignored." She lifted her palms in the air. "And now they're happily married."

"Just like that?" He fixed his eyes on her and let them speak for him. Full of skepticism.

She'd already learned to read his eyes. "You doubt me?"

"Not doubt, exactly. It just sounds like you're crediting forgiveness with your friend's happy-ever-after ending."

"I do. I'm not saying it was easy, but forgiveness set things into motion for them."

While Brynn had been talking, TD had been absentmindedly folding the customer receipt left by the waiter. It ended up as a little paper ring, with one edge slotted into the other almost like a dovetail joint. He held it out to her on his open palm and flashed her a sudden, startling smile. "For you. A memory of our wonderful day together."

She picked it up and fit it on a finger on her right hand. She wondered if she had said too much, gone too deep too fast, if maybe he had tuned her out while she'd been chattering away about Dawn and Kevin's story. She thought it was an incredible love story all woven together with forgiveness, but maybe he didn't see it that way.

And then he surprised her.

"There's a family gathering coming up," TD said. "I've been on the fence about going, but you've got me thinking I should reconsider." He put his hand over hers, the one with the paper ring on it, and she felt her pulse leap. "Maybe"—he flashed a smile—"you could come with me."

Her eyes widened a little. "Me?" To meet his family?! That seemed like a huge step. Not that she wasn't interested—she was. "Me?"

"You. You're in Boston, right? So am I." His face as he looked at her was tender, solicitous, and she felt a yearning within her. His touch, his smile, his everything. "Until today, I don't think I've realized how lonely I've been, or how long I've been lonely. I'd like you with me. Maybe you're right. Maybe a miracle will happen." He squeezed her hand, the one with the paper ring. "I have a hunch you seem to have a knack for bringing out the best in people."

His fingers tightened over her hand, and for a moment she forgot about everyone else in the restaurant. It was only the two of them. Everything intensified, every nerve in her body was tingly, the air was electric. Her heart was thundering so loudly that she was sure he could hear it pound. He leaned slightly toward her to cradle her cheek tenderly. "You are so beautiful," he said, before he kissed her. No passionate kiss, this, but a tentative, gentle touch. He kissed her again . . . lightly . . . lightly . . . the brush of a butterfly wing. And suddenly the waiter was back at their table, clearing his throat in a loud way.

They got the hint. They had left the restaurant and strolled down the street, hand in hand.

Slowly, sadly, she slipped the little paper ring off her finger and put it back in her makeup bag. Dawn's question kept circling, buzzing like a mosquito. *TD hasn't tried to find you, has he?*

No. No, he hadn't. And she would be easy for him to find. He held the marriage certificate. He knew her last name. He knew of the engineering company she worked for. It wouldn't be hard to call her office and ask them to forward his information to her. If he'd wanted to find her, he could've. Would've.

Maybe Dawn was right. Maybe Brynn had been duped by TD's charm and good looks. Maybe he was a complete fraud.

She curled into a ball on the bed, miserable.

● ● ●

Callie
How's that Double-Fold Vanilla coming?

Dawn
Six quarts made and in the freezer. Why are you still up? It's nearly one in the morning.

Too much to do! Plenty of time to sleep after the wedding.

Well, I'm going to bed.

Before you go, one last thing . . . I know I asked for 30 quarts. I think we're going to need more.

CALLIE! We can talk about this in the morning. I'm going to bed. You should go too!

Chapter
THIRTEEN

> When I was a kid, I used to think, "Man, if I could ever afford all the ice cream I want to eat, that's as rich as I ever want to be."
>
> —country singer Jimmy Dean

Thursday, June 30

It was early, only five thirty in the morning, yet Marnie could tell they were in for a scorcher. The air was so still that even the bugs weren't chirping, the birds weren't singing. Life didn't sit well with her when the thermometer climbed over ninety-five, especially when the humidity was high too.

A long day of scooping ice cream lay ahead of Marnie, all alone in the shop because Callie's, Dawn's, and Brynn's time was completely booked up by Ashleigh Hayes's lavish wedding reception. She felt very sorry for herself and decided to go to the beach before breakfast. A walk along the ocean would help reset her bad mood.

As she tied the laces on her sneakers, she thought about texting Linc to see if he could join her. It was a regular tradition of theirs, those early morning beach walks, but if he didn't answer back or, worse, texted that he was too busy, it would only add to her crankiness.

Bear Hayes was the reason for the mood she was in. To think that he had the gall to bump Linc from his role of walking his only daughter down the aisle. How dare that boy! Who did Bear think he was?

Good grief. Why didn't Lincoln stand up for himself? After all, he was still Bear's father. He was Ashleigh's father. He was trying to make up for years when he let work override family time.

Yeah, Marnie probably shouldn't try to contact Linc this morning. She would say too much. She pulled an elastic band around her hair to form a ponytail and opened the bathroom door just as Brynn opened her bedroom door. "You're already dressed? It's not even six o'clock!"

"I'm due at Callie's. More baking. Hopefully, I can finish the baking this morning and then start icing cakes this afternoon." She followed Marnie down the narrow stairs.

"I didn't even hear you come in last night."

"I arrived just as Dawn was finishing up. That reminds me." She went to the freezer and opened it. "I should take a carton or two of vanilla to do some trial runs with the cakes." She grabbed two containers. "Callie is rather keen on trial runs."

Marnie went into the broom closet and came out with a small cooler. "You're working very hard for someone you don't even know. I'm a little concerned that you've taken time off to try to sort out your life . . . and you've been roped into baking all day, every day."

"I really don't mind." Brynn closed the freezer door with her hip. "In fact, just the opposite. Being busy with something I love to do is just what I've needed. I've always enjoyed baking, and this is an incredible chance to learn from Callie. And it's helped to keep my mind off of . . . things."

Marnie took the ice cream quarts from Brynn to set inside

and close tight. She might not have Dawn's ice cream making talent, but she knew that keeping ice cream frozen was critically important. "So about that *thing*. What's been happening?"

"Nothing. Well, nothing except my denial. I know I need to deal with it sooner or later." She lifted her eyebrows. "Dawn will see to that."

Oh dear. Marnie could easily imagine how Dawn might spearhead a resolution to Brynn's twenty-four-hour marriage. She would go full steam ahead as a means to protect her friend.

Brynn walked to the back door holding the cooler in one hand. "Do you think I'm making a mistake by putting it on the back burner for now?"

"Do I think it's a mistake to set it on the back burner? No. Just the opposite. I think time can provide a needed perspective. I hope you won't let Dawn talk you into anything you don't want to do."

"She's not. I definitely need to take care of this."

"Maybe a starting place would be to have a long talk with your groom."

That word made Brynn twitch, almost as if she'd been stung by a bee. Interesting. Until just this minute, it hadn't occurred to Marnie how carefully Brynn avoided mentioning his name or talking about their brief wedding as anything more than a *thing* that needed legal attention. "Brynn, what do you think made you say yes to marrying TD?"

Brynn had been in the middle of reaching up to grab her purse off the wall peg and stilled at the question. "I've given that some thought and decided it was attraction. A powerful one. But attraction isn't real love."

"Even in the best of marriages, real love comes later."

Marnie couldn't see her face, but she hoped she was listening. "Brynn, this marriage happened for a reason. Slow down and find out why."

Brynn turned, looping her purse strap over her shoulder. "I'll try." She opened the door to leave.

"You can take my car. I don't need it today. I'll be manning the shop all day."

"Thanks, but I can use the exercise. It's really not far to get to Callie's. Everything and everyone in Chatham seem pretty close."

In one way, that was true. In another way, Marnie felt very far away from Lincoln.

Halfway out the door, Brynn turned back. "Sure you'll be okay in the shop all alone today? I feel a little guilty."

"Don't. I'll be fine." Just as the door nearly closed, Marnie called out. "Brynn. Hold it a second. Has it occurred to you that your heart might be trying to send you a message?"

Brynn's face went flat. "My heart? It's talking to me?"

"Yes. Your heart might be trying to get through to you. Call it your heart, your gut instincts, your bone-deep feelings."

"Honestly, Marnie, I have no idea what you're trying to say."

Marnie knew just what other thoughts were flitting through Brynn's mind, because the expression on her face was so like Dawn's. *Sounds like one of your hippy-dippy sayings.* Well, too bad. Someone needed to say those kinds of things. "I can't help but think there is a good reason you married this guy. Some bone-deep feeling that told you this was the right man for you. For one brief moment in your life, your gut instinct overruled your logic. And now you're trying to smother it."

"Smother it?" Brynn seemed thoroughly baffled. "Can you smother your gut instinct?"

"Oh yes! Women do it all the time. We smother it, ignore it, override it. You and Dawn are particularly good at it. Callie, too, but she's gotten much better at listening. You should ask about her story sometime—how she ended up here."

"Dawn told me. Callie poisoned two hundred people at the Food Safety Conference."

Marnie frowned. "Not *that* part of her story. The part about how the whole experience brought her to a better place. How she learned to listen to her heart. Not just listen, but act on it.

Brynn, I truly believe God has given everyone, women especially, a wonderful intuitive sense and we just don't listen to it."

"But . . . how do you listen to it?"

Brynn had just raised an excellent question. *Now* they were getting somewhere. "It takes practice. Lots and lots of practice. But once you start, you'll get better and better at it. It's all about trust."

"Trusting your intuition?"

"Well, yes. But better still is to realize the intuition is a gift from God. Meant to help, guide, protect. God is at the source of that intuition. That's what I believe."

Brynn looked like she was actually considering Marnie's remarks. She opened her mouth to say something, but then a text chirped from her Apple watch and she looked at it—and the moment was lost. "Callie's waiting for me. I need to dash."

Marnie was left in the kitchen, frowning. Technology! It could give good things, but it was a thief too. It had just stolen a near-breakthrough moment for Brynn. She had dipped a toe in the water of faith, only to draw it out. Marnie had noticed this before in Brynn. She would spend Christmases and Easters with the Dixons, attend church eagerly, listen attentively—far more than Dawn did! Afterward, she would ask Marnie all kinds of questions about the significance of the holidays. But then she'd return to her daily life and set aside deeper matters. Important things.

This time, Marnie thought as she locked up the Creamery to go on her walk, *this time I'm going to pray that the Lord won't let deeper things in Brynn's life get set aside. Not this time.*

● ● ●

"Your heart might be trying to send you a message." It was a comment only Marnie Dixon would make, and it went straight to Brynn's soul. Did the heart really work that way? Or was Marnie right—that God was the source of intuition? Brynn believed in

God, vaguely, but she had never imagined him to work that way. Nudge people if they're going the wrong way. What did that say about choice? Yet something about the thought of a God who guided was very comforting, very reassuring. She looked up at the bright blue morning sky. "Well, if you're up there, you're invited to take the lead down here. I'm open to advice."

Light was just starting to fill the morning sky as Brynn walked along Main Street. She passed window boxes full of red geraniums—her favorite—admired big bushes of blue and pink hydrangeas that hid a building's foundation, ducked under cheerful flags that hung near thresholds. She loved the weathered silvery-gray shingles of most cottages' exteriors. Chatham seemed to have gathered all the best things about New England to showcase them. She wondered what it was like to live here year-round, if it still felt as magical in January and February. Probably, she thought. Even if it was quiet and peaceful, it would still be Chatham, a little town by the sea.

Why not live here?

What? Where had that thought come from?

You want to live in Chatham.

No I don't! I have an enviable life in Boston.

Enviable to whom? If you're not happy, why stay there?

She stopped abruptly. This was ridiculous. She was arguing with herself. She was losing her grip on reality.

This was probably how it started. One impulsive, irrational decision. Then another. Before you knew it, you were heavily medicated and watching *Bonanza* reruns all day long.

She turned a corner and nearly bumped right into a man trying to straighten a real estate For Sale sign by his mailbox. "Sorry!"

The man barely glanced at her. "No problem." He looked up at the little house and sighed. "It'll sell fast, which is just as well. The missus already bought a place in Florida."

"You're moving to Florida?"

"Retiring. Permanently. Me and the missus have been spending our winters down there, and she says it's time to hang up my rolling pin." He shook his foot. "It's the gout. Too hard to stand on my feet all day."

At that, Brynn's head snapped up and she stared at the little house. It might look like a little house, but it was actually a bakery.

● ● ●

Dawn put a hand out on Kevin's side of the bed, but it was empty. Cold too. She lifted her head. What time was it? The clock read eight o'clock and she groaned. She should've been up an hour or two ago. She needed to hurry to the grocery store and resupply the Creamery with milk, cream, and eggs. She'd made a dent in the batches of Double-Fold Vanilla per Callie's orders, but she hadn't had time to make enough ice cream for the shop's to-go freezer today. She'd noticed it was low in stock, which was good news for the shop. Bad news for the ice cream maker. She jumped out of bed and hurried to change.

Kevin came in with a cup of coffee for her. "You're finally awake. I thought you could use this."

It was a sweet gesture, but Kevin's coffee was awful. Just awful. She waved a hand in the air. "Thanks, but I need to keep moving. I have to get to the Creamery before Mom opens the freezer and realizes we don't have enough ice cream to last the day."

He swirled the coffee mug, then took a sip. "What do you think about adding hand-hewn beams in the kitchen?"

She frowned. "I loved exposed beams, but that kitchen already has such a low ceiling. Sometimes I think all the colonists must have been short like me. Bruno stopped by the other day to drop off Leo for a few hours, and he bumped his head on the doorframe. Coming in and going out."

"I was thinking of maybe . . . raising the kitchen ceiling. Opening it up to the roof rafters."

"Would that be historically accurate?" That was Kevin's constant drumbeat.

"It's the exterior that matters most. Like Callie's cooking school. The interior has wiggle room."

She hid a smirk. Then why wouldn't he agree to converting the fireplace to natural gas like the one at the Creamery? On a cold winter day, it was a gift to just flip a switch and see flames ignite. "Raising the kitchen ceiling would delay every other project on this house, wouldn't it?" Not that much progress was happening this summer. Kevin was thoroughly absorbed with finishing up another renovation to get it on the market before winter, which meant any project started for this house had been put on hold. It meant living with plywood flooring and no door on the bathroom. It meant living with open stud walls. That old saying "cobblers' children have no shoes" still rang true, Dawn rued. She didn't share that thought out loud.

Kevin leaned his back against the wall, one ankle over the other, sipping his awful coffee. "Your cell phone has been ringing. Someone in Hyannis has been working hard to get hold of you." Out of his pants pocket, he took her cell phone and handed it to her. At the door, he turned. "So what's going on in Hyannis?"

"Hyannis?" She busied herself with tying her sneakers.

"Yes. Hyannis. I happened to notice the caller ID."

"Oh?" She kept her head down and rummaged around her brain for excuses.

"Don't even try. You're a terrible liar."

That was true.

"Dawn. Look at me."

She kept tying her sneakers.

"You went to the fertility clinic, didn't you?"

Busted. With a sigh, she nodded. "Just for a consultation. Just to see what kind of options I might have."

"I thought this was a team effort."

Slowly, she sat up. "It is. I wanted to get some information, that's all. Knowledge makes me feel better. More empowered."

He gave her a "not buying it" look. "Knowledge makes you feel like you're in control. But this is a situation you can't control."

She sat on the edge of the bed. "Look, I know you think that we should give this time, but you aren't seeing it from a woman's point of view. Time is not helpful when it comes to trying to conceive a baby. Time is a thief."

"It's not just time that we should give. It's trust. Trusting God will bring us a baby at the right time. Trusting each other in this process. It always circles back to trust. And sneaking off to Hyannis to meet with a fertility specialist strikes me as the opposite of trust."

She looked up at him. He was right. She knew that. He always had a way of bringing her back to where she should've been in the first place. Their eyes held for several electric beats. "I'm sorry. I shouldn't have tried to keep this from you. I just feel so . . . panicky. I'm so afraid that I'll never be able to have a baby."

He sat down on the bed next to her. "I'm sorry too. I wish this were easier on you. I admit that I don't understand how the biological clock might feel as it ticks away." He shifted slightly on the bed and made her lift her chin to look at him. "So let's make a compromise."

"Like what?"

"Wait a year until we start the infertility process."

"A year from six months ago?"

He smiled. "Fine." He leaned over and kissed her lightly.

She waggled her eyebrows in her best come-hither look. "You missed my sloppy joes hint."

He scrunched up his face. "What hint?"

"See? You missed it again."

Slowly, understanding dawned in his eyes. "Sloppy joes is your hint for sex? Really? Wow. I will never look at another one in the same way." His face registered pleasure. He tucked both arms around her and gently pushed her backward on the bed. "There's no time like the present."

"Hold it. What about ice cream?"

Hovering over her, bearing his weight on both elbows, he kissed her on each cheek, then on the tip of her nose. "Ice cream," he said, kissing her on her lips, "can wait."

• • •

While Callie taught a cooking class about making French patisseries, Brynn remained at her workstation in a corner, near the ovens, mixing batter for the remaining cakes. Callie had said Didi promised her that the deadline had passed for any additional changes by the bride's mother, so they could carry on without worry. Brynn wondered. This mother of the bride seemed to take a devious delight in throwing curveballs, and Didi accommodated every pitch.

This afternoon, Brynn and Callie would start assembling the cakes into mini-tiers, then carve out a middle portion to fill with Dawn's Double-Fold Vanilla ice cream. The last step would be icing them.

Such intricate work! Brynn loved every minute of the detail work, which endeared her to Callie, as did her willingness to be taught. "You'd be surprised," Callie said, "how few students actually listen to me and take instruction to heart."

Brynn did. All morning long, she kept thinking about how much she was learning from Callie. About how much more there was to learn from her! Baking was manual labor, but there was also artistry involved. Creativity. Romance. Baking satisfied her in a way that she could never seem to make her parents understand. Or Dawn, either. All they saw was the manual labor, the low wages, the lack of formal education, the job insecurity.

She took a bowlful of cracked eggshells to the trash and saw it was overflowing, so she picked it up to take to the outdoor garbage bin. While there, she lifted her face to the sun for a pause.

What if . . . ?

No. Don't even open the door to that line of thinking.

What if I . . . ?

No. No, no, no, no, no. Don't say it.

What if I bought that little bakery?

She squeezed her eyes shut. *Ridiculous! First of all, I don't have ready cash and the baker's wife wants an all-cash offer. Second of all, my baking skills are pretty basic.*

Her eyes opened. *But look how quickly I learn! And when have I ever felt so satisfied with work?* A bone-deep good feeling, to borrow a Marnie-ism.

She closed her eyes again. Dawn would say she was just running away from her problems. From blowing things with TD, from feeling too embarrassed to return to work.

But she wasn't happy with her job. Not really. There wasn't much more to learn at work. She had even grown weary of living in Boston and fighting traffic and the cost of living and the crowds. Urban living took a toll.

What if—

"Brynn, are you all right?"

Her eyes popped open to find Callie standing in front of her, eyes filled with concern. Brynn's cheeks grew warm. "I'm fine. Just . . . enjoying the sunshine."

"As the class was leaving, I looked out the window and thought maybe you were having a stroke or something."

"No, no. Nothing like that." As they turned to head back into the cooking school, Brynn said, "Callie, do you think it's necessary to go to culinary school to run a bakery?"

"Not at all. You'd be surprised how few people in the food industry have gone to culinary school. I think you just need to be prepared for long hours and a lot of hard work." They walked a few more steps and then Callie stopped abruptly. "Get OUT!" Her face lit up. "Are you thinking of starting a bakery? Where? In Boston?" Her big brown eyes went wide. "Wait. Hold the phone. HERE? In Chatham?"

Brynn froze. She hadn't even officially formulated that thought into words—it had just been a feeling, a vague idea. Her mind spun as she tried to think of a way to deflect Callie's interest. But not denying it quickly just fed into Callie's suspicions.

"You are! Brynn, that would be so awesome!"

Too late.

"Chatham needs another bakery! There's one that's not bad, but he's always heading off to Florida. I tried to see if he'd bake Ashleigh Hayes's wedding cake and he turned me down flat. Said he was suffering from . . . what did he call it? A bout with the gout."

Brynn wasn't sure if she should end the conversation right now . . . or continue it. The need to confide in someone won out. "I had a chat with that very baker this morning on my way to your place. There was a new For Sale sign out in front of his bakery. I suppose that's what's got me dreaming."

"I love dreams! The bigger the better." Callie clapped her hands in happy little pats.

This woman's enthusiasm was dangerous, but exciting. More exciting than dangerous. "I love to bake, but running a bakery requires entirely different skill sets than civil engineering."

"You can take classes at the 4Cs. I can ask Bruno to bring home a catalog of classes." Her mouth formed an O. "Here's an even better idea! Negotiate with the baker so that he stays on a while to train you."

Brynn was starting to panic. Callie had already pushed this train out of the station. "Wait a minute. There's more to consider than my lack of experience." She rubbed her fingers together. "Money. The baker's wife wants an all-cash offer."

Arms folded, head leaning to one side, Callie gave this predicament serious thought.

At least she was slowing down. Brynn took the opportunity to present another point of view. A rational, clearheaded one. "Dawn would say that this is crazy. Impulsive. Foolish."

"Well, sure. Of course Dawn would say that. But she's also

running an ice cream shop. Don't forget that. She gave up her big-shot career in Boston to live in Chatham. So did Kevin, for that matter. He's got a master's degree in historical restoration and is flipping houses for a living. All risky moves. But I don't think they've regretted it for a second. I know so. They don't regret it."

Quietly, Brynn said, "They listened to their hearts."

"Exactly." Callie nodded vigorously.

"Is that how you opened your cooking school? Listened to your heart?"

"Absolutely. That, and one other thing. Here's the way I've learned to look at everything. If I knew I had only a year or two to live, what would I regret not doing while I had the chance?"

Brynn felt a chill run down her spine. Had she said yes to TD because she knew she would've forever regretted saying no?

"And you can afford this, right? I don't mean to pry, but Dawn has hinted you're a trust-fund baby."

Brynn opened her mouth to object, to minimize the question, but why bother? "Yes, I have the means to afford it. But I won't have access to the trust fund until I turn thirty-five." Her grandparents had set up her trust fund with that limitation because of her father's multiple divorces. Her father had blown through so much money that the grandparents put a stipulation on Brynn's inheritance, just in case.

Callie tapped her jaw with her finger. "So you need a bridge loan. I think I can help with that."

"Oh, Callie, no. I can't ask you for that."

"Me?" She placed her palm against her chest. "I didn't mean me. I would if I could, but I'm strapped with the cooking school. Barely keeping on top of things. But I do know of someone who might be willing to help you."

"Who?"

Scallop shells crunched as a car pulled into the parking lot. Callie's husband, Bruno, and Leo waved to them from the open car windows. Callie gave Brynn's upper arm a little squeeze.

"Leave this with me for now." She hurried over to meet them, and Brynn watched the little family gather, a pang in her heart. What was that feeling?

She saw Bruno give Callie a peck on the cheek, and she saw Leo show her his baseball cap.

A stab of envy pierced her. Now she knew what that feeling was. Envy. Brynn wanted the life that Callie had made for herself. She wanted all of it.

* * *

Callie
Do you know of a good realtor in Chatham? Really good. The kind who can seal the deal. I need one right now. Pronto!

Dawn
Yes. I'll send you his contact info.

Thanks!

Why do you ask?

Pause.

Callie?

Chapter
FOURTEEN

It was the color of someone buying you an ice cream cone for no reason at all.

—children's book character Lemony Snicket

Today was even busier in the Main Street Creamery than yesterday, which shouldn't have surprised Marnie and Dawn, not with more tourists arriving for the Fourth of July weekend. Dawn was in the kitchen, making batch after batch of ice cream, as Marnie manned the front of the shop. There was hardly a break, all day long, and as Marnie turned the POS tablet around for a customer to sign, she thought again of how Lincoln had been the one to create a point-of-sale system for the shop. A day like this would have been a nightmare had Marnie kept the old-fashioned register the way she had first planned.

"Mom, I need to make a run to the store for more ingredients. Do you need anything?"

"Maybe a sandwich or yogurt? Something to eat fast, in between customers."

"Will do. I'm going to make a quick stop at the cooking school to drop off some cartons of vanilla ice cream."

"Are you feeling okay? You look beat."

Dawn yawned. "I went to bed way too late last night. A nap sounds nice, but it's not going to happen today. Or tomorrow. Not until this wedding is over. Did you hear that Callie volunteered us to work the wedding?" She yawned again. "All of us."

"Me?" Her voice raised an octave.

"You get a pass as Linc's date. According to Brynn, Deidre Klassen came to the cooking school today distraught because her hourly hires bailed on her. Something about a Taylor Swift concert. Suddenly, Super-Callie stepped in to rescue her. My words, not Brynn's. Apparently, Callie is now scrounging Chatham for servers and parking valets, and she told Brynn that she's going to need all of us to work the wedding. Even Leo."

Marnie was relieved to be on Callie's exempt list. She'd been hoping to sit with Lincoln at the wedding. To eat with him. To dance with him. She wondered if Linc even knew that the Dixons were now going to be working the wedding. Probably not. She wondered how Bear might feel about that. Actually, she thought he might enjoy it. She gave Dawn a distracted wave and turned her attention to a couple who had just come in for ice cream. As she rang up that customer, the door opened and in came Lincoln. He waited until the couple left and turned to Marnie.

"Hi there, stranger," she said. "You look hot."

His face glowed red, shiny with sweat. "Hot as hinges out there."

Was that all it was? He seemed to be a little breathless. And close up, she noticed how tired he looked. Terribly tired. "Everything okay?"

"Everything's fine. Quick question. Dawn's friend, she's very important to you, isn't she?"

"Brynn? Of course. She's like a daughter to me. I adore her."

"I thought that's what you said. Like a second daughter."

"Why do you ask?"

He hesitated, just long enough for the bells on the door to chime as a group of teen girls walked in. "Thanks again for everything you and the others are doing for Ashleigh's wedding." He gave her a quick wave. "I'll get out of your way." And he was out the door as quickly as he came in.

You're not in the way, Lincoln, she wanted to say. *You've never been in the way.* But she did wonder why he had asked about Brynn. Had something happened at the cooking school? Had cakes not risen? Gone flat? She hoped not. Brynn was putting her whole heart into baking those mini–wedding cakes.

Her whole heart.

Marnie watched the teen girls as they studied the chalkboard with today's flavors. She had noticed how girls, in particular, were notoriously slow to decide what flavor to order. They would choose a flavor and look to a friend to confirm it, then change their mind based on the friend's response.

This!

This was exactly what she was trying to explain to Brynn. She took a deep breath. "Girls, I want your attention. All eyes, on me." They looked at her, surprised. "I am going to give you some of the best advice you've ever been given. Pick the flavor of ice cream that you most want to eat. You do not need your friend's approval. You be you. It's a huge life lesson that most women take decades to figure out, if at all." She covered her heart with both hands. "Learn to listen to your heart."

The girls' eyes went wide, their mouths dropped to an *O*. The front room was completely silent. An eerie quiet.

Uh-oh, Marnie thought. She had just freaked out eight teenagers by giving words of wisdom that their adolescent brains were incapable of comprehending. She had an instant flashback to doing something similar as a Girl Scout leader—letting the Brownies give full vent to their artistic expression by painting their arms and legs—and afterward learning she had been replaced as the leader by another mother. Dawn, a rule abider, had been mortified by the whole incident.

One small girl, who had struck Marnie as the most insecure of the pack, stepped forward. "I'll take Lemon Basil."

"I want to try Blueberries and Greek Yogurt."

Emboldened, the girls made their orders, each one different than the others. As Marnie scooped ice cream into cones, she couldn't stop smiling. She couldn't even charge the girls for their ice cream cones. She was too pleased with herself.

● ● ●

Dawn planned to make a quick stop at Callie's cooking school before she went to the grocery store for ingredients. As she pulled into the parking lot, she was glad to see the lot was empty but for Bruno's car. That meant she wasn't interrupting a class. Time was of the essence for ice cream, and she wanted to get it from one freezer to the other as fast as possible. She didn't want to risk any chance of it melting. Worse still, melting and refreezing.

As she lugged in a heavy cooler full of ice cream containers, Bruno met her at the door of the cooking school and reached to take the cooler out of her arms. "Actually, there's another one in the car. If you can get that one, I'll start putting these in the freezer." The giant commercial freezer that Callie had spent an absolute fortune on.

Opening the freezer, Dawn noted how well organized everything was. So Brynn was right. Anyone could come into this kitchen, open up the freezer, and immediately find what they were looking for. Dawn sighed. Such organization must have been taught at culinary school. One shelf was filled with Brynn's mini-wedding cakes on trays, sorted by varieties, carefully wrapped in shrink film. Chocolate, vanilla, carrot cake, and red velvet that nearly glowed with its red vibrancy. She had to give props to Brynn; the cakes looked perfectly baked. While some bakers excelled in taste, others excelled in looks. Brynn had always been able to nail both.

Dawn thought back to Brynn's cookie business that she had started in college. She really had no skills to start with, but within a few weeks, her cookie business became so successful that Brynn had started talking about leaving college to attend culinary school. Brynn's parents, with Dawn's help, talked her off that ledge and back to engineering. Way too risky.

Below the cakes was an empty shelf with a clear-as-could-be note: *Dawn's Double-Fold Vanilla Ice Cream 6/30.* She started stacking the ice cream as Bruno brought in another cooler from her car. "Thanks," she said, smiling at him, though he only gave her a nod in return.

Bruno and Callie were such an interesting couple. Complete opposites. If Bruno was a still pond, Callie was a raging waterfall. If Bruno was softly smoldering coals in a fireplace, Callie was bright fluorescent overhead lighting. But Dawn couldn't deny that their relationship was an impressive one. They accepted each other without trying to change the other. There were moments when she thought her own marriage could use a little more unconditional acceptance. If she wasn't trying to get Kevin to see things from her point of view, he was trying to push her to rely more heavily on faith. Push, pull. Their relationship had a lot of that. The upside was that they made each other better people. The downside was that they butted heads a lot. Quite a lot.

Bruno started handing her containers to stack in the freezer. "Where'd Callie and Brynn go?" She would've thought they'd be cooking or baking or icing. The countdown had begun. The wedding was only forty-eight hours from now.

"I'm not entirely sure. Callie was all excited about a building that just went up for sale and dashed off to go meet someone."

Dawn paused. "A building for sale? In the historic district?" Maybe she should call Kevin. Those sales were few and far between. Usually, they went through private hands, off market.

"Not sure. Something about a bakery."

"Is Callie thinking of expanding?" Is that why she had asked for a good Realtor? Dawn knew the cooking school was doing well, but she didn't think it was doing *that* well.

Bruno reached into the cooler for the last few containers. "Not Callie. This was for Brynn."

Dawn gasped. "What?" Her voice sounded shrill. "What is Callie up to?"

Bruno bypassed Dawn to put the last few containers in the freezer and close the door. "Honestly, I'm not sure what the excitement was all about. Maybe I shouldn't have said anything."

Leo walked in the door, with Callie following behind, her arms full of grocery bags. Dawn marched right over to her. "Where is Brynn?"

Eyes wide, Callie took a step back. "She's . . . talking to someone."

"Who?"

Callie cast a questioning glance at Bruno, who shrugged his shoulders in a guilty way. She sidestepped Dawn to set the grocery bags on the kitchen counter. Without looking at Dawn, she put on her chef's coat and slowly buttoned each button.

Dawn knew this was an avoidance tactic. "Callie, what have you done?"

"I haven't done anything." She busied herself with pulling out bowls from the open shelves under the counter.

"Where is Brynn?"

"I'll tell you," Leo said.

Dawn's head jerked around. Leo looked different. Older. On his head was a Chatham Anglers baseball cap. "Leo, what's happened to you? Where's your cowboy hat?"

"I'm not going to be a cowboy anymore. I'm going to play baseball, just like Bear Hayes. Did you know he was a baseball pitcher?"

Dawn's jaw dropped. "Please tell me you're kidding."

Solemnly, Leo shook his head. "I'm not kidding."

Frowning, Dawn turned to Bruno. "But he's always wanted to be a cowboy. Always."

Bruno shrugged. "It's his life to live."

But he's only seven, Dawn wanted to say. *Can't you do something? Can't you keep him a little boy . . . just a little longer?* But she didn't say any of that. There was a bigger problem at hand. With a dispirited sigh, she asked Leo where Brynn was.

"She's at the baker's. He has gout."

Dawn knew all about the baker's gout. Everyone did. They also knew that because his gout attacks kept shutting down the bakery, his wife was furious that he hadn't sold his business yet. They had no backup baker. Customers had gone elsewhere. There was no thriving business to sell anymore, just a hollow bakery. Had he sold last year, like his wife had wanted him to, they could've retired in Florida in high style. Now, his wife said, they would have to live in low style. Still, she was quick to point out, they could live all year in Florida on what they paid in taxes to the Commonwealth of Massachusetts.

Dawn's eyes were on Callie, who was suddenly very occupied with the contents of the refrigerator.

Why would Brynn be at the baker's unless she was making an offer on it? And why would she do such a thing unless Callie had talked her into it? Pure panic washed through Dawn. "Callie, stop what you're doing and look me in the eyes. Tell me you haven't spun your Callie magic."

"Callie magic?" Callie didn't even turn around. "What is *that*?"

Bruno picked up his keys and crossed the room to put a hand on Leo's shoulder. "I think this is the moment when Leo and I will exit stage left. We'll be at home if you need anything."

Leo had been watching Dawn and Callie with great interest, sensing the tension spiking in the room, and he didn't want to go. Bruno had to steer him out the door.

Dawn walked around the large counter to stand near the refrigerator. "Callie magic is your ability to persuade people to do things they shouldn't be doing. So did you encourage Brynn to do something reckless?"

Callie set some ingredients from the refrigerator on the counter and looked at Dawn. "Reckless, as in, opening an ice cream shop without any prior food industry experience?"

Touché. Dawn frowned. "At least tell me where Brynn is."

Callie wasn't paying Dawn any mind. Instead, her head was in the freezer and she was counting Dawn's containers. She turned her neck slightly toward Dawn. "I'm going to need eight more containers."

"Eight!"

"Yes, eight. And I need them as soon as possible. This afternoon's task is to finish the mini–wedding cakes."

"Why so soon?"

"So tomorrow can be devoted to every other aspect of the meal." Callie closed the freezer, opened the refrigerator, and took out a carton of eggs. She set them on the counter, next to a stack of room-temperature butter. Without missing a beat, she put butter in the mixer and started to crack eggs into a bowl. As flustered as Dawn felt, she had to admire how seamlessly Callie worked. She cracked two eggs at a time, one in each hand. They slid into a bowl so she could fish out any eggshells before adding to the butter. But that extra step wasn't really necessary. There wasn't going to be a single eggshell in that bowl. Callie's work habits were impeccable.

She glanced up at Dawn. "Remember, if we do this right, it's going to be good business for all of us, including the Main Street Creamery."

Dawn opened her mouth to give her a piece of her mind, but Callie had turned on the mixer to the highest speed. In other words, talking was over.

Fine. Just fine. Be that way. Dawn picked up her empty coolers and left the kitchen in a huff. In the car, she tried calling Brynn, but her phone went right to voicemail. She texted her, waited, but got no response.

Fine. Just fine.

She had ice cream to make.

• • •

Nanette burst into the Main Street Creamery, cutting through a line that wove out the door. She didn't care. She was full of news. "Yoo-hoo! Don't mind me." She went right around the counter to stand beside Marnie as she scooped ice cream. "You won't believe what I just saw! With my own two eyes!"

Scooping the last of the strawberry balsamic into a cone, Marnie barely glanced at her. "I hope you saw Dawn returning to the shop to make ice cream." The freezer was getting uncomfortably empty.

"I didn't see her." She drew a little closer. "I saw her friend. That cute little friend of hers."

The woman she'd been serving handed Marnie a twenty-dollar bill, and she had to sidestep around Nanette to make change at the register. "Nanette, I'm a little busy right now."

"I won't stay but a minute."

"Then, can you help? I need more cardboard containers from the storage closet." Nanette scampered away and Marnie waited on the next customer. Too soon, Nanette returned with her arms full of small cardboard containers. "Thanks. You can put them on the back shelf."

Nanette set them down, stacking them neatly, then she sidled over to where Marnie stood, scooping ice cream. "I was in the bank again with another batch of Michael's pennies. Turns out he had another shoebox full in the closet. Can you believe—"

Marnie rolled her eyes. She didn't have time for this! She did what she often did with Nanette—tuned her out. She smiled at the next customers—a dad with his two little boys—and asked what they'd like. Nanette didn't even notice that Marnie wasn't listening. She just kept droning on and on about Michael's penny collection in her tinny, loud voice, getting in her way as she scooped ice cream. One customer, two customers, three, four, five . . .

"—so your little friend is buying the bakery."

Marnie froze. Slowly, she turned. "What in the world are you talking about?"

Nanette's eyes were dancing with excitement. "Your little friend! She's putting in an offer to buy the bakery."

Marnie stopped everything and turned to Nanette. "You must be mistaken."

"I'm not! I heard it all. I saw it all. And guess who else was in the bank? Lincoln Hayes!"

"Lincoln?"

"Yes! He was getting a cashier's check drawn up." Nanette leaned in close. "A whopper."

"Well, he is putting on a very elaborate wedding. No wonder he needed money."

"He wasn't there because of the wedding. He was buying the bakery for your little friend!"

Marnie didn't know where to start. "What makes you think that?"

"Because that's what they were talking about! Lincoln was ponying up the cash so your little friend could buy the bakery."

Facing Nanette, Marnie stilled. "He wouldn't do such a thing." Or would he? Is that why Linc had stopped by the Creamery this morning to ask how Marnie felt about Brynn? Like a daughter, she had told him.

Nanette lifted her spindly wrists. "That little friend of yours promised to pay him back. I heard her say that."

"The bank wouldn't let him just hand out money like that."

A deep male voice cut into their conversation. "More appropriately, the bank *shouldn't* let him hand out money like that."

Slowly, Marnie lifted her eyes. There was Bear Hayes, standing at the counter, stony-faced, imposing eyes narrowed at her. When had he come in? Why did this keep happening? He kept showing up at the worst times! She hadn't even noticed he was standing in the long line. She had no idea what to say. Shockingly, even Nanette seemed to be at a loss for words. There'd been a normal buzz of conversation among the customers, but they seemed to catch the tension in the air. The shop was as quiet as outer space. Every customer's eyes were fixed on Marnie and Bear. Or maybe it just felt that way.

Nanette scampered around the end of the counter. "I think I'll just scoot on over to the T-shirt shop."

Marnie looked past Bear to the line of customers patiently waiting for their turn. Now wasn't the time to address anything more, plus she needed to gather facts. "Bear, have you decided?"

"Yes, I think I know just what I want," he said, and stepped out of the line to leave the shop.

And he did not mean a flavor of ice cream.

• • •

Brynn felt ecstatic. With the help of Marnie's very good friend Lincoln, she was able to make an all-cash offer on the bakery. Taking Callie's advice, she had asked the Realtor to negotiate having the baker stay on for six months to work side by side with her. She couldn't think of any other way to speed up the process of acquiring the baking skills she would need for success. Culinary school just took too long.

So the offer was on the table, though she knew the baker's wife didn't like the idea of delaying their move to Florida. It might not work out. But, as Callie said, it might. The real estate agent told Brynn that he would have an answer for her soon. Either way, she and Callie had agreed to keep it quiet. No need to get anyone else's opinion on the matter until . . . there was a matter to discuss.

If this worked out, she had to give credit to Callie. Her excitement was contagious. She told Brynn, "Well, what's the worst thing that could happen? Sell the bakery and go back to engineering. But at least you tried. At least you dared to try. So many people don't."

That was the clincher for Brynn. If she went back to a career in civil engineering, that wouldn't be such a bad option. She liked her work. She could always go back again. But she also liked to bake. In fact, she loved to bake. She just had to give this a try. Driving past the Creamery, she decided to pop in and get her phone charger. The long line out the door gave her a stab of guilt for not helping Marnie this week like she said she would. But she really needed to get back to the cooking school and start icing and filling those cakes. It was going to be a long night ahead. And she didn't mind! She really didn't mind. She used to dread late nights at the engineering firm.

She slipped in the back door and saw Dawn at the ice cream machine, pouring a base into the hatch. She tiptoed past and went up the stairs, cringing when she stepped on the squeaky step. She stopped, held her breath, and let it out when the swirling sound started in the ice cream machine. She hurried up the last few steps, went into the bedroom, and found her charger. Behind her, the door clicked open. Brynn spun around to see Dawn, a weird look on her face.

"What have you done?"

She held up the charger. "Forgot my charger. My phone's about to die."

Dawn closed the door behind her. "Did you buy the bakery?"

Oh man. Brynn wasn't prepared for a confrontation with Dawn. A Dawn-frontation. "Where did you hear that?"

"I went over to the cooking school to drop off ice cream."

"And Callie told you I bought a bakery?" Not fair! It was going to be kept under the radar. They'd agreed.

"No. Callie wouldn't tell me anything . . . which only made me very suspicious. I had to piece it all together. So tell me the truth. Did Callie talk you into buying the bakery?"

"Relax." Brynn lifted her palms like a stop sign. "I haven't bought anything." Not yet. "And Callie did not talk me into doing anything." Nothing she didn't want to do.

Dawn's head tipped slightly. "Brynn, you did. I can see it in your eyes. You bought the bakery."

"I didn't!" She looked away. Why did she feel the need to hide this from her best friend? This was exciting news! Dawn should be happy for her. "I . . . only put an offer on the bakery. I'm waiting to hear. It's not a done deal." Not yet.

Dawn's face went chalk white. "Brynn! What in the world is happening to you?"

● ● ●

Kevin
I heard there's a house for sale in the historical district. Any chance you can spare a few minutes to check it out with me?

Linc
Sorry, no time to spare today. Where is it?

It's the bakery. That baker with the gout.

Pretty sure there's already a sale pending.

What? Why am I always the last to know?

About this? Or about everything?

Everything.

Chapter
FIFTEEN

A day without ice cream was a day wasted.

—author Iain Pears

On the way back to the cooking school from the Creamery, Brynn called the Realtor to see if she could yank her offer off the table, but the Realtor said he had already submitted it.

"Not to worry," the Realtor said. "Your offer is probably going to be rejected." He had just learned of two other offers getting presented to the baker today. "When a building pops up in the historical district, it gets snatched up."

"Do you know anything about the other two offers?"

"One wants to turn it into a hair salon and the other wants to open a dog accoutrement store."

To Brynn, that only meant she had a better-than-not chance of getting the bakery. She and the baker had shared a "moment" early this morning. They both loved to bake. By asking him to stay on and mentor her through the process, she just had a feeling that she had most likely sealed the deal.

But now she regretted it. Deeply. Dawn was right. She had no business giving up her thriving career to start something brand new, something risky, in a tourist town. Brynn felt cold all over, though the day was steamy. What was happening to her? She was making rash, impulsive decisions, one right after the other. First, she'd married a man she'd known only a few hours. Then she ran away from him, from the possibility of a life together. Days later, she put in an offer on a bakery in a beach town. She squeezed her eyes shut. And now she was back to marinating in regret and wanting to erase it all. Was she coming unhinged? Dawn certainly thought so. The troubled look on her face said that and more.

What if Brynn couldn't erase this? What if she was stuck with the bakery? What if she wasn't in love with baking like she thought she was?

That's what Dawn believed. She told Brynn that she only enjoyed baking because it wasn't her full-time work. "Trust me on that, Brynn. I'm speaking from the experience of making ice cream all day, every day. It's hard work! It's not the romantic image you have in your mind. Don't give up your engineering career. Your big salary. Your 401(k). Your annual vacation."

Of course. Dawn had experience in this area. She could see things Brynn couldn't see.

Then again, Callie had made an interesting point about Dawn. She did seem much happier making ice cream than she ever had working as a CPA. Brynn remembered how wound tight Dawn used to be, how serious. Joyless. Grim.

Still, Dawn's dire warning unnerved Brynn. That was why she had called the Realtor to cancel the offer . . . only to find out that she couldn't. She had set things into motion and it wasn't easy to undo it. Just like she'd done with TD.

She arrived at the cooking school to find the parking lot was full, which meant there was a class going on. She could slip in, unnoticed, and get to her workstation in the corner, back to baking those wedding cakes. Fifty more to go! Then came the hard part: carving out an interior section to fill it with ice cream. Dawn said she was coming to help because she was worried the ice cream would start to melt while they were working. That girl got twitchy about melting ice cream.

Brynn went right to her corner and pulled out everything she needed to make carrot cake. She'd kept this batter for last because it took more time and was a little trickier than the other more straightforward recipes. The mix-ins changed the texture of the cake, and if she wasn't paying close attention to measurements, she'd end up with an overly dense crumb. Fortunately, it was her favorite cake of all. Peeling and grating carrots, she felt anxiety slip away. Stirring the spices into the batter, she felt calm return. She did love this work. She did! Working with her hands, using all her senses, tapping into creativity. She'd always felt delight that her baked goods brought joy to people. An indescribable happiness filled her—the same euphoric feeling she'd had when she'd been with TD.

She stilled.

Into her mind floated an image of the two of them driving in the desert, the convertible top of TD's rental car down, the highway empty. It felt like they were the only two people on earth. "Tell me about your perfect life," TD said. "If there were no obstacles, what would you do differently?"

He surprised her, the questions he asked. So curious, with such a sincere interest in hearing the answers. She liked that quality about him. "You go first," she said. "What's your perfect life?"

He grinned. He had a way about him, she'd already discovered. A dimple would crease his cheek when he was about to say something she wouldn't have expected. "My perfect life is to have a wife I adore and a bunch of kids. We'll create all kinds of family traditions, like cutting down our own Christmas tree, and making gingerbread houses, and giving each other homemade gifts. And not just Christmas traditions, but year-round ones, like pizza and movie nights on Fridays. Getting donuts on Sunday morning. Camping trips every summer. The works." He couldn't help but laugh. "I have a whole laundry list of family traditions I want to establish."

She stared at him, overwhelmed with emotion, her eyes stinging with tears. She had grown up *longing* for that kind of family life. Hungry for it. She didn't know someone else might feel the same way, especially a male someone.

When she didn't say anything, he glanced over at her. When he noticed she was wiping away tears, he pulled the car over and turned it off. "Did I say something wrong? Tell me."

It took her a while to pull herself together. "Your perfect life is all about relationships." A husband, a dad. He wanted to be a family man.

He gave that some consideration. "Relationships should always come first. Frankly, family should always come first. I suppose I want to give my family everything I missed out on. And one thing I have promised myself—I will never ever get divorced. No matter what. I'm all in for life."

Brynn was hit with another wave of being overwhelmed. She almost had to pinch herself. Was he for real? TD was everything she'd been looking for in a man and had never found. Never even came close.

She was quiet for so long that he reached over to squeeze her hand. "Everything okay?"

"Sometimes . . . I wonder if I've made the right choices in my life, you know?"

"As a matter of fact, I do." He still held her hand in his. "So what does your perfect life look like?"

"Well . . ." she coughed a laugh. "Well, my perfect life doesn't sound nearly as profound as yours."

"Try me."

"I want to live in a small town."

"That's it? No family?"

"Oh, most definitely with a family." She grinned. "Goes without saying. I want to have two, maybe three children. And a very nice husband." One who is completely committed to his wife and children. She took a deep breath. "And there's one other thing I imagine in my perfect life."

He had shifted in his seat to face her, one arm slung over the back of her seat. He smiled and she was struck by what a lovely, gentle smile it was. His chiseled features could be a little fierce looking, but when he smiled, everything softened. "Imagine away. Remember, there are no obstacles to this perfect life. You can have anything you want."

"Someday . . . I want to own my own bakery."

Jolted back to the present, Brynn gasped. She had never said that out loud to anyone. But she had felt safe enough with TD to tell him her secrets. And owning a bakery had always been one of her best-kept secrets. Until today. It was out in the open today for all to see, to comment on, to cheerlead (Callie) or criticize (Dawn).

As she slipped the carrot cakes into the oven, she remembered how TD had responded to her secret. "I think," he said, as he leaned close to smooth away some strands of hair from her cheek, "that a perfect life is within reach, if only we're brave enough to go after it."

Looking back, that comment, right there, was probably what set them both up to pass by a wedding chapel a few hours later and walk right in. Crazy! Crazy . . . and brave. Bold. Daring. They were willing to go after that perfect life. Both were all in.

Until the next morning, when Brynn freaked out and ruined everything.

She peeked into the oven to see if the cakes were starting to rise. She hadn't ruined everything. She hadn't ruined *this*. She still had a piece of her perfect life to go after.

In her pocket, she felt her phone vibrate with an incoming text. She washed her hands and pulled it out of her pocket. It was the Realtor.

Brynn, you've got yourself a bakery!

What? Seriously?

The baker's wife loved the all-cash offer.

No countering?

Well, just a small matter. Baker's wife says no to the apprentice overlap. I agreed to that.

Brynn's eyebrows shot up. Shouldn't she have had a say-so? How could she start a bakery without any experience? Without credentials? Without a mentor? She could feel her heart start pounding right out of her chest. Somebody needed to stop her, to save her from herself!

Paperwork coming. Stay tuned. Start your ovens!

● ● ●

Marnie thought about Maeve's advice to say nothing to Linc about Bear's accusations, but she just couldn't not tell him. She'd texted Linc all afternoon without a response. Normally, he answered back just as soon as she finished texting him. She tried calling him, but the phone went straight to voicemail.

Finally, she called again and left a message. "Linc, there's something I need to tell you. I was hoping to see you this afternoon to talk to you face-to-face, but the day is getting late. Your son Bear has been . . . expressing some concern that our family has taken advantage of you. Of your generosity. We can talk about that some other time, but in the meantime, I heard through the grapevine that you're financing Brynn's offer on a bakery and Bear found out about it and . . . Linc, as kind an offer as it is, I think you should tell Brynn you can't help her. Not right now. Not if it creates more tension between you and Bear. This time is so important for you and Bear and Ashleigh. As kind as you are to squeeze in help for Brynn, you really need to put your own children above everyone else. That's what I needed to say to you. Please call me as soon as you get this message. Okay?" She let out a sigh. "Okay, goodbye."

She ended the call all churned up inside. Just as churned up as she had been when Dawn confirmed everything Nanette had overheard at the bank today. This was yet another undocumented loan that Bear Hayes could use against Linc. She wasn't sure what Bear might do, but she'd heard stories of adult children who'd used legal means to put financial handcuffs on their elderly parents. Linc was not elderly, and he certainly wasn't suffering from dementia—only careless generosity.

Dawn walked into the front room with a stricken look on her face. "Callie just texted." She held up the phone to read. "Brynn bought the bakery." She dropped the phone to her side. "She added dancing emoticons and chef's hats." Her voice was flat.

Marnie blew out a puff of air. "So, it's a done deal."

"Very done. Overdone. Brynn asked the baker for six months' overlap to apprentice her, and his wife said no to it. So Callie told Brynn not to worry, that she'd teach her everything she needed to know. The two of them are suddenly BFFs."

Add that to Dawn's growing list of frustrations. Marnie remembered something that Maeve had noticed about her husband Paul's three daughters—one of them was always on the outs. Two against one.

Dawn crossed her arms against her chest. "You and Callie should be ashamed of yourselves."

"What? Callie and me?"

"Brynn came here for some needed guidance to fix one problem, and what she got was a cheerleading squad that encouraged her to create yet another problem for herself."

"A cheerleading squad."

"You with your 'trust your instincts' peacenik advice. Callie with her 'dream big' philosophy. Don't even try to deny it, Mom."

She wasn't. There was no denying it. But Marnie wasn't taking the blame. Brynn was the one who had made these decisions. After all, Marnie knew about them only after the fact. "I still say there's a reason Brynn has made such big decisions."

Dawn let out a snort. "I'll say. Brynn is losing her ever-loving mind. On Saturday, she meets and marries a stranger. On Thursday, she buys a bakery." She put her hands on her hips. "Come on, Mom. Even you have to admit this is not the behavior of someone who is emotionally stable."

"There's another way of looking at this. Brynn is finally making some decisions on her own terms."

"Finally? Then, whose terms has she been making decisions on? Her parents have always been checked out. Completely self-absorbed. Brynn hasn't had a boyfriend in years. If she hasn't been making decisions on her own terms in all these years, then whose?"

Marnie stayed quiet. Thirty seconds passed, a minute. She remained utterly silent.

A funny look came over Dawn's face. "Hold it. Wait just a minute." She patted her chest. "You mean me? You think I've been making decisions for Brynn?"

Bingo. "Well, you've always had a very strong influence on her."

"That's because I want the best for her! I've always wanted her to reach her potential. She's talented and capable and smart."

"And surprisingly insecure."

That stopped Dawn short. A long moment passed. Suddenly Dawn looked fifteen years old and upset that her mother was late to pick her up from high school. "If I had married a stranger, wouldn't you be concerned?" Her voice was a knot of petulance.

"You keep calling him a stranger. Brynn must have had some pretty strong feelings for him."

"In less than a day's time? Those aren't feelings. That's a school-girl's crush."

"I don't deny that it was impulsive."

"Reckless."

"Reckless? Now that I don't know. And the same for the bakery. Impulsive, yes. Absolutely. But Brynn is not an impulsive person. I wonder if her heart made those decisions and if it might have been the first time she was led by her heart. I just don't think we should interfere." Other than trying to get Lincoln to stop financing the bakery . . . but that was obviously a moot point.

Dawn scowled at her. "And you're implying that I discourage Brynn from listening to her heart? What about her mind? Her logic? Reasoning? She is on the brink of throwing away everything that she's worked so hard for!"

"And for what, Dawn? She's alone, in a studio apartment in Boston, working at a job that she's not passionate about."

"What makes you think she isn't passionate about her life in Boston? Her friends? Her civil engineering career? You'd be shocked at her salary. I'm shocked."

Oh Dawn. You miss so much. "Because Brynn is here, in Chatham . . . and she just bought a bakery."

The look on Dawn's face! Completely befuddled.

• • •

Marnie
Have you ever known someone who is extremely capable, thorough, high achieving in almost every area of their life, but they always overlook the obvious?

Maeve
Yes! Many people. Most husbands. I've come to realize that a high IQ doesn't always mean a high EQ. Often, it's just the opposite.

Chapter

SIXTEEN

I'm skipping dinner and going straight for the pints.
—Unknown

This wasn't exactly a golden moment for Dawn. She didn't know what was worse. Brynn's alarming departure from reality or her mother's dismissal of it. Mom minimized the situation with her irritating "live and let live" philosophy. Worse! She flipped it around and put the blame on Dawn. Not fair! How was it Dawn's fault that Brynn married a stranger and wanted a divorce? How did buying a bakery out of the blue have anything to do with Dawn? She didn't even know the sale was going on!

The churning of the ice cream machine changed to the sound of tennis balls in the dryer, and Dawn knew the ice cream was just about done. She took out containers and their lids, dated and marked them with the flavor: Atlantic Sea Salt with Chocolate Swirl. It was a favorite among the locals. Mom had said the frozen display freezer in the shop was getting perilously low of grab-and-go pints, and she wanted Dawn to stock up before the three-day weekend. As she waited for the timer to go off, her thoughts drifted back to college.

Brynn had been baking, decorating, and selling cookies, and toyed with the idea of baking full-time. They'd had long talks about the pros and cons of leaving college to go to culinary school. Mostly cons. Brynn had come to the conclusion that she could always dabble in baking, but she couldn't dabble in engineering. It required a full commitment. And the rewards were abundant, unlike an insecure job in the food industry. Dawn vividly remembered where they were sitting in their apartment as Brynn said that very thing.

That was Brynn's decision. Right? Yep. Pretty sure that was all Brynn.

Or was it? It did sound like something Dawn would say. Even more so like what her dad had told her when she was still in high school, kicking around the idea of culinary school instead of college because she enjoyed making ice cream so much.

Well, it was definitely good advice. For Dawn as her dad steered her back to the college path. And for Brynn, as she settled into a degree in civil engineering. In fact, Brynn had received solid recognition in her field, she'd gotten promotion after promotion, she was highly respected. Yep. Definitely the right decision.

After Dawn emptied the barrel of the ice cream machine and put the containers in the freezer, she checked off her list and felt a wave of fatigue. Still so much to do! This whole week, she had felt a little off. There'd been so much going on—Brynn's unexpected arrival and the shocking reason as to why she'd come, something that still needed sorting out. And now the bakery fiasco. Dawn should've found a lawyer right away and started the process to dissolve Brynn's marriage. She didn't know any lawyers, but she vaguely remembered that Linc had said his son was a lawyer. Bear Hayes certainly acted like a lawyer. Suspicious. Distrustful. Skeptical. Maybe she should ask him if he could help Brynn, or if he knew who to ask for help. Maybe he'd warm up a little if she sought out his advice.

A yawn escaped. She still had batches of Double-Fold Vanilla to make for Callie this afternoon. Another yawn. She couldn't wait for this wedding to be over. No wonder she felt so tired. So easily bothered. The whole fertility thing kept nagging at her, bothering her more than anything else.

The clinic!

She had completely forgotten to return their call. She grabbed her phone and went up the stairs to her old bedroom to listen to the voicemail. "Hi, Dawn. This is Alicia from the Hyannis Fertility Clinic. You had asked me to put you on the waiting list in case of a cancellation. I just had a spot open up for next Wednesday so I've got you penciled in. If I don't hear from you, I'll assume you're ready to begin the process of fertility testing. If not, call and cancel the appointment. You can just leave a message."

She held the phone in her hand. Should she cancel?

But she wanted to keep it. She was ready to start the process, even if Kevin wasn't.

Should she keep it?

She didn't feel good about going behind Kevin's back, but she also felt he just didn't understand.

The clinic had stressed that it was best to start the process together, to rule out any issues.

But if she found out the problem rested with her, like she thought it might, she wouldn't even have to involve Kevin. And then he would be grateful that she had handled this without him.

With a sigh, Dawn clicked off her phone. Suddenly, she felt very tired, more tired than she'd ever felt in her life. People problems were exhausting. All she wanted to do was to lie down and fall asleep forever.

She flopped back on the bed, just for a minute. Just to rest her eyes.

• • •

Brynn took the carrot cakes out of the oven and set them on racks to cool. Gently, she pressed a finger onto one and watched it spring back. Perfect. Follow the recipe and it would turn out.

If only love had a recipe. Love was a hot mess.

Dawn had accused Brynn of using the bakery as a distraction tool to avoid the unresolved issue of marrying TD. "And what will be next? What'll be the next distraction?" Exasperated, Dawn had put her hands on her hips. "Brynn, here's an illustration from engineering that you've taught me. If the foundation of the building isn't level, the whole building will end up crooked. Everything builds on each other."

It was hard to argue with that. Foundations were critical.

Brynn's silence gave Dawn the impression that her logic was starting to make a crack in her bakery-buying decision. Dawn could have stopped there, but she was on a roll. "Consider yeast in a dough. If it's gone bad, the dough won't rise. You don't keep baking. You stop, toss it in the bin, and start again with the right ingredients."

Brynn was starting to wobble. "Now you're saying that TD was bad yeast?"

"Well, you still haven't heard from him, have you?"

No. Not a peep. He'd made no effort to contact her. But she hadn't either.

Satisfied that she had done what she'd set out to do, Dawn put her hands on Brynn's shoulders. "Don't you worry. I'm going to help untangle this new mess you've gotten yourself into. That's what a best friend is for."

Brynn knew Dawn was trying to help, but somehow, she had only made her feel worse. More confused.

She took the last mini–wedding carrot cakes out of the oven and set them on racks to cool. While that batch had been baking, Brynn had cut holes in some of the other cakes and filled them

171

with Dawn's Double-Fold Vanilla, then slid them back into the freezer, covered with shrink wrap. She was working as quickly as she could so the ice cream wouldn't melt.

Tomorrow, twenty-four hours ahead of the wedding, Brynn would add a crumb coat on each mini-cake. Crumb coating, a thin layer of icing spread over a cooled cake, kept the moisture in and helped that final decorating layer to go on smooth and easy. The morning of the wedding was set aside to ice all two hundred mini-cakes.

In between classes, Callie had spent some time late this afternoon doing a couple of options for icing. Didi Klassen had stopped by the cooking school to make the final selection, but she came in during a class, so Brynn met with her. She wondered if she might have news of more mother-of-the-bride changes to the wedding, but so far, things were static. Tomorrow, Callie was expecting a delivery of forty pounds of salmon. Didi crossed her heart and promised no more changes. "And if there are," Didi said, "Bear said to add them to his father's bill." She leaned close to Brynn. "No love lost there."

"Bear?" Brynn said. "Lincoln's son is named Bear?"

Didi shrugged. "Apparently it's a family nickname. He definitely does not look like a bear." She lifted her eyebrows up and down. "He's a hottie." She giggled. "If I were only ten years younger . . . and single." She pointed to Brynn. "You're single, aren't you? You two should hook up." Her phone buzzed and she yanked it out of her pocket, hurrying outside to answer it.

No thank you, Brynn thought. First of all, she wasn't single. Not really. Maybe? She didn't feel single right now. And she was definitely not interested in a son who dissed his father, Lincoln, the very man who had gone out of his way to help her purchase the bakery today. Brynn was beholden to Lincoln. So no, she had no interest in meeting his son. Not anyone's son. Not now. She might not feel married, but she wasn't exactly single.

Her mind drifted to TD. This afternoon, she had given some

serious thought to trying to find him and for the strangest reason too. After the real estate agent texted that her offer for the bakery had been accepted, he was the first person she wanted to tell. An odd thought, considering most likely he felt nothing but contempt for her.

Brynn shook off that unsettling thought and tried to focus on the work in front of her. One hundred and ninety mini-cakes to hollow out and fill with ice cream before they melted. As she took out another tray of cakes from the freezer and pulled away the shrink wrap, she felt that Zen-like focus return. Baking. It always did this for her. Calmed her soul.

* * *

Friday morning, July 1

Dawn slept so hard during the night that she felt groggy in the morning. At Kevin's insistence, they went for a run along the beach. Sort of a run. More like a slow trot. Dawn's energy was still zapped. Brynn's issues, she thought, were the culprit. So much to worry about! As they ran, she filled Kevin in on the latest news. "So I don't know how to get her out of the bakery deal."

"Isn't there a twenty-four-hour buyer's remorse clause in the contract?"

"Is there such a thing?" Dawn stopped short. "Then why didn't we use it for my mom when she bought the Main Street Creamery?"

"Because that was a private sale." A moment later, jogging in place, Kevin said, "You don't regret buying the Creamery, do you?"

No, she really didn't. "That was different. Mom and I were in it together. Brynn's all alone in life. She needs my help to undo everything."

They started their slow jog again. "I don't think you should be messing with her marriage to this guy."

She rolled her eyes in annoyance. That was Kevin's first reaction when Dawn told him about Brynn's impromptu marriage. *Don't mess with this, Dawn.* Men could be so clueless. "I'm not messing with anything. I'm helping Brynn sort out her life."

"But she hasn't asked you to sort out her life."

"Kevin, she's here! She's baking ridiculous mini–wedding cakes in Chatham when she should be in Boston."

A runner sprinted past them. Kevin stopped abruptly and turned around. "Bear!"

Bear Hayes stopped running when he heard his name and turned, then walked toward them, breathing hard.

"Didn't mean to break your pace," Kevin said, all smiles.

Bear used his T-shirt to wipe off the sweat from his face. "Sorry," he said. "The day's already hot."

Dawn and Kevin hadn't broken a sweat. "I don't think you've met my wife Dawn."

"Actually, we did meet," Bear said. "In the hardware store."

Yep. Dawn remembered. "Everything coming along for the wedding?"

"To be honest," he said, "I'm trying to stay clear of wedding details. I've never been a fan of big, fancy weddings. You know how the saying goes. The bigger the wedding, the shorter the marriage."

Not so much for Brynn, Dawn thought, a little sadly. That was the shortest marriage on record.

Bear misread the look on her face. "Sorry. Guessing you had a big wedding."

Kevin scoffed a laugh. "Just the opposite. It was tiny. Held in the ice cream shop."

When Bear's eyebrows shot up, Dawn added, "It was perfect." She probably sounded a little defensive, but this guy made her feel like she should defend herself.

She was ready to part ways with Bear, but Kevin, apparently, had a different idea. "Say, Bear, you're an attorney, aren't you? If you have a little extra time today, would you mind sitting down with Dawn's friend? She's gotten herself into some trouble this week."

"Kevin—" Dawn's voice had that *Bad idea!* warning to it.

Even Bear looked hesitant. "I'd like to help, but I'm not a criminal lawyer."

"Criminal?" Dawn said. "No, no. Nothing like that. She's just made a few impulsive decisions lately—some messes, big ones, that need to get undone. Mistakes . . . which she regrets."

"What kind of regrets?"

"Real estate regret," Kevin said.

"I'm not a real estate attorney," Bear said. "But if there are any contingencies, she might be able to get out of the contract without too much difficulty. At the worst, she'd probably just lose her deposit."

Kevin turned to Dawn. "Think there are any contingencies?"

"I have no idea."

Bear had been looking past them at the lighthouse. "Tell you what. If she has a copy of the contract, I can look it over. Later this morning is best. In the afternoon, I've got plans with Leo Bianco."

"Cowboy Leo?" *My Leo?* Dawn's eyes slightly narrowed.

Bear smiled. "We're going to a Chatham Anglers game."

"How did that come to be?" Dawn felt protective about Leo. Why was Bruno letting this near-stranger take his child off for a day? Wrong, wrong, wrong! Warning bells went off in her head. Didn't people listen to the news? Terrible things happened!

"Leo's dad asked if I could watch him for a few hours while he's teaching a class and Callie is cooking away for Ashleigh."

"I can watch him," Dawn said. She wasn't exactly sure how she could fit that in with all the ice cream making she had to do, but she'd figure it out. After all, Leo was part of her family.

"Thanks but no thanks," Bear said. "I've been wanting to see a baseball game while I'm here."

"That's awesome," Kevin said. "Leo's a lucky boy."

"I'm the lucky one." Bear put his hands on his hips. "It's fun to see Chatham through the eyes of a little boy. Makes me want to relive my childhood."

For just a brief moment, Dawn saw something light up in Bear's eyes—tenderness? longing?—but it vanished before she could put a name to it.

"I spent most every summer here until I went off to college. Then I came back and played one summer of baseball with the Anglers."

"No kidding?" Kevin's admiration was obvious. "I've always wanted to go to one of those games."

Bear grinned. "Then come with us."

Kevin was just about to say yes when Dawn stepped in. "Thanks, but we've both got a full day of work ahead." *And why aren't you running ragged with wedding tasks like the Dixons are? That's what she wanted to say to Bear, anyway.*

"So," Bear said, looking straight at Dawn in that way that made her feel like she was on the witness stand and just about to get grilled, "I'd be happy to see if I can help your friend untangle her regretful decisions. Sounds intriguing."

This was a terrible idea. Terrible! Dawn tried to think of a graceful way to get out of it. On the other hand, Brynn needed help and she needed it now. But where? Not the cooking school or the Creamery. Coffee shops and restaurants were packed with crowds this week. "Let's meet at the library. Would eleven o'clock work?" She hoped she could snag Brynn away from Callie's lengthy to-do list. "It shouldn't take long. Ten or fifteen minutes, tops."

"I'll be there." Bear lifted a hand in a wave and jogged off, picking up his pace until he was back at his full run.

Kevin watched him go from a canter to a full gallop. The morning sun was behind Bear now, turning his body into a silhouette. "There goes one cool cat." His voice oozed with admiration.

Dawn turned to him, amazed. "If I didn't know better, I would think you have a man crush on Bear Hayes."

The lightness slipped off Kevin's face, replaced with a scowl. "That is a very juvenile remark, Dawn."

Not really. Kevin acted nervous and insecure around Bear. Like Bear was the quarterback on the high school football team and Kevin was the water boy.

Off in the distance, Bear was hardly visible now. Clearly, he took physical conditioning seriously. Kevin and Dawn, not so much. "We should work out more," she said. "Maybe we should join a gym."

Kevin rolled his eyes. "Maybe we should just try jogging a little faster." He started off down the beach.

It took her a while to catch up with him, and by the time she did, she was huffing and puffing. "Why are you mad at me?"

"Because you have a tendency to spoil things."

"Are you talking about Brynn? Because as I recall, you were the one who just now invited a lawyer to meet with her to untangle the messes she keeps making in her life."

He stopped and stared at her. "It's not a bad idea to get some free legal advice from a lawyer. But it should be Brynn who leads the discussion. Not you telling Brynn what she should do."

Dawn's eyes went wide. "I am only trying to protect my friend!"

"It's not your job to fix Brynn."

"Yes, it is! It's what friends do for each other. I was the one she turned to when she was in Las Vegas, scared and uncertain about what to do next. I'm the reason she came to Chatham in the first place. She wanted my help."

"You are trying to control things," he said, his voice rising in frustration. "It's your default path. If life doesn't meet your high expectations, you go into control mode. You did it with our first wedding, you did it when your mom bought the Creamery, you did it when Callie came to Chatham and you made her go to that Happiness class. You're doing it with Brynn. And you're even trying to do it with our baby. You can't just let nature take its course, can you? You have to decide everything for everybody. You can't leave well enough alone."

By now, Dawn was sputtering with righteous indignation.

Kevin started a slow run, but turned around to add one more thing while jogging backward. "I haven't made a lot of friends in Chatham, in case you haven't noticed. You have your mom and Callie and now Brynn, but I only have Bruno and he hardly talks. A guy like me needs friends. Just because I found someone I'd like to be friends with, it doesn't mean I have a man crush." He pivoted and took off at a fast pace.

Dawn could never catch up with Kevin now. It didn't matter. She didn't want to. She was furious with him! His accusations were way too hard on her, not at all fair. In each situation he mentioned, she'd only been trying to help. Kevin had it all wrong. As for the baby, she was only trying to *have* a baby! She felt defensive, resentful and . . . embarrassed.

Embarrassed because she'd never thought about Kevin's lack of friends in Chatham. She'd never even noticed. He was right when he said that he was the type who needed friends. He'd always been surrounded by a lot of them. It wasn't easy to build a community of friends in Chatham—the population was like an accordion, swelling in the summer and contracting in the winter. Most locals were on the older side. Some were ancient.

Discouraged, Dawn felt hot and sweaty and tired and mad. She spun around to head toward home. She had work to do—to figure out some way to get Brynn to the library at eleven o'clock to meet Bear Hayes.

● ● ●

Marnie
Linc, did you get my voicemail from last night?

One hour later.

178

Lincoln

Sorry to be MIA! Busy finding solutions to problems. Deidre Klassen's party supplies rental company fell through. Scrambling to find a replacement.

But did you listen to my voicemail?

One hour later.

Just listened now. Don't worry about Bear. His bark is worse than his bite.

Was it? That only made Marnie worry more.

Chapter
SEVENTEEN

There are problems that only coffee and ice cream can fix.

—author Amal El-Mohtar

Brynn was in high-efficiency mode, covering each wedding cake with a crumb coat like she was a machine. Callie had shown her some tips and then left her completely alone, which was an indication to Brynn that she was doing a good job.

These last few days, she'd gotten to know Callie well enough to realize that she was the hovering type. She seemed to have a sixth sense whenever a cooking student wasn't following directions to a T. She would suddenly be by their side, showing them how to do it properly—whatever it was. This morning, it was mincing garlic. A woman kept whacking garlic cloves incorrectly and they would go flying off in the air, hitting other cooking students. Callie stepped in and showed her how it was done, then stayed by her side until she could hit it correctly, using the palm of her hand on the blade of the knife to mash it. "If you keep doing it the way you're doing it," Callie warned, "you will slice your hand wide open. I've seen it happen. Blood spurted everywhere. Covered the entire kitchen."

Terrified by that visual, the woman adjusted her style quickly to match Callie's expectations. That was the thing about Callie—she knew what she was doing. You could learn a lot from her love of principles. It was refreshing to Brynn to see how success played out. So much of her engineering work focused on fixing problems. Most problems could be avoided if things had been done right the first time.

Like now. Brynn's critical crumb coats were picture-perfect. So when Dawn texted to meet her at the library at eleven o'clock to meet with a lawyer, she texted back,

Can't. Too busy.

She saw the bubbles start bubbling and braced herself for Dawn's reaction.

It won't take long. It's just to get a plan started
on how to move forward to dissolve . . . things.

Brynn wondered what things Dawn thought needed to be dissolved—the impulsive wedding or the purchase of the bakery? Both, knowing Dawn. She knew that Dawn was worried about her. She was trying to help. It wasn't like Brynn to make radical, life-changing decisions, and now she'd made two in one week. She didn't know what to think about the first impulsive decision, other than shame for leaving TD the way she did. Dawn's doubts about TD's character kept stirring in her. If he was as committed a guy as he had described himself to be, why hadn't he tried to contact Brynn by now?

But the second impulsive decision that she'd made this week . . . that she had no doubt about. She was going to buy that bakery, no matter what this lawyer had to say.

Dawn
So you'll come?

181

Brynn

It's just that . . . there's so much to do here.

Fifteen minutes, tops! And the library is walking
distance from Callie's.

Who is this lawyer?

Lincoln's son.

Seriously, Dawn? I haven't heard very good
things about him.

A pause, which meant that Dawn didn't disagree. Nobody
seemed to like Lincoln's son.

Well, Kevin adores him. So does Leo. And it's
free legal advice.

Ten minutes, tops.

Perfect! I'll be right out front of the library
waiting for you. Eleven o'clock. Don't be late!

● ● ●

At ten minutes to eleven, Brynn took off her apron. Callie was
out back, arguing with the fish guy about the delivery, so Brynn
left a note on the counter where it would be easy to find:

Be back soon. Meeting Dawn for a quick errand.

She went out the front door and checked her GPS on her
phone. Dawn was right, it was quicker to walk to the library
than to drive. She hurried from one shade tree to the next in an
effort to dodge the beating sun, but it did feel good to get outside.
There'd been a lot to think about lately, a ton of decisions to make,
and she kept pushing things to the back of her mind while she was
baking in the cooking school. Delightfully so. But as she walked

down the sidewalk, buried concerns came to the forefront. When should she tell her boss that she was leaving the firm? Or should she just take an extended leave of absence? Maybe she should. After all, as Dawn had reminded her, what if the bakery failed? She should have a plan to fall back on.

Callie would tell her not to allow failure to enter her mind in any way, shape, or form. She would say that having a backup plan meant she wasn't all in.

Should Brynn call her parents and let them know anything about this week? She wasn't even sure if they were in the country right now. Her father's business took him to Asia for long periods. Her mother's work took her to Europe. They never seemed to be on the same continent at the same time, which might have been intentional. She didn't even know how they'd respond to the news that she was opting out of the brainy engineering world to labor away at a bakery in a small town.

Actually, she did know how they'd respond. They would put the blame on Marnie and Dawn and their ice cream shop. They would insist that the Dixons were influencing their daughter to give up on high-achieving values and settle for mediocrity. They'd always felt miffed that Brynn preferred spending holidays with the Dixon family over flying off to meet her mother or father somewhere in the world, staying in a hotel, watching movies alone because they were busy at work.

Imagine how they'd react when she told them she had gotten married . . . and then left the groom. They would have plenty to say about that.

So no, she decided with a sigh. She would not tell her parents about the recent upheavals in her life until everything was figured out. Sorted. Resolved.

She turned the corner and saw the sign for the public library. Her gaze swept the area to find Dawn, but there were people everywhere, coming in and going out, probably to get out of the heat. An incoming text made her phone vibrate. She grabbed it out of her pocket and had to shield the phone's face with her hand, even with her sunglasses on, because the sun was so bright.

Dawn
Running late. Traffic! Parking! Tourists! Be there asap.

Fine, Brynn thought. Just great. She would have to explain her situation to this Bear guy without Dawn's steady editing.

She stopped. Hold it! Maybe this was her out. This guy didn't know who she was. She had no idea who he was. She could just tell Dawn that she couldn't find him without her (true!) and she decided she needed to get back to the cooking school (also true!). She slipped her phone back in her pocket and made an about-face to retrace her steps.

"Brynn? Is that you?"

She spun around to see a man stride toward her. Between his baseball cap and sunglasses, she couldn't see his face, but his voice, his walk, all struck a familiar chord. Brynn looked at him, her heart pounding like she was about to jump out of an airplane. As he drew closer, she felt goose bumps rise, spreading over her entire body. For several long inescapable seconds, her heart thundered.

About ten feet away, he stopped abruptly.

"You came!" Brynn said, her voice shaking with emotion. "I knew you'd find me. I just knew it!" She ran toward him and threw her arms around him. TD had come!

Chapter

EIGHTEEN

Ice cream is duct tape for the heart.

—Unknown

On a typical winter day, the drive from the Main Street Creamery to the library would take just a few minutes. On a typical summer day, it took Dawn over half an hour to drive the short distance and another ten minutes to find a parking spot. She hit her forehead with her palm. She should've walked! The Eldredge Public Library was *on* Main Street! What had happened to this morning's resolution to get in better shape? It didn't even occur to her to not drive. That had to change, she decided right now. She needed to work out more. She was appalled at how out of shape she'd become—huffing and puffing all the time. Lately, she just felt blah. Tired. So tired she wanted to pull the car over on the side of the road and drop off for a short nap. She turned the air conditioner on full blast and that helped wake her up.

When she finally found a parking spot, she ran two blocks to get to the library, nearly knocking over a stroller in her haste.

"Sorry, sorry!" she called out after the mom yelled an unrepeatable name at her. The July sun beat down, burning the back of her neck. As soon as she reached the library's property, she cut off the sidewalk to cross the grass. This building, on the National Register of Historic Places, was one of Kevin's favorites on the Cape. Built in the mid-1890s in a Romanesque/Revival style—one of the few such buildings in Barnstable County. The architect had designed it using many local materials: Quincy granite foundation, West Barnstable red brick and pink mortar for the structure, capped off by a slate roof with eyebrow dormers. If the exterior was stately, the interior was grand. Lavish oak wainscoting, a fireplace with a mantel of carved oak, floors of marble and oak, and two stained-glass windows.

She shielded her eyes and looked around for Brynn and Bear, but there was no sign of them. Too hot to wait outside, she guessed, so she started up the steps to look for them just as Mrs. Nickerson-Eldredge came through the large doors, pointing a finger at her. "Did I see you cross over on the grass?"

Dawn cringed. Mrs. Nickerson-Eldredge had more airs than a duchess. She saw everything . . . and spoke with authority. Her voice sent a cold shiver down Dawn's spine.

Mrs. Nickerson-Eldredge pinned her with two beady little eyes. "The grass is off-limits. It's very difficult to keep grass growing well when people think they can just stomp all over it."

"I'll remember that." Dawn could barely resist an eye roll, but she did. "I'm, uh, looking for someone," she stammered. "We were supposed to meet out front."

"Bear Hayes was looking for you."

Dawn's eyebrows shot up. "You know him?"

"Of course I know Bear. I've known him since he was a boy. He was charming then and he's even more so now."

Good grief. Mrs. Nickerson-Eldredge had a soft spot for Kevin, and it seemed like she had the same tender feelings for Bear. She had grown to like Dawn's mom. But for Dawn? She remained unimpressed. New England chilly. "Well, I'll just go inside to find him." She wiped her damp forehead. "Sure is hot out."

"He left."

"He left? Where did he go?"

"I don't know. I don't track people's comings and goings."

Don't you? Dawn had to work hard to keep a straight face. "Did you happen to notice if he was with someone?"

"Yes. That friend of yours."

Interesting. "But they left the library?"

"That's what I said."

"Okay. Well, thank you." Dawn started down the steps. "I'll stay off the grass!" She hustled down the sidewalk, feeling better than she had felt in a few days. Ever since Brynn's arrival, she'd felt anxious, overly sensitive, irritable, extra tired. She was worried about her friend! But now she felt proud of Brynn for finally being willing to take some initiative to untangle her problems. See? Kevin was wrong. Mom was wrong. All along, Brynn had just needed a little pressure from a well-meaning friend.

• • •

Sitting in the passenger seat of TD's car, Brynn tried to get her head around what he'd just told her. *Oh no. Oh no.* A feeling of dread sank in her stomach, cold and hard. "So then . . . you *didn't* try to find me?"

"No." He kept his eyes facing forward.

When she had thrown her arms around him in front of the library, he didn't return her embrace. He carefully peeled himself out of her hug and said, "Let's go somewhere we can talk in private." He didn't say another word. He just started walking toward the parking lot and she watched him go. She caught up with him and grabbed his arm. "TD, wait. I know what I did must have hurt—"

Stone-faced, he kept his stride.

"I'm sorry! I am!"

He pulled his arm away and kept walking as she watched him go, her body leaden, crushed by his coldness, his abruptness, his pushing her away.

Not knowing what else to do, she followed him to his car. He opened the passenger side for her, avoiding any eye contact with her, and closed it gently after she got in. Then he came around the front and got in the driver's side. He turned the car on so that they'd have air-conditioning, but he kept the car in park. "So . . . your friend is Dawn."

Gone was the warmth and affection, the sizzle of electricity that had been between them right from the first moment they'd met. In its place was a strained guardedness. She felt his coldness like a slap in the face. "Yes. But . . . how do you know Dawn?"

He didn't answer her question. "Just to be clear, Brynn, I did not come here to find you."

"Hold on. First of all, could you please take your sunglasses off and actually look at me. And second, if you're not here for me . . . then . . . why *are* you here?"

He pushed his sunglasses to the top of his head and looked at her with those beautiful dark eyes of his. "I am here for my sister's wedding."

Wedding. His sister's wedding. For a minute, Brynn couldn't find any words. She shifted on the seat to face him. Her eyes widened in disbelief. Her heart went crazy. The very air in the car seemed to spin while she stared at him, shocked. *What is happening? Oh God-help-me-help-me-help-me.* "You're . . . Bear Hayes?" She stammered in a choked voice, as if trying to recover from having the wind knocked out of her. And she was! "You're the Bear Hayes no one likes?"

"That's me." He cast a sharp glance at her. "Though I didn't know everyone didn't like me . . . until just now."

She felt the blood rush to her cheeks. This couldn't be! She pinched her eyes shut, then opened them wide. "But you told me your name was T. D. DeLima. I saw you sign the wedding certificate." She gasped. "You lied to me?" So Dawn *was* right . . . he *was* a sketchy dude. A complete fraud.

"No. I didn't lie to you. I never lie." He said it staccato-like, definitively. "During my senior year in college, I changed my name to DeLima, my mother's maiden name. It was the year my grandfather died and I felt closer to him than I ever did to my father. TD is for Timothy David. When we were kids, my sister Ashleigh turned it into TD, which evolved into Teddy Bear, which eventually shortened into Bear. So that's what people in Chatham know me by. Bear Hayes."

"But . . . you told me you lived in Boston."

Her mind was having trouble piecing all the details into place over the ringing in her ears. *This can't be happening.*

"I spent every summer of my childhood on the Cape. Right here in Chatham."

"And your father . . . that's Lincoln." The man whom TD had spoken of with such disdain. Her gaze traveled over his features. *Oh my goodness.* The high forehead. The Roman nose. The shape of the eyes. Why hadn't she noticed the similarities between Lincoln and TD before now? They shared a strong resemblance to each other, clearly father and son. No wonder she'd felt so fond of Lincoln.

Then it dawned on her. "This wedding!" She clapped her hands to her forehead. "*This* was the family event you said you were dreading. Your sister's wedding!" She stared at him in bewilderment.

The silence stretched out. "You've obviously met my father. That brings up another matter. From what I understand, my father is bankrolling your purchase of a local bakery."

"How do you know about that?" She shook her head. "Never mind. It doesn't matter how you know. What you should know is that he's *not* bankrolling it. He's bridging a loan for me until my . . ." Dawn's warning ran through her head and she stopped herself from saying trust fund. This was the first time she'd sensed the need to keep information about herself hidden from TD, and she wondered if it would be the first of many. "Look, I plan to pay him back. Every penny."

He regarded her coldly. "No interest on this loan, I gather."

"Well, no. Your father was adamant about that. But it's just a bridge. Short term. The baker would only accept a full-cash offer. No contingencies."

She got the distinct impression that he wasn't interested in the details of the sale because he had something else on his mind.

"These undocumented loans with the Dixons and my father are out of control. It has to stop. Whatever it takes, it has to end." His words were rushed, as though they'd been pent up.

"TD, slow down. We have a lot of things we have to talk about."

He turned slightly to look at her, but his face showed nothing of what he was thinking. "No, Brynn, we really don't have anything to talk about. There is nothing we need to discuss. You made that perfectly clear when you left me the way you did."

She needed to explain that she had woken up to the cold light of day and panicked. That she wished she hadn't just . . . left him like that. That she felt ashamed of herself for doing such a thing. She opened her mouth to start, but he cut her off.

"Your friend Dawn verified that by asking me to untangle the legal messes you've gotten yourself into. Mistakes. Ones you regret. That's a direct quote, by the way."

"Wait. Let me explain!"

"No need. There's nothing we have to talk about."

She stared at him. "So that's it? TD, this is serious!"

He straightened, staring outside, putting even more distance between them. "I've never been more serious." He wasn't looking at her anymore, but she saw his Adam's apple rise and fall as he swallowed hard.

Suddenly she remembered that Adam's apple rising and falling as they said their vows. Maybe he was more nervous right now than he let on. "You're honestly going to pretend that nothing ever happened? Like we never met . . . never had such a wonderful day"—her voice broke, fighting tears—"never went into that chapel . . . and . . . we . . ." She stumbled into silence.

A moment passed when she didn't think he would answer her at all. He kept his gaze fixed on the windshield. "Yes. After the dissolution takes place, then that's exactly how it will be."

She felt tears push against her throat and behind her eyes. "Just like that."

"Like we never met." He turned to look at her. His dark eyes held no warmth or emotion, just an unfeeling detachment. "Like this *mistake* never happened."

Mistake? Was that what he thought of her? Of them?

She had no idea what to do next, what to say, and suddenly she knew she was close to a full-on breakdown. She had to get out of this car before the tears started coming. She wasn't going to let this cold man see her cry. She reached for the door handle, hoping he would ask her to stay, to talk it out. But he kept his face straight ahead, all business. She got out of the car, and when the door clicked shut, she stepped away. He backed up his car and drove off without a second look. It wasn't that he peeled away, he didn't. It's just that he drove off definitively. No turning back.

Slowly, she walked out of the parking lot, keeping her head down to avoid eye contact with people. She reached the sidewalk and stopped, trying to remember if she should go left or right. Which way was the cooking school? She couldn't remember! She felt shaky, wobbly, like she might faint right there on the hot sidewalk, in front of all these people who had come to Cape Cod for a vacation.

Her phone vibrated and she glanced at caller ID. *Dawn.* She couldn't handle Dawn right now. She couldn't bring herself to say that Bear and TD were one and the same, the man she thought she had fallen in love with. She could imagine the look on Dawn's face, trying so hard to hold back an "I told you this was a mistake" look. She let the call go to voicemail and turned off her phone.

Walking on the sidewalk, she struggled for self-control, lost it, regained it, lost it again. She couldn't seem to stop the flow of tears. She could feel them, big and wet, running down her face. TD had hardly looked at her in the car, had taken great care to not touch so much as her fingertips. She thought of how tenderly, how lovingly he had touched her last weekend. He hardly looked at her now. She couldn't believe he was the same man. He showed no desire to work anything out between them. He cut her off when she tried to explain why she'd left. He gave her the same cold shoulder that he'd given to Marnie and Dawn and everyone else. Like she was nothing to him.

All she could think was to get back to baking. Get back to the cooking school. Get back to the wedding cakes. To her crumb coating. It was the only way she could settle down her desperate, bouncing thoughts. But as she drew near to the cooking school, she saw Callie out in the parking lot, talking with a delivery man. Food orders were coming in for the wedding, one right after the other.

Brynn stopped in her tracks. She just couldn't face Callie quite yet. Callie would know something was wrong and not let up until she told her everything. Then she would try to fix it. So like Dawn!

Brynn pivoted on the sidewalk, causing a man walking his dog to veer into the road to avoid bumping into her. She decided to go to the Creamery for a few minutes, just to wash her face, regain her composure. She had to keep moving. It was the only way she could keep from breaking down in a major crying jag right on Main Street in Chatham. She picked up her pace until she broke into a jog, then into a run.

Now she knew why nobody liked Bear Hayes.

Bear looked like TD. He dressed like him. He even smelled like him—a clean, soapy aftershave scent. But this was not the same man she had married.

● ● ●

Marnie heard the back door open and knew Brynn had returned to the Creamery. She saw a flash of her pink top as she made a dash up the stairs, and it gave her a funny feeling. As soon as there was a customer lull, she locked the door and set a "Back in 10 Minutes" clock on the door.

She hurried upstairs and knocked on the bedroom door, then cracked it open without waiting for an answer. Sitting on the bed, Brynn stared woodenly at the wall. She looked pale and shaken.

"Something's happened," Marnie said.

"I don't even know where to begin."

"Start in the middle." Marnie could piece it together. She was good at that kind of thing.

Brynn blew out a puff of air. "Bear Hayes . . . is T. D. DeLima. One and the same."

Whoa. Whoa whoa whoa. Marnie had to sit down. So many questions were coming so fast that her mind didn't even finish one before another supplanted it. How could this possibly be? How could those two have met in Las Vegas and never realized the connections they had to each other? TD was Bear? That was mind boggling. How could Brynn have been drawn to someone so harsh? So unforgiving? That was even more mystifying.

And suddenly Marnie had a different view. It was an unlikely scenario. Only the Lord could have brought those two together in such a way. She felt her skin tingle at the eerie coincidence. God was up to something! "This is . . . a miracle."

Brynn coughed a laugh. "But aren't miracles supposed to make you feel happy?"

"Maybe it's hard to understand while you're still in the middle of the story."

Brynn studied her for a long moment, a quizzical look in her eyes, before she spoke. "The thing is, I'm pretty sure this particular story has ended."

"Were you able to talk about . . . what happened between you?" *Like, your marriage?* "Was he understanding?"

"Understanding? Marnie, he hates me." Brynn tightened her lips to keep from crying.

"He doesn't hate you."

"Leaving him like that . . . it was a terrible thing to do."

With a single finger Marnie lifted Brynn's trembling chin and looked into her troubled brown eyes, her lashes spiked with tears. "So you experienced a moment of doubt. And then you panicked. It's an understandable reaction."

"You didn't see the look on his face . . . oh, it was just awful." Brynn dissolved into a pool of tears. "I hurt him. The same way his father had hurt him. He won't ever forgive me."

She gently rubbed Brynn's back and waited until this wave of crying stopped. "From what Lincoln has described, Bear . . . or TD . . . has reason to be angry with his dad. His complaints are justified. Lincoln was a mostly absent father. He missed much of their childhood and he's trying his best to rectify that. Ashleigh's been open to forging a new relationship, but Bear refuses."

Brynn's eyes filled with fresh tears. "See? That's just what I mean. He'll never forgive me."

"No marriage can survive without a lot of forgiveness. You can trust me on that."

"So you think I should take Dawn's advice and start the process to end things?"

"I didn't mean that! I just meant that even the best marriage requires forgiveness. And forgiveness takes practice. It comes in fits and starts. It's a lifelong work. Sometimes I think we're all beginners at it. But as long as you're trying to forgive, you're forgiving. It's only when we don't even try that bitterness sets in."

"I've only added more reasons for TD to be bitter."

A light went on in Marnie's head. "I want to tell you something that you might not like to hear."

She wiped a tear off her cheek. "What?"

"It sounds to me that maybe you care more about him than you think you do."

Brynn shook her head tiredly and leaned her forehead on the heel of a hand. "Honestly, I don't know what I think anymore. Or what to do about TD. Or the bakery. Or my life."

"Maybe," Marnie said, "you have to do what your heart tells you to do."

Brynn's red-rimmed eyes lifted. "At this point, I think I'm afraid of listening to it."

· · ·

Callie
Where's Brynn?

Dawn
She isn't back at the cooking school yet?

No. She left a note that she was going on an errand for you. That was over an hour ago.

True. But it was a very important errand. I'm sure she'll be back as soon as she can.

The wedding is tomorrow! Didi and The Knot photographer are on their way over for beauty shots. What errand could be so important?

Let's just say, it should give Brynn a needed perspective.

Chapter
NINETEEN

Ice cream soothes the soul.

—author Adrienne Posey

Saturday morning, July 2

The sun beat down on Chatham on Saturday, making the day hotter than the ones that preceded it. Heat shimmered off the waves of the Atlantic Ocean, the air grew steamier with each passing hour. But a heat wave wasn't going to stop Ashleigh Hayes's wedding from happening. The day was finally here. And today, Marnie was going to meet Lincoln's ex-wife Jeannie for the first time.

She was a little disappointed that she hadn't been invited to last night's rehearsal dinner. Linc had assumed she was invited but, apparently, Jeannie had specific plans in mind for the rehearsal dinner. Like, who was invited and who wasn't. Linc apologized profusely, but Marnie told him not to feel badly, that it was just as well. And it did turn out to be just as well. She had the shop to take care of until closing time, and then she hurried over to the cooking school to help the girls cook into the wee hours.

Marnie zipped up the back of her dress. She had taken great care in choosing her dress, making sure she didn't wear anything that Dawn would say made her look like a flower child from the 1960s. It had to be pink, Linc's favorite color on her. She chose a flowing pink maxi dress that he particularly liked.

In the bathroom, she put her face right up to the mirror. *Is that really me?* Where did those wrinkles come from? When had they arrived?

She smoothed down her hair, wishing she'd thought to make an appointment at the hair salon to get a stylish updo. She had planned on wearing her hair pulled back with a barrette, but today's steamy humidity made it bushy. It looked ridiculous. She pulled out the barrette and sprayed her hair down with hairspray, hoping it would weigh down the ends so she didn't have a pyramid-shaped head.

She wasn't sure why she felt so nervous. Actually, she did know why. It felt as if something wasn't right between her and Lincoln, though she didn't know what. She understood that he had a lot going on at the cottage, a lot of moving parts. But in a week's time, they'd gone from daily habits of starting the morning with a walk on the beach together, ending the day with a text or a phone call, seeing each other multiple times throughout the day . . . to almost no contact. She didn't know what he was learning about his daughter's fiancé, or if he'd had any conversations with his prickly son, or what it was like to have his ex-wife in town. A week ago, they would've talked everything through, anything important, and lots of unimportant things. Suddenly, it was like a tap had been turned off. Marnie missed him, and she felt oddly insecure about their relationship.

Strange, she thought, leaning toward the bathroom mirror to brush mascara on her eyelashes. There was no doubt that she was getting older—the cold light off the mirror confirmed that. But given the right set of circumstances, like today, she was sixteen years old again, getting ready for a date and feeling stomach-twisting insecurity.

She put the wand back in the mascara tube and took a deep breath. A Bible verse Lincoln often quoted popped into her head: "Boldly approach the throne of grace." *Lord,* she prayed, *I'm not sure of what today will hold, but I'm asking for an extra measure of your grace today. For Lincoln, for myself, for all those involved. Let me go through this day knowing you're right there with me.*

She took in a deep breath. This was the difference between being sixteen years old or sixty. She knew where to find the peace she needed.

She pulled her hair back into a ponytail and slipped it underneath and through to hide the elastic. Better, she thought. Not great, but better. Dawn would roll her eyes at the thought of a ponytail at a wedding, but it would have to do. She glanced at her watch, realizing she should've left ten minutes ago.

She opened the bathroom door to overhear Nanette's loud, tinny voice downstairs, and she cringed. Nanette had volunteered to man the ice cream shop during the wedding and reception. A very kind offer, but it came with Nanette-style complications, like how distracted she could be. Last time, she ran across the street to tell her husband Michael about something, leaving the shop with a line of confused customers.

Worse still, Kevin had asked Mrs. Nickerson-Eldredge to come help. Marnie was speechless when Kevin told her. She knew that Mrs. Nickerson-Eldredge adored Kevin and would do anything for him, but the older woman wasn't exactly front-of-the-shop material. She had very little patience for indecisive customers, especially the type who liked to sample each flavor. She had much less patience for Nanette.

Still, the only other option was to close the shop, and that would've meant a loss of significant revenue. Marnie had plenty of doubts about the capabilities of the two women, but having them there was better than not having them. Still, before she left for the wedding, she wanted to spend some time with them reviewing basic instructions, like . . . Don't leave the shop unattended. Dip each scooper in water between scoops so that the ice cream rolls right off. And don't bicker with each other.

She grabbed her purse and went downstairs. As she reached the bottom step, the back door opened and Bear Hayes burst in, wearing his tux. Marnie's first thought was: *Wow, Bear is an extremely handsome man.* Her second thought was: *Why is Bear here instead of at the cottage?* And then her third thought: *Why does he look so upset?*

Bear's gaze skimmed the kitchen, then he looked past Marnie to peer into the ice cream shop. "Where is he?"

"Who?"

"My father. Where is he? No one's seen him all morning. His car is gone. He's not answering his phone. He's already missed the pre-wedding photographs."

"I don't know where he is."

He gave her a look like she was hiding something. "I thought the two of you were pretty tight."

"Bear, I don't know where he is. I haven't heard from him today. Not since yesterday afternoon." And that was a very unsatisfying text too. Just a brief *One more day til the wedding!*

Bear looked around the kitchen in a distracted, irritated way. "This is so typical of my father. Any time you think you can count on him, he's gone. There's always something more important than his family. I thought this one time . . . for Ashleigh's sake . . . he would come through. But no."

"He's probably getting some last-minute errands done."

"There are no last-minute errands to do."

There were *always* last-minute things to do before a wedding. But Linc was cutting it close. The wedding was supposed to start within a few hours. "Why would you think he'd be at the Creamery on his daughter's wedding day?"

Bear's eyes drilled in on her. "I figured that's where he'd be. It's pretty obvious you're more important to him than his own family."

Marnie ignored that dig. "I know your dad would not miss Ashleigh's wedding."

Bear coughed a laugh. "Then you don't really know him." He pulled out his phone. "Can't you find him on your phone? The Find Me app?"

"No." Marnie was a very low-tech person, and she felt as if that phone feature was an invasion of privacy. Right now, she wished she'd been a little more open-minded. "When did you last see him?"

"Last evening at the restaurant. The rehearsal dinner. There were a lot of people there. I wasn't paying much attention to my father."

More likely, Bear hardly acknowledged his father's presence. "I'll find him. You go back to the cottage."

He gave a slight nod and pulled out his phone. "I'll share my contact info with you so you can let me know when you find him." He handed Marnie his phone so she could enter her number, then took it back, tapped on his phone, hit send, then slipped it back in his tuxedo pocket. "Look, this wedding will go on, with or without him."

"I'm sure it will be with him."

"Are you sure?" Bear lifted his fingers in an air quote. "'Something came up' is what we plan to put on my father's tombstone. Something *always* comes up. We're used to managing without him."

It was hard to believe he was describing Lincoln. Marnie couldn't imagine managing without him. "I understand how you feel."

At the door, Bear stopped and turned to look at her, a slightly puzzled look on his striking face. "Do you? How could you possibly know how I feel?"

Because I know so much more about you than you think I do, Marnie wanted to say. *Because I know you're hurting and you've been hurting for a very long time. Because I know that being here in Chatham brings to the surface a lot of buried pain. Because I know that when you married Brynn, you had hoped for a happily ever after story and the opposite has happened.*

All those thoughts were running through her mind, but she didn't say them aloud. She didn't voice them because he didn't expect an answer. He was already in his car and backing out of the driveway as she reached for her phone to call Lincoln.

No answer. It went straight to voicemail.

Where could he be? She texted Callie and Dawn to see if they'd seen Linc this morning, but they both texted back no. What about Brynn? She wondered if something might have come up with the bakery. She texted Dawn to see if Brynn might be with Linc.

Dawn
Brynn's right here with me. She hasn't seen Linc. Why? What's going on? The wedding is still on, right?

Marnie
Everything's fine. Just had a question for him.

Like, where'd you go?

* * *

Deidre Klassen's promise to find warming ovens and small freezers for Ashleigh Hayes's wedding didn't materialize. Dawn knew that every wedding had its unexpected glitches, that they often made for good stories later on. What she didn't expect was to see Callie pivot so quickly under pressure. Nothing, so far as the food was concerned, was going to derail this wedding—not a merciless heat wave, not a wedding planner who spent more time schmoozing with *The Knot*'s photographer than doing her job. Callie was going to deliver the goods.

Last night, Callie, Brynn, Dawn, and Mom stayed up way past midnight, preparing and cooking all the food for the wedding that could be made the night before, from canapés to salads to entrées, for two hundred guests. A wide variety of appetizers that Brynn thought she could live on: potsticker dumplings, maple bacon, seared tuna with wasabi seaweed salad, lamb meatballs with rosemary yogurt, locally grown tomatoes with fresh mozzarella, tempera green beans with spicy mayonnaise. Each entrée cost as much as gold. At first, Brynn held a knife in her hand, nervous about making a mistake. Callie laughed at her timidity. "At the end of the day," she said, shaving a truffle like she was grating Parmesan cheese, "it's all going to be consumed."

Maybe, but each mouthful cost a pretty penny. Seared bluefin tuna (!), grilled filet mignons (Japanese Wagyu!!), a Croatian truffle (!!!), mushroom risotto as a vegetarian option, a salad of greens with slivers of fennel and segments of peeled grapefruit. Knotted bread rolls with thyme and rosemary, butter flavored with sea salt.

It wasn't ideal, Callie said, to prepare some of the food this far ahead, but she had plenty of industry tricks up her sleeve. No one, she insisted, would ever know. The two-sided refrigerator was packed full but, typical of Callie, in time-sensitive organization. No hunting would be necessary. Each course, whether cold or hot or room temperature, would be delivered just in time for waitstaff to serve. The cottage's kitchen and pool house would serve as staging areas for the food. Callie planned to stay at the cottage all throughout the wedding, supervising and coordinating every aspect of food. Coordinating just about *everything*, from what Dawn had observed. Deidre Klassen seemed far more concerned with how she would be portrayed in *The Knot* than in actually managing this wedding and reception.

Brynn volunteered to stay at the cooking school all day to handle reheating the food. Dawn offered to take her place, but she had barely gotten the words out of her mouth and Callie—far across the kitchen—shouted, "No!"

Aaaand that was that. Apparently, reheating food was a big, big deal, and Callie trusted only Brynn to do it correctly. Only Brynn.

Annoying! It irked Dawn that Callie's faith was in Brynn, a rookie to the food industry, over her. She ran an ice cream shop! Who knew more about the importance of keeping food at its proper temperature? Dawn could manage that task in her sleep.

But the talk with her mom yesterday had hit a nerve. First, she was miffed, then as her emotions settled down, she decided there was probably some truth to Mom's advice. Dawn could work on being less of a know-it-all with others, even when she did know better. She reminded herself that Callie still suffered PTSD after accidentally poisoning two hundred people at the annual Food Safety Conference. Fine. If she only wanted Brynn in the kitchen, then so be it.

It did surprise Dawn that Brynn had volunteered to stay behind at the cooking school and miss a chance to see the wedding. After all, Lincoln's cottage was over-the-top swanky. Definitely worth seeing. But Brynn didn't care to see it, and that was a red flag to Dawn. Her worry about Brynn kept growing. All last evening, as they chopped and cooked and washed dishes at the cooking school, Brynn hardly said a word. She acted subdued, sad. When Dawn asked her how the meeting went with Bear yesterday, she said she didn't want to talk about it. When Dawn pushed, Brynn said he was no help at all and it was a terrible idea to meet him and please stop nagging her. She snapped! Brynn *never* snapped. Dawn blamed Bear Hayes. He seemed to bring out the worst in everyone.

As soon as she could, Dawn was going to track down a lawyer for Brynn. But that would have to wait until after the Fourth of July weekend. Until after this ridiculous wedding.

Callie relegated Dawn to Bruno's team for the day. That meant schlepping. Back and forth, from the cooking school to Linc's cottage, she and Kevin in their cars, Bruno and Leo in another, with trays of food in large, insulated bags. Lucky Mom had been given a pass so she could attend the wedding as Linc's date.

Dawn drove slowly along Shore Road, so slowly that old ladies honked at her to pick up her pace. Not a chance, Dawn wanted to shout. She was hauling precious cargo. A week of her family's life had gone into preparing and delivering this food.

By early afternoon, Dawn was ready to call it a day. Not Callie, though. She could be found in either the cottage kitchen or the pool house kitchen, supervising the waitstaff and kitchen help that Linc had scrounged up after Deidre Klassen said it had been impossible to find anyone. (What planning had Deidre Klassen actually done for this wedding? Dawn had noticed a pattern occur often enough that she wondered if it was her schtick: Deidre would burst in frantically, wailing about a forgotten task on the to-do list in such a way that some kindhearted soul jumped in to rescue her. Oozing gratitude toward whoever saved her from a sizable chore, she would dash out. If it was a schtick, it was pretty clever. *That*, Dawn smirked, certainly wouldn't make it into *The Knot*'s feature.)

Callie, by contrast, took everything in stride. Dawn had to hand it to her—whenever she brought in the latest load, she noticed Callie was cucumber cool; her voice never rose in frustration, she never showed the slightest bit of stress. Clearly, she was accustomed to such a demanding pace.

Dawn wasn't. She was tired. So tired she wanted to find a spot where she could just lie down and sleep. But she couldn't. She had more round trips to make from the cooking school to the cottage. Drive there, drop the food, turn around, and head back to the cooking school for another load. Callie had said she wouldn't let Dawn peek while the wedding was taking place. Or the reception. She said it was extremely unprofessional at an event to see the kitchen help unless they were actually serving a guest. Deidre Klassen happened to be striding through the kitchen at that very moment and stopped to high-five Callie. "Amen to that, sister."

Fine. Just fine.

• • •

Marnie had scoured Chatham, driving to every spot Lincoln might have gone to. She really didn't know where to start or where to end, she just had to keep trying. She even went to the beach near the Chatham Lighthouse, his favorite place to walk with Mayor. She should've asked Bear if Mayor was gone too. She felt ridiculously overdressed in her pink maxi dress as she plodded through the sand, looking for a sign of him. She drove to the community center, to the library, to the church, to his favorite coffee shop. No one had seen him.

Back in the car, she put her forehead on the steering wheel and closed her eyes. She was going about this the wrong way. She was letting Bear influence her to think that Lincoln had blown off his daughter's wedding. He just wouldn't do that. She knew he wouldn't. Something *must* have happened to him.

She pulled out her phone and googled the phone number for Cape Cod Hospital in Hyannis. With her hand shaking slightly, she asked, "Do you have a patient named Lincoln Hayes?" *Please say no*, she prayed. *Say no.*

The operator tapped on her computer. "There's a Lincoln Hayes in the emergency room."

A cold shiver went down Marnie's spine. "What's happened to him?"

"I'm not able to give out patient information."

"Please," she pleaded. "I've been looking everywhere for him. His daughter is about to get married. Please tell me. Is he all right?"

"Are you a family member?"

"Yes," Marnie said, cringing at the lie. She never, ever lied.

There was a long pause. More tapping. "You'd better get down here."

● ● ●

Bear
Still no sign of him?

Marnie
I found him! But he won't be at the wedding.
Will explain when I find out more.

No surprise. Of course he won't be at his
daughter's wedding. Something always comes
up.

Chapter
TWENTY

Ice cream makes gray days brighter and sad people happy.
—Unknown

Panic swamped Marnie. She sat in the ER waiting room of Cape Cod Hospital, hardly aware of how crowded it was, fighting a dread that kept sending chills down her spine. All she'd been told when she arrived was that Lincoln had come to the ER at dawn experiencing chest pain. The receptionist wouldn't give her any information on him, which felt ominous. What could that mean?

She thought back over the last week, of noticing how pale Linc had looked, how often she'd thought he was having a sharp pain. Once or twice, he had seemed short of breath. Another time, he had suddenly leaned a hand on the doorframe to steady himself, as if he were dizzy. She wondered if what she'd seen in him this last week were signs of an impending heart attack. He was so physically fit. How could a man in his condition be having a heart attack?

She felt troubled by the length of time Linc had been in the ER. When she first arrived at the hospital, she thought he might be having a panic attack. Callie had suffered greatly from those when she first moved to Chatham. Marnie knew the symptoms could mimic a heart attack. Terrifying.

But Linc wouldn't still be in the ER if he were having a panic attack. He would've been given a sedative and sent on his way. She glanced at the clock. What was taking so long? Every time a door opened, she practically jumped. She wondered if she should text Bear, or anyone else, and let them know about Linc . . . but what did she really know about his condition? Not much. And it was the middle of the wedding. She decided to wait until she had news.

Sitting here in the hospital, waiting, made her nerves feel raw. She rubbed her face with her hands. This moment turned the clock back to three years ago, when she'd gotten a call from the hospital in Needham to come immediately, that her husband Philip had an accident at work. That time, she remembered sitting in the emergency room, waiting and waiting, confident he'd be fine. She hadn't even been overly worried as she sat patiently, waiting to hear how he was doing. Philip was a highly regarded electrician. He knew his way around power and its dangers and was extremely careful and thorough in his work, much like Dawn. But when the doctor came through the doors and walked toward her, he had a look on his face that told her everything. They'd been unable to resuscitate Philip.

Marnie fought a terrible dread. Worrisome thoughts barreling at her, way too fast. Was today going to end in the same way? Were they working on Linc, trying to keep him alive? Philip's death had been shattering enough. How would she survive losing Linc? Grief was so all consuming, so raw. Her mind raced with all kinds of scenarios. *Stop*, she told herself. *Stop and pray*.

"In everything give thanks," Paul told the Philippians. This lesson needed constant reminding, over and over. Giving thanks was the lifeboat in any crisis.

Marnie leaned forward in her chair, resting her elbows on her knees and face in her hands, doing some mental digging. Little mercies started to come to light. Linc was here, in the hospital, getting excellent care. What if he'd been driving and had a heart attack? Or what if the heart attack had happened during Ashleigh's wedding ceremony? Worse still, what if Linc had been alone, unable to call for help? Giving thanks slowed her mind's anxious downward spiral. Next, she gave thanks for the doctors and nurses who were treating him, and asked for the peace that passed all understanding to fill Lincoln's mind. For her mind too. She prayed there would be purpose in this health crisis, that God would bring good out of it.

There's so much work for love to do, she reminded the Lord, as if he needed reminding. *Please don't take Linc yet.* He still had to make things right with Bear, with Ashleigh, maybe even with the mysterious ex-wife whom Marnie had yet to meet. She glanced at the clock. And, whom she would probably never meet. By now the wedding was over and the reception was underway.

So Marnie prayed for Callie, Brynn, and Dawn, and all the work they'd done the last few days to make this wedding feast a success. *Bless them, Lord. Give them energy to manage the day. Smooth out any troubles. And Lord, if you could create a private moment for Bear and Brynn to connect, please do.* She wanted them to talk before Dawn was told that Bear and TD were one and the same. And she definitely wanted Brynn and Bear to talk before lawyers got involved. Just to talk.

"Mrs. Hayes? Mrs. Hayes?"

Consumed by prayer, it took a while for Marnie to realize she was the one being called. She took in a deep breath and rose to face the doctor.

● ● ●

The last tray of food went out the door with Bruno and Leo and Dawn. Brynn cleaned up the kitchen and looked around the room, satisfied. She'd done her part. She'd done everything well. Even Callie had said so. She'd texted throughout the late afternoon, sending thumbs-up emojis. The wedding reception had been a success.

This had been a good day to be mostly alone, because it gave her time to think. She had a lot of things to sort out, and she was thankful Callie and Dawn were thoroughly preoccupied. They both had very strong personalities, and Brynn felt like she was caught in a tug of war between them. Callie's cheerleading was contagious, but so was Dawn's practical pessimism. Brynn needed to clear her mind from their input.

And that was only about the bakery! Imagine if they knew the alter-ego of Bear Hayes and what he meant to Brynn. She shuddered at the thought of when that headline got revealed. It was inevitable, but for today, she had time to think. To mull and ponder.

She still struggled to absorb the shock of seeing TD. Of learning that he was Lincoln's son, the unlikable Bear Hayes. She had no idea what to do next—to start the ball rolling to dissolve the marriage or let him take the lead. He certainly seemed angry enough to start the process.

She sighed. What a mess.

Today, just today, the future between them could be set aside. Yesterday's conversation with Marnie kept buzzing in her brain. Thankfully, Marnie seemed neutral about the buying of the bakery—neither for it nor against it—but she kept circling Brynn back to the same theme: Listen to your heart.

That kind of thinking was counterintuitive to Brynn. She didn't trust her heart to make decisions. Only her logic. She'd watched her parents experience one disaster after the other by listening to their hearts. Brynn had always wanted to live out a life completely opposite that of her parents. It's one of the reasons she had nearly Velcro-ed herself to Dawn in college, and then to her family. She liked the way Dawn thought about things: solid, logical, predictable. She had felt like she'd won the lottery when the Dixons invited her for holidays. She loved being scooped into their tight family circle.

Marnie, she'd always enjoyed, but it was Dawn's dad, Philip, to whom Brynn looked for advice. Dawn had kind of dismissed her mom, and Brynn didn't question that opinion. Marnie was a free spirit. Like, really into church. Church was kind of her answer to everything.

Whenever Brynn visited, Marnie would encourage her to come to church, and sometimes she would say yes, but just to be polite. Afterward, they'd talk about the sermon and Brynn found them interesting. At every transition point—college graduation, promotions—something kept nipping at her heels, jabbing at her to ask, Is this all there is?

This week, she was gaining a new appreciation for Marnie Dixon's hippy-dippy advice.

Listen to your heart.

Marnie had questioned if Brynn tended to stifle God-given intuition. "Your instincts," she kept telling Brynn, "are there for a reason. They're meant to lead you to good decisions." Even an impulsive marriage to TD came about because some right-brained instinct broke through, giving her the confidence to put her trust in him.

That remark had startled Brynn silent. She knew how Marnie felt about Bear Hayes—yet, even so, she was able to keep her own feelings out of it because *she* trusted Brynn's instincts.

How could she? Brynn didn't trust her own instincts!

Listen to your heart.

If Brynn were to listen to her heart, really listen, then what it was telling her was pretty clear. She *wanted* to own that bakery. She really did. No matter what anyone else thought about her decision. She wanted it.

Wow! Another bold decision that she was making for herself! And while it might not make a lot of sense to someone like Dawn (or to Brynn's parents), she wasn't going to let it slip away.

Yes. She was going to keep the sale on track, even if Dawn was appalled by her lack of baking experience, even if TD accused her of taking advantage of Lincoln.

She heard a text ding on her phone and crossed the large kitchen to check it.

Marnie
Brynn, I need you to find Bear and tell him to go to Cape Cod Hospital. Please do it quietly so no one else knows.

Brynn
Knows what?

That Linc is in serious condition.

What? Oh Marnie, I'm so sorry. But can't I ask someone else to get Bear?

I tried but no one is answering their phones. Please, Brynn. It's an emergency. Just let him know. Bear needs to get here as fast as possible. Take Callie's car to Linc's cottage.

Brynn closed her eyes. Only for Marnie would she do this. She yanked off her apron and grabbed Callie's car keys. Near the key rack was a spare white chef coat, hanging on a hook. She grabbed that, too, and slipped it on as she headed to the car.

● ● ●

Twenty minutes later, Brynn drove up to Lincoln's cottage and handed her keys to a parking valet. She told him she was the wedding cake baker (true!) and to keep the car available for a fast exit. The late afternoon sun was still high in the sky, providing plenty of light for Brynn to see the grandeur of this home. A cottage? She coughed a laugh. Seeing where Lincoln lived made her feel better about accepting his financial help with the bridge loan, and on the heels of that thought came guilt. *Brynn*, she

212

chided herself. *That poor man is lying in a hospital bed in critical condition!*

She wove her way through the kitchen and asked a server where Kevin and Bruno and Dawn were. Kevin and Bruno were washing dishes in the pool house, he told her. He hadn't seen Dawn in a while.

"What about Callie?"

"She's around here somewhere."

Brynn headed out of the kitchen and into the backyard, then stopped to glance around. Like the house, this yard was breathtaking. There were wide-open French doors all along the back of the house. Inside, a band was playing "Cowboy Up" by Jill Johnson and young people were on the dance floor. Older guests had spilled outside to sit at tables under the soft glow of strung lights. The air held the sounds of celebration: music, people chatting and laughing. Brynn had to smile. Clearly, this event was a success. It made her feel pleased for Callie, for Didi, for everyone.

An enormous sparkling swimming pool covered half the yard and was full of floating candles, all lit. She paused, searching for the best path to get to the pool house without being noticed in her borrowed chef's coat. She hoped Callie might be able to send someone in to find TD, but suddenly, there he was. Not ten feet away, TD had come out to the patio to teach Leo cowboy line-dancing steps. Three walks forward, heel, heel. Three walks backward, stomp, stomp. Over and over they practiced, both of them laughing through the steps. Brynn ducked behind a porch column, observing them with a lump in her throat. There was just something about a man with a child—carrying a sleeping child out of a restaurant or pushing a baby in a stroller—that melted her heart. She'd always thought it was the sign of a good man.

She watched TD, struck by how attractive he was. The black tuxedo, his chiseled features. She had no idea he could dance like that. And Leo—who really shouldn't have been out mingling with the wedding guests—was determined to follow along but kept mixing up the heel and the stomp part. TD encouraged him to try and try again. Over and over. She watched their feet move in sequence—TD's glossy black shoes next to Leo's beat-up cowboy boots, and her heart melted all over again.

This was the man she had fallen for.

She felt eyes on her, and when she glanced up, she realized TD had spotted her. Slowing to a stop, the lighthearted look on his face faded, then flattened as he stared squarely at her. And then she could see the moment he found his place in the dance steps again. The music ended and TD crouched down to tell Leo something, giving him a tousle of his hair. Leo darted away to the pool house, where he was probably supposed to be in the first place. Brynn waited by the porch column, hoping TD would come to her. And he did.

Behind the column, he stood nearly nose to nose with her. A muscle ticked in his jaw. "What are you doing here?"

"Marnie Dixon asked me to come find you. Your father is in the hospital and she said you need to get there. Right now."

He stared at her, and she knew his thoughts were volleying back and forth between disbelief and belief. Finally, he said, "So, then. Let's go."

• • •

Dawn
Mom, how's the reception going? Make sure you get pix of you and Linc. You're not wearing that hideous pink maxi dress, are you?

Thirty minutes later.

Just delivered the mini–wedding cakes. Are people talking about the ice cream?

Another hour later.

Mom? Yoohoo.

214

Chapter

TWENTY-ONE

The only emperor is the emperor of ice cream.

—poet and lawyer Wallace Stevens

After the final delivery of food to Linc's cottage, Dawn was driving past the Chatham Bars Inn on Shore Road when she heard a text come in on her phone. Thinking a text finally came from Mom, she turned off the road and into the round circle drive of the inn to read it.

Dawn had a soft spot for the Chatham Bars Inn. She and Kevin often stopped in for a drink, to sit by the fire in the beautiful living room. They had some of their best heart-to-heart talks here. Maybe, she thought, she should bring him here to talk about joining her at the fertility clinic for next Wednesday's appointment. Maybe here, he'd be more open to starting the process with her. Less resistant. It's not that she didn't agree with him about the need to trust God for the timing of their future babies, but she didn't think it had to be all or none. All trust, no action. Kevin accused her of all action, no trust. Maybe there should be both. Trust God *while* starting the process of fertility treatments.

The parking circle was empty and she didn't see an attendant on duty, so she turned off the car and read the text on her phone.

Callie

Great job, everyone! What a team! Start to finish, the food was a huge hit. The waitstaff returned empty plates to the kitchen—solid evidence to a chef. Kudos to you both, Brynn and Dawn. Didi said the mini-wedding ice cream cakes were DA BOMB. (Direct quote!) She said to buckle our seat belts . . . The Knot's feature will be life changing!

Dawn closed her eyes, basking in the praise. There was a reason a third of all the ice cream sold in the world was vanilla. And then there was her Double-Fold Vanilla. She had known it would be the cherry on top of the entire meal. It was *that* good. She yawned once, then twice, and drifted off to sleep.

She woke with a start, completely disoriented, when someone rapped on her car window.

"Lady, you okay?"

It was the parking attendant for the hotel. Dawn blinked a few times. "I'm fine. Just . . . resting my eyes."

He looked at her suspiciously, like he was assessing her for signs of driving under the influence. "You been here a long time. You sure you're okay? Maybe I should call someone to come get you?"

"I'm fine." Dawn yawned. "Just had a really busy day today." She started the car, waving to the attendant, who looked like he still doubted her ability to walk in a straight line.

As she waited at the edge of the parking lot for a car to pass, she tried to remember what came next. Where was she supposed to be? Dishes. That's right. Callie wanted her back at the cottage to help Brynn with the dishes. She yawned again. Just a few more hours and this wedding would be history.

216

● ● ●

The news Marnie had been given by the doctor wasn't good—Linc had come into the ER early this morning with radiating chest pain, and while getting set up on monitors, he had coded. A full cardiopulmonary arrest. He'd stopped breathing, his heart had stopped. They performed CPR, then shocked him, and the good news, the doctor said, was that he had a full neurological return.

He'd been rushed to the cath lab for angiography where a cardiac interventionist had placed a stent over the culprit lesion. The doctor said Linc was in the right place at the right time for a heart attack. "The door-to-needle time had to happen in ninety minutes or less," he said. "Which it did. He'll be sound as a bell in no time."

Marnie wasn't quite sure what any of this meant—it was mostly new vocabulary for her—but the doctor seemed pleased and not at all worried. Then again, he was an ER doctor. Life-and-death emergencies were his life work; he saw them every day.

She sat in a hard plastic chair, eyes closed, praying constantly for Linc. No wonder he hadn't seemed like himself lately. He'd probably been feeling symptoms and ignoring them, pushing himself to see this wedding through. She fought a growing resentment toward Lincoln's ex-wife. That woman had made this wedding as excessive and unreasonable as she could. And for what? What had she hoped to get out of it?

Ten minutes ago, Brynn had texted that she and Bear were on their way. Marnie hadn't expected Brynn to come *with* Bear—only to deliver a message to him. Was this good? Could it be an answer to prayer? Or . . . maybe a hint from above *to* pray for them? So she prayed for this unexpected time in the car together, that it might be beneficial for them. Romans 8:28 promised that God could bring good things out of everything. Her friend Maeve reminded her that verse didn't mean immediately . . . but eventually.

Even this? she wondered. *God, can you bring good out of a heart attack?*

Bear had yet to make peace with his father, and he had no idea what he might be losing.

*   *   *

Brynn had been willing to deliver the message to TD that his dad was at Cape Cod Hospital, but she hadn't expected to be his driver. She hadn't prepared herself for spending time alone in a car with him. When she told him that she wasn't planning to go with him, he said that he couldn't get his car out of the garage, not with that tangled mass of parked vehicles. Brynn thought about just handing him the keys to the car, but she knew that wouldn't go over with Callie. It was a new car and Callie was a little nutty about it. So she walked over to the driver's seat and got in. "You'll have to navigate. I don't know where I'm going."

"So very true," TD said.

That made Brynn's back stiffen. Now was not the time to discuss their situation. The day had started with his sister's wedding and it was ending with his father in the hospital. She could find it within herself to keep her mouth shut. She concentrated on the driving.

"Tell me what you know about my father. Was it an accident?"

"All I know is that Marnie said you needed to come to the hospital right away. You can read the texts she sent."

"Not necessary." TD's eyes stayed fixed on the windshield.

"I don't even know what to call you. TD or Bear?"

Carefully schooling his reaction, he didn't answer her question for the longest time. So long that she asked it a second time. He shifted in his seat. "Does it matter?"

"Well, yes. Of course it does. A person should be called what they want to be called."

He remained silent, not really answering her. Now and then

he would point to give her directions until she reached Route 28. "Stay here until Hyannis," he said.

The traffic was bad for a holiday weekend, but Route 6 would've been worse. They crept along slowly, and a very awkward, uncomfortable silence filled the car like a balloon, almost palpable. And just like that, TD popped it. "Tell me the truth. Was it all a game to you?"

Every muscle in her body tensed. It felt like a blade went through her heart. She sat in the driver's seat, stuck in terrible traffic, unable to swallow what he was accusing her of. She choked down a retaliation, which would have been futile, and gripped the steering wheel so tightly her knuckles turned white.

He mistook her silence for assent. "So when, exactly, did you figure out I was the son of Lincoln Hayes? At what point did you join the Dixons in their plot to take advantage of my very wealthy and apparently very gullible father?"

With that insult she came out of her stupor, incensed. "I had no idea that you were the son of Lincoln Hayes until the day I saw you in front of the library," she said tightly. "I didn't even meet your father until this last week. And the Dixons are not taking advantage of your father! They're not like that. You'd know that if you'd only spend time to get to know them."

He paused, as if putting aside that topic before confronting another. "Well, you certainly wasted no time finding a new life for yourself."

"I don't need your father's money. Other than this bridge loan to buy the bakery—which he offered to me, by the way. I have plenty of money." *Don't say it, Brynn. Don't say it!* "In fact, Dawn thinks *you're* the one who's after my inheritance! She thinks you set everything up . . . like a con man."

He looked at her like she might be crazy, and a part of her couldn't blame him. She did sound like a crazy woman! But she wasn't about to let him continue with those icy insinuations.

"A few days ago," he said in a cold voice, "I went to Hyannis to meet with a divorce attorney. You can expect to hear from him soon."

The traffic started moving and nothing more was said. There was really no talking to him. She thought of something she'd heard long ago: You never really knew someone until you'd seen them mad.

It dawned on Brynn that she really knew very, very little about this man who called himself T. D. DeLima. She might have thought she did, but she was dead wrong. She did know one thing. She would never again think of him as TD or call him by that name. Bear was the perfect name for him.

* * *

Through the window of the waiting room, Marnie could see the tension between Brynn and Bear as they walked from the parking lot to the emergency room as vividly as if it were visible. Brynn held her elbows tightly against her abdomen, Bear stood ramrod straight, his hands shoved tightly in his tuxedo pants pockets. Marnie had worried about asking Brynn to deliver the message to Bear, but she had no other option. Someone from the Hayes family needed to be here.

She went to meet them at the door. As soon as Bear saw her waiting for them, he picked up his stride. "So what's going on?"

"Early this morning, your father came to the hospital with chest pains. He coded while he was here."

"Coded?"

Marnie paused. "His heart stopped."

For just a brief second, Marnie saw fear in Bear's eyes. It was there. There, and then gone. Brynn was the one who acted more visibly shaken by the news. She grabbed Marnie's arm. "How is he?"

"It was a godsend he was at the hospital when it happened. He had to undergo a procedure to help him."

"Procedure?" Bear said. "What kind of procedure?"

"They've put a stent in his blocked artery to reestablish the blood flow. The doctor said that he expects a good outcome."

Once again, a flicker of emotion lit Bear's eyes, then it was gone. "Then, all is well. The crisis is over." He glanced at his watch.

"Well, not quite," Marnie said. "They told me he'll be in ICU for twenty-four hours. But family can visit, they said. Bear, I thought you should be the first one to see him."

"Not necessary," Bear said. "And I'm going to head back to the wedding."

Marnie's eyes went wide. "You don't want to see him?"

"Dad's a tough guy. I'm sure he'll be just fine." Bear cleared his throat. "Besides, I should get back. Ashleigh will be counting on me."

Marnie exchanged a shocked look with Brynn. "Bear, your father nearly died today." She didn't even want to think about what might've happened had he not come to the hospital this morning.

"But he didn't."

A nurse interrupted them before Marnie could respond. "Mrs. Hayes? You can see your husband now."

Bear's eyes narrowed. "Sounds like you've got everything covered, Mrs. Hayes." He cast a glance at Brynn. "I'll take an Uber back." He strode out the way he came in.

Brynn and Marnie watched him go. When the doors closed behind him, Brynn turned to Marnie. "I know," she said. "I know." She breathed in a deep breath, then let it go. "I'll be right back. There's something I need to do." And she hurried down the hall and out the door.

• • •

Something had just slipped into place for Brynn, as clearly as if a door had opened, spilling light into a dark room. She rushed outside to where Bear was texting for an Uber. "Your father nearly died today and you're acting like it was nothing."

Startled, he looked up, then back at his phone. "He doesn't

need me to just sit around. Marnie Dixon has everything covered."

"You're lashing out at everyone. Especially the Dixons."

He swung around to stare at her. "And why would I be doing that?"

"Because you're mad at me." And he grew cold when angry, she was discovering. Cold and hard. His dark eyes were as tough as granite. "Everything between us . . . it just went too fast."

"Too fast is right. Our formal engagement lasted under fifteen minutes."

"But I will not agree to a divorce."

He dropped his arms, shocked. "What?"

"I married you because I believed you were the one. Everything I said to you during that ceremony was what I believed to be true. Divorce is not an option."

"What are you saying?"

"That you will have to figure out how to get an annulment if you want to dissolve our marriage."

"What does it matter whether it's a divorce or an annulment?"

"To me, it matters. It matters a lot. I never would have married you if I thought it would end in divorce."

"And yet you're the one who left."

"I panicked. I admit that. Marriage is terrifying to me, and the realization that I had just entered into one . . . the way we did . . . well, I just freaked out. But I did not marry you with divorce in mind. To me, marriage is a promise. I made that promise to you in good faith."

TD put his hands to his forehead in exasperation. "You fled the scene!"

Well, blast it! She wasn't a saint. She'd felt scared and overwhelmed by poor judgment only to make another mistake of poor judgment. "I'm here now," she said, in a voice she'd never heard before. A decided one. "And I'm not going anywhere. I'm resigning from the engineering firm." She wasn't just going to take a leave of absence. She was wholly embracing this new chapter. All in. "I bought a bakery. I'm staying in Chatham." She was starting to make decisions for herself, and it felt pretty darn good. "So the ball is in your court. If you want to annul this marriage, you'll have to prove to the judge why it should be annulled. Because I won't agree to an uncontested divorce."

He looked at her as if she was crazy. "You don't have to agree to a divorce. It can still happen even if one partner doesn't agree the marriage has ended."

"Well, that's on you, then."

"'That's on me,'" he replied in a mocking tone. "Brynn, why are you making this so difficult? It could be a piece of cake."

Without meaning to, he couldn't have chosen better words to use on someone who had just bought a bakery. It added just the right amount of fuel to her small inner fire. Stubbornly, she stood her ground, crossing her arms over her chest. "So we both agree that things went fast between us. Way too fast. But we did talk about how we felt coming from divorced families and how we did not want that for ourselves." She saw the Uber driver turn in the U-shaped hospital entrance, looking for his rider. Their time was short. "That was a promise we had made to ourselves . . . and to each other."

"Yet you were the one," he said, his voice cracking, "who broke that promise by leaving."

That crack in his voice had lasted only a matter of seconds, but it gave him away. Remorse spread through her, and with it came the sting of tears. She no longer wondered how much she'd hurt him by leaving that morning; she'd cut him to the quick. He was suffering, the hurt and simmering resentment he felt for his father had only compounded, and it was all because of her. A well of sympathy rose in her, and she had a sudden overwhelming need to comfort him. She *ached* to put her arms around him. To help start the process of healing. She swallowed her pride. "I did break that promise to you." She laid a hand on his arm and felt his muscles tense beneath her touch. "And that's why . . ." A softness crept into her voice. "That's why I would like to ask for your forgiveness."

When he didn't respond, she looked up to find his eyes filled with pain and longing. For a moment, neither of them moved. Their eyes held for several beats, until the Uber driver pulled up. Bear got in the car, his face turned away from Brynn.

● ● ●

Marnie followed the nurse to the ICU room where Lincoln had been moved. "Your husband woke up briefly," the nurse said, "asked if you were here, then drifted off again."

Marnie's eyes started to sting with tears. She hoped the nurse told Linc that she was right there, waiting. That she wouldn't be anywhere else.

The nurse stopped at the door to Lincoln's room and handed Marnie a mask to put on. "He had to be sedated for the procedure, so it'll take a while for those to clear his system. He'll probably be sleepy. Also, he's going to be sore. CPR can be hard on a body. Often, it breaks ribs. Not in your husband's case," she hastened to add as Marnie's eyes went wide with alarm. "But his chest will be sore and red from the defibrillator. A little burned."

Marnie must have still looked shocked, because the nurse then said, "Look on the brighter side. He's feeling a whole lot better than he did when he came in here this morning."

As Marnie saw Linc lying there, unconscious, wires everywhere, oxygen prongs in his nose, her stomach went weightless with alarm, then dropped with a thud. She bit her lips and felt tears begin to swell as the fear of helplessness began to take hold. *Marnie Dixon, don't you go to pieces now!*

She went to the opposite side of the bed, away from the machine that was tracking Linc's vitals. His right hand had a pulse ox on his finger to monitor oxygen and an IV, his wrist had a tight band for the incision sight, his arm had a blood pressure cuff. She watched the steady beating of his heart on the machine, listened to the blood pressure cuff tighten and release. She pressed a palm to his temple and forehead, trying to control the fear that made her hand tremble and tightened the muscles in her chest. He looked so vulnerable. And she felt so vulnerable. Tears were falling now. She silently told him he was loved. Oh, but how he was loved. She'd known for some time that she loved him, but she hadn't realized how much until this moment. What would she do without him?

She sat beside him for a while as he slept, which was good in a way because it gave her time to pull herself together. *No more crying, Marnie Dixon.* The late afternoon light coming through the window seemed suddenly flat and dull. A whole day had passed by and she had hardly been aware of it.

His eyes fluttered open, closed again, then slowly opened. His gaze swept the room, then landed on her. The look of love and relief in his eyes made her tear up again. "Hi," he whispered.

"Hey you," she said in as sturdy a voice as she could manage. She tried to smile, but she knew it came out all wrong.

"Pink. My favorite."

She looked down at her pink dress. Had it really just been a few hours since she'd gotten dressed for the wedding? It felt like days had passed.

"Will you," he said shakily, "help me break out of here?"

Such an unexpected comment had her smiling through a prickle of tears. "Not a chance. You're right where you need to be." She reached over the rail to take his wire-free left hand in hers. It was so cold. She cupped his hand with both of hers.

"So sorry," he said, his voice hammered thin. "About all of this."

"Don't be sorry. Just focus on recovering." She brushed the

top of his forehead with the back of her hand. "So you woke up in terrible pain?"

He nodded. "I didn't sleep much last night. Kept feeling like an anvil had been dropped on my chest." He swallowed with effort. "As the pain traveled down my left arm, I knew it wasn't going away this time."

"This time?"

"Like it did last week."

She squeezed her eyes shut, trying not to cry. "Oh Linc . . ."

"A few days ago, I had some discomfort in my chest. But after a while, it went away."

"But you didn't see a doctor?"

He gave her a weak smile. "It's been so busy. I didn't want to spoil Ashleigh's special time." He closed his eyes. "The wedding," he said, his eyes opening wide. "I missed it. I missed the whole thing."

Was he serious? Marnie had to shake her head. Did he not realize how close he came to losing his life today?

"Did you get to go?"

She could tell he was fighting to stay awake. "I . . . well . . . no. This morning, Bear couldn't find you, so he came to the Creamery. I told him to stay focused on the wedding and I'd find you. Which I did." Tears pricked her eyes, and she paused, swallowing. "I'm confident the day was a success. I have no doubt Ashleigh's wedding was everything she hoped it to be."

Linc looked away. "Except for the missing father of the bride."

"That couldn't be helped. You tried, Linc." He tried so hard to be there that he jeopardized his own well-being. "Everyone understands." Or would, when they learned that Linc was recovering from a heart attack.

"Not Bear."

"He was here. He came to see how you were."

Linc's eyebrows lifted. "He's here now?"

"As soon as he knew you were okay, he went back to the wedding."

Now his eyebrows were down. "Bear's angry."

Angry. Bitter. Hardened. "Your son . . . he has a lot to work through." Now wasn't the time to let Linc know about Bear and Brynn and their twenty-four-hour marriage. Nor was it the time to tell him that when Bear had come to the Creamery early in the day to search for him, he had assumed Linc had more important things to do than to be at his only daughter's wedding. Marnie didn't say any of the things crowding her heart. Not how frightening this day had been, how difficult the waiting was, or how much she loved him. Instead, she plastered on a big fake smile. "I have a bone-deep feeling that something good is going to come out of all this."

Linc turned to her, his eyes full of tenderness. "I love you for saying that," he said with feeling.

His eyes drifted shut again, just as a nurse poked her head in. She checked the band on Lincoln's wrist and released it slightly. "He's out cold," she said. "Your husband is going to be sleeping for a while, which is just what his body needs. Why don't you go home and get some rest? Leave your cell phone number at the desk and I promise you'll be called if there's any change."

Marnie didn't want to leave the hospital room, but the nurse was probably right. Linc needed rest, and she needed to check on the ice cream shop. Brynn had texted that she would relieve Nanette and Mrs. Nickerson-Eldredge, but she should get back and see how those two had fared. What a day. She kissed Linc on the forehead and left the room, but her heart stayed put.

● ● ●

Callie (group text)
Heading back to the cooking school with the surplus food. Who wants to come help put it all away so nothing goes to waste?

Twenty minutes later.

Hello? Hello? What's happened to my team?

Ten minutes later.

Bruno
We've all gone to bed. Night.

Chapter
TWENTY-TWO

Life would be vanilla ice cream without 31 flavors of in-
dividuality.

—blogger Heather King

Sunday, July 3

Sometime in the night, an immense clap of thunder shook the
old house, waking Dawn out of a sound sleep. Kevin, a sound
sleeper, slept through the whole thing. Dawn got out of bed to
open the window and let the cool air in. She stood by the window
for a long time, watching the lightning bolts illuminate the night
sky, before she finally went back to bed and listened to the rain
pound the roof. She tried not to think of leaks in the attic. Instead,
she focused on the delightful realization that the heat spell, at
last, had been broken. The thunderstorm moved on and Dawn
drifted back to sleep.

The next morning, she remained snug in her bed, drowsy, dozing, a rare gift. Kevin had woken her at six to say he was leaving
to head to Truro. One of the waitstaff at last night's wedding had
given him a tip on a poorly maintained historic house that might

be coming on the market—one with exposed gunstock beams wedged in the corners and a large open hearth with "hangey things" (Dawn's term for cauldron hooks or for Betty lamps)—all nods from colonial days. Kevin wanted to talk to the owner before the house was listed, to convince him to sell it to him so that he could preserve the house's architectural integrity. Anyone else, especially a general contractor, would look at a historic house in bad shape and consider it a knockdown. Not Kevin. He wanted to buy it before a bulldozer could get to it.

Dawn stretched out in bed, thinking of how well suited Kevin was for his work as a preservationist architect. His favorite hobby had always been to search out period features in old homes. The quirkier, the better. The central chimney house they were living in now and slooooowly renovating had been built in 1745 and bore all kinds of unusual characteristics. Wooden pocket shutters, for example, that slipped into the wall next to a window. Some called them Indian shutters, based on a legend that they were created to protect the early English settlers from tensions with the Native Americans. Kevin dismissed that as a myth. More likely, he said, pocket shutters were a practical invention to block light and wind.

Kevin's latest favorite discoveries were small doors that hinted of a slightly more recent era than colonial days: milk doors—small wooden openings where the milk man would pick up empty bottles and leave fresh ones. Or coal doors—iron openings that allowed the coal delivery man to shovel coal down a chute directly into a basement.

He'd invited her to come with him, but after such a long day yesterday, she had no interest in doing anything but sleeping. She dozed off and on again for another hour or so. When she was finally ready to get out of bed and start the day, she reached for her phone.

"Morning!" she said after Brynn answered. "Want to come to the house for coffee? Kevin found Betty lamps in the attic."

"What's a Betty lamp?"

"It's a lantern that people would hang on their hearth. People would burn fish oil with wicks of twisted cloth."

"And it's named after some lady named Betty?"

Dawn laughed. "According to Kevin, who knows these things, Betty morphed from the German word *besser*. Meaning 'better.' Better light. Not necessarily a better smell, though. I can still smell the fish oil. Want to come over for coffee and get a tour of our house? You haven't seen it yet. It's still pretty torn up, but it's fun to see the before and hope there will be an after."

"Thanks, but it'll have to wait for another time," Brynn said. "I'm going to church with your mom."

What? No one looped Dawn in? "I go too. Same church. Let's meet and have lunch afterward. I've been giving your life some thought. I have a new idea to untangle things."

"Dawn, I appreciate it. I do. I know you want to help, but I don't want you untangling my life. In fact, I don't need anyone's help untangling my life. Because I know just what I'm going to do."

Dawn sat up straight. "So you were able to pull out of the bakery sale? Good for you! I knew there was a loophole you'd be able to find." She gave a fist pump in the air.

"No. I'm going to keep the bakery."

Dawn hung her head. Callie! She'd gotten to Brynn. Spun her Callie magic over the fantasy of having a bakery.

"Before you say anything, let me tell you this. I'm good at engineering and I made a lot of money at it, but it was never a perfect fit. I love to bake. Something inside me stepped up and said, 'Yes, this is what you're meant to be doing.'"

Dawn closed her eyes in defeat.

"I don't even have to see you to know what you're thinking."

"What am I thinking?"

"That I have no experience running a commercial bakery. That I'll be heavily dependent on Callie to gain skills. That the risk is too great for the reward—which, at its best, will be low. That I'm giving up a promising career in engineering. That my 401(k) will be quickly emptied out. That my trust fund will be drained." She let out an eloquent pause. "Am I close to what's running through your mind?"

Dawn cleared her throat. "Maybe." Definitely.

"And you know what? You're absolutely right. I have no experience. I will be heavily dependent on Callie, which isn't fair to her. She's got enough on her plate with the cooking school. You're right about every single thing, but you forgot one important thing."

"What did I forget?"

"That baking makes me happy. The same way that making ice cream makes you happy."

Dawn opened her mouth to object, then closed it. She couldn't think of an objection. Making ice cream did make her happy. Even during a week like she'd just had, she still felt a great satisfaction in her work.

"But I'm not crazy. I know where the problems are. So here's what I've decided to do."

Dawn leaned forward on the bed. "What?"

"Cookies. I'm going to turn the bakery into a cookie shop. I know cookies. I bake great cookies. The location of the bakery is ideal for foot traffic. I might not be ready to churn out a big variety of baked goods on a daily basis, but cookies, those I can do."

She could, actually. This plan made sense. A lot of sense. "I suppose," Dawn said slowly, "you could always increase your inventory as you gain skills."

"Maybe. Yes, I probably could. But selling cookies might be good enough. I am confident I could make a success of it. I have five basic recipes that work every time."

Repeatable. Consistent. Dependable. All good.

"And I've been watching people in Chatham. They like to picnic. They like to eat on the beach. Cookies are very transportable. Very shareable. Cookies would work here."

Dawn pulled the phone away to look at it. Who was this woman? A new and improved Brynn Haywood. She'd never, ever heard Brynn sound so clear and determined. Creative too. Yet she also saw Brynn's engineering logic woven into this plan. Five basic, reliable recipes. A transportable product. Dawn felt so proud of her. Logic had returned. Brynn had come back. "So what about TD?"

"What about him?" Her voice went flat.

"How are you sorting out that sticky situation?"

"Working on it. We, um, we'll have to talk today. After church. There's something I need to let you know."

"What do you mean?" Dawn went on high alert. "Has something happened with TD? Have you heard from him?"

"I'd rather explain in person. Not on the phone."

"Can't you just give me a headline?"

"Not really," she said, but then she paused for a minute. "Well, yes. Here it is. I have heard from him."

"What? When? How could you not have told me? This is front-page news."

"That's exactly why I didn't want to tell you until after the wedding. Look, I'd better get going. I heard a car door slam and I think that means your mom just got back from seeing Lincoln at the hospital. I want to hear how he's doing."

"Wait just a minute! Why is Lincoln in the hospital?"

"You haven't heard? Better call your mom." Brynn hung up.

What in the world had happened since yesterday? Dawn was usually right on top of everything. She called her mom, but it went straight to voicemail. Huffing, she threw off the bedcovers and scooted out of bed to change clothes. She was going to meet Mom and Brynn at church and get the latest scoop. As soon as her feet hit the floor, she realized she'd gotten up too fast. She sat right back down on the bed until the room stopped spinning.

● ● ●

The car door Brynn had heard belonged not to Marnie but to Nosy Nanette from across the street, a person she had quickly learned to avoid. Once Nanette started talking, she did not stop. Twice now, Brynn had been trapped by this tiny woman with spiderweb hair. Firehosed by whatever happened to be on her mind at the time. An endless stream of consciousness.

So when Brynn saw it was Nanette's car and not Marnie's, she closed the door quietly to remain unseen. It was such a beautiful summer morning that she decided to head down to the beach and get a run in before church. She jogged past the bakery and slowed, pleased to see the For Sale sign had a big SOLD slapped across it. She had hesitated before turning the corner, worried the sight might terrify her, but it truly made her happy. *Why, that's me*, she thought. *I'm the reason it's been sold.*

She decided to take her delight in the Sold sign as evidence that she was trusting her own instincts, like Marnie had encouraged her to do. Marnie believed that God had given Brynn those instincts, and she was starting to agree. Something was definitely stirring in her, and she couldn't quite explain what, but she was leaning into it and not avoiding it like she'd done in the past.

When she reached the road, she crossed and went straight to the water. The sun was already up, reflecting brightly off the Atlantic. Cooler today than it had been the last few days, after a thundershower in the middle of the night cleared the air. The tide was heading out, and she walked along the water's edge, breathing deeply of the salty air. Someone's dog barked, and another barked back, and she started to jog slowly up the beach. Suddenly a big golden retriever was beside her, jogging along as if he'd been sent to guard her. "Hey there, pup. Wait, I know you. Aren't you Mayor?" Lincoln's dog. She stopped, and the dog stopped. And suddenly, there was Bear.

He was in shorts and a T-shirt. A scruff of stubble rimmed his cheeks. "I guess we had the same idea this morning."

"I guess so." Awkward silence. "Did Ashleigh get off on her honeymoon?"

"Yes. They left for Tahiti last night."

She squinted in the morning sun. "From one beach to another?"

"I know. Crazy, right?" Their gazes met momentarily and a soft smile curved his lips. "Not what I would want for my honeymoon." For one split second, his guard was down, but then he realized what he'd said and back up it went. More awkward silence.

She searched for something to say to avoid all the unsaid that hovered between them. It was hard to believe that it had once been so easy to talk to each other. "Did Ashleigh get a chance to see her dad before she left?"

"No. I didn't tell her why he'd missed her wedding."

She flicked him a glance. "Why wouldn't you tell her?"

"Because she didn't ask. I suppose we're just used to him not showing up."

"Having a heart attack isn't the same thing as unexpected business."

"No?" He sounded unconvinced.

This conversation had taken a wrong turn. A pair of screeching gulls arced overhead, but she barely noticed them. "Are you going to see your dad today?"

"Wasn't planning on it."

She planted her hands on her hips. "Aren't you even wondering how he's doing?"

"My dad spent my entire childhood not at all concerned about his two children. Why should I suddenly start caring about him?"

"Because he's trying! He's doing all he can to make amends."

Bear coughed a laugh. "A little late for that."

"You're wrong. It's never too late."

Aggrieved, he turned and started walking away.

"Hey!"

He stopped abruptly but didn't turn back.

"You just won't let anyone off the hook, will you? One mistake and you cut people off for good!"

He spun around to face her. "One *mistake*?" He said the word like it was poisonous. "Do you have any idea how it felt when I realized you'd left? You'd think a lifetime of disappointments with my father would have inured me to more of them, but nothing"— his voice split on the word and he paused to regroup—"nothing felt as harsh as waking up to find you'd left. No word from you. Not a single effort to reach me."

She could feel the heat rise in her cheeks, could feel the pulse pound in her throat. She swallowed and swallowed again, unable to get her bearings. What could she possibly say to that? It was a fair indictment. "Bear," she whispered, her eyes wide, her throat hot and tight. "I am sorry. Truly sorry. Please try to understand—"

"I don't understand it. And I don't want to understand it. Frankly, it really doesn't matter why. The point is that you made your choice. You left." He whistled to Mayor and the two started down the beach.

Tears made the sight of them running in the distance swim before her, and she hunched a shoulder and blotted her eyes on her sleeve. She took in a deep breath, steeling herself, trying to gain a grip on her emotions. As if clouds cleared to reveal the sun, she knew exactly what the problem was between them. It was the echo of another story. And suddenly, she felt *mad*. So angry that she took off after them. "Hey! Hey, Bear. Stop! Stop!"

Hearing her, Mayor danced around on the sand and hurtled back in her direction. Bear slowed, then stopped, turning, waiting until she caught up to him.

"When I married you," she said, breathing hard, feeling a rush of conviction, "I thought I knew you. But I certainly didn't know this corner of your heart. I never would have said yes to you had I known."

"What are you talking about?" His forehead wrinkled in confusion. "What corner?"

"The dark corner of unforgiveness." In a flash, she saw his face tighten like a fist. With that, she turned and jogged off.

• • •

Marnie had gone to the hospital as soon as she got the call that Linc was awake and asking for her. She wanted to be as close as possible to him, to see for herself how he was doing. The nurse at the station desk told her that he'd had a pretty good night, all things considered.

Relief flooded through Marnie. "So he's going to be all right?"

"We'll be watching him carefully for the next few days, just to make sure the stent is restoring blood flow to the heart like it's supposed to do." The nurse winked. "Don't you worry. Your husband will be back to work on his honey-do list before you know it."

Marnie knew she should come clean about not being Linc's wife, but for now it provided a clear benefit: insider info about his condition. "Can I see him?"

"Go on in."

She knocked gently on the hospital door and opened it. Linc was sleeping, so she tiptoed in and sat by his bedside. Wires were still attached all over, but a normal color had returned to his face. She settled back in the chair and used the time to pray for him, to thank God for Linc's survival, for his recovery. And to ask for healing between him and his son.

Ten minutes passed, then twenty, and finally he stirred. His eyes opened and, like last night, landed on Marnie with a smile. "Did you come to take me home?"

She laughed. "Not so fast, my friend. But I'm glad your spunk is back."

"The nurse thinks we're more than friends. She keeps referring to you as my wife."

Marnie scrunched up her face. "They assumed . . . and I didn't correct them."

He reached out to take her hand. "I like the sound of it."

So did Marnie, actually. Quite a bit. After Philip died, she thought she'd never marry again, but she'd never imagined meeting someone like Lincoln Hayes. "So, your heart's been giving you some trouble."

He let out a sigh. "So they say."

"How long had you been experiencing symptoms?"

"Not too long."

She tipped her head in doubt.

"A few weeks."

"And what kinds of symptoms?"

"Shortness of breath. Chest pain. Fatigue after exertion. But it eased up when I rested."

"Isn't that a sign of angina?" She had been googling.

"I thought it was just stress. But then, yesterday morning, I remembered what you said."

"What did I say?"

"That if I was in persistent pain, I should get to a doctor. So I did."

She squeezed her eyes shut. "And you drove yourself to the hospital." The very thought of it sent a cold shiver down her spine. The nurse had told her that he had coded soon after arriving at the hospital. It could've easily happened while he was driving. He could've died on the way. He could've caused an accident for someone else. *Thank you, thank you, thank you, Lord, for protecting him.* She wasn't even sure Linc knew he had coded. If so, he seemed pretty matter-of-fact about the whole thing.

"I've been trying to figure out how this could have happened to me. I exercise, eat right, keep to a low weight. How could someone like me have had a heart attack?"

Marnie had given that some consideration. What about stress? she wanted to ask. What about trying so hard to take care of everybody? What about the toll a bout of cancer took on your body?

But those thoughts, like others, could wait for another day. Timing was everything.

Linc yawned. "I thought you said Bear was here yesterday, but then I realized I must've been dreaming. He would've been at the wedding."

"You weren't dreaming. He was here for a few minutes. As soon as he knew you were all right, he returned to the wedding."

She could see Linc's eyelids grow heavier. She wanted to tell Linc about Bear and Brynn, but not now. Linc didn't need to be overloaded with problems. One at a time was plenty. What she really hoped was that Lincoln and Bear would have an opportunity for a heart-to-heart talk before Bear left the Cape. But she also knew she needed to leave that hope in God's hands. The Holy Spirit could arrange the timing of that conversation.

She was conscious of overstaying. She rose from the chair and planted a kiss on the top of Lincoln's head. "Sleep in peace, God is awake."

His eyes fluttered open. "Victor Hugo."

Was that who said it? She never did know. She only knew she loved it and planned to teach it to her grandchildren one day, if she ever had some. Leave it to Linc to know the source of the quote. "I'm taking Brynn to church. Then I'll come back afterward."

"Before you go . . . any word about how the wedding went?"

"Great. Everything went perfectly." At least, as far as all the food went. So great that Deidre Klassen was over the moon. Something about a feature on a big, important website that was going to *change their lives*. She was excited, Callie was excited. Marnie didn't think life needed any more excitement.

● ● ●

Brynn was the one who had asked Marnie if she could go to church with her. Surprised by the question, Marnie had a look on her face like she could barely hold back from shouting "Hallelujah." She didn't, though. But she did ask Brynn why she wanted to go to church.

It took Brynn a moment to gather her response. It wasn't easy, this soul-searching stuff. "I keep feeling a longing for . . . something more. Something that glimpses possibilities far beyond facts." The more Marnie had talked to her about trusting her instincts, about listening to her heart, the more she pointed to what was behind that. Or rather Who.

Marnie said that longing was evidence of God at work, whispering to her heart. She'd never given much thought to pursuing God, but she'd never had to either. Life had seemed pretty predictable to her. Hard work equaled success. Treating people well brought its own rewards.

Suddenly, life wasn't so simple. This last week, she had felt small and very, very alone. She needed help. Guidance. Peace of mind. If going to church could do that for her, she was willing to go.

The music was pleasant, the sermon was nice enough, but there came a moment in the service that nearly undid Brynn. Communion. It wasn't new to her, but this time it hit her.

She wondered if it had something to do with the bakery—she was now wholly committed to those humble, basic elements, to transforming them into something nourishing and sustainable.

Or maybe it was that she connected the breaking of bread to putting trust in Christ. Maybe it was both—after all, buying the bakery was a giant leap of faith. Whatever it was, whatever it meant, as she dipped the bread in the cup of wine, a well of emotion rose up inside her and tears started pouring down her cheeks. For the first time in her life, she had a quiet certainty that God was with her. She wasn't alone.

She couldn't even return to her pew. She went straight to the restroom to mop her face, and only when she felt like she had regained control did she return to Marnie's side. The pew was full of Dixons—Dawn and Kevin, Callie and Bruno, and Cowboy Leo, who was now wearing a baseball cap. She was pretty sure that Lincoln would be here, too, if he weren't in the hospital. Joining this family whom she loved started her tears all over again.

But they weren't sad tears. A deep sense of peace filled her, from top to bottom. On this beautiful Sunday morning on Cape Cod, there was no place else she'd rather be, no other people she'd rather be with. But a little part of her heart kept poking at her, as if to remind her that someone was missing.

Lord? What are you going to do about Bear?

It was Brynn's first prayer.

●　●　●

Maeve
So how did everything turn out yesterday?

Marnie
Much much much differently than expected.

???

Too big a convo for texting. Maybe we can talk?

Yes! But not sure when I can get free. Super busy weekend here, as you well know.

241

Chapter
TWENTY-THREE

Sometimes life is what it is, and the best you can hope for is ice cream.

—author Abbi Waxman

Right after church, the hospital called to let Marnie know that Lincoln was undergoing an echocardiogram to see how much damage had been done to his heart. Most likely, afterward he'd be moved out of ICU and into a regular room. Marnie smiled with the news, and Kevin told her to go, that he would man the Creamery counter for a few hours until she got back.

She found Linc in his new room, sitting up in his bed, leaning against pillows, still wired to a machine but nothing like in the ICU. His face lit up when he saw her, and she smiled in return. Amazing, what just-in-time medical care could do.

She pulled up a chair and sat beside him. "You look like you're feeling a lot better."

"I am." He reached out to take her hand. His felt much warmer than yesterday. "Still grieving that I missed my daughter's wedding."

"I know. That's going to take some time to get over." She covered his hand with both of hers. "I'm kinda sorry I never met Jeannie."

His eyebrows lifted. "Did you want to?"

"Yes, of course. She's the mother of your children. She'll always be important."

He took that in for a while. "There's something about a brush with death that gives God an opportunity to deliver a needed wake-up call. The first time I was in this spot was when I had cancer and realized I had no one to put down on my emergency list. This time, my wake-up call is about unfinished business."

"How so?"

"I sense God wants me to take a good hard look at the mess I've made with the family he entrusted to me. And to do something about it." He paused, as if gathering his thoughts. "This wedding . . . it's obvious that Jeannie's angry with me."

Marnie wanted to lift her hands and shout *Amen!* She didn't, but she wanted to. Prudence kept her quiet. The way this wedding had unfolded throughout the week was very troubling to her. Clearly, Linc's ex-wife was going to make it as expensive, as lavish, as difficult and detailed as possible. As Deidre Klassen told Callie, who told Brynn who told Dawn who told Marnie: "That woman has an axe to grind."

"I've been thinking . . . maybe I should apologize to Jeannie. Though, after all these years, I'm not sure it would change anything for her."

"Apologies don't have an expiration date."

"You're right." He smiled at her. "You have such a wonderful way of phrasing things. At least I could tell Jeannie that now I see how lacking I was as a husband and father." His eyes grew glassy with tears. "All those years, she tried to tell me."

"Tell you what?"

"That I was missing out on so much. That one day I'd regret it."

"You didn't believe her?"

"I think . . . I just didn't see it for what it was."

How sad, Marnie thought. No wonder Bear couldn't get past his childhood hurts. No wonder she had sensed his simmering resentment toward her and Dawn. For Bear to see Linc embracing Marnie and the Dixon family—strangers to him—in the loving way he'd longed for from his father . . . well, she was starting to understand his prickliness. His inability to forgive. "Linc, what made a career so important to you? Was it money?"

"Partly. My own father skipped out when I was around Cowboy Leo's age. Just left. My mother worked herself to the bone to provide for us. I saw the shame in her eyes when she handed over food stamps to the grocery clerk, and I promised myself that when I became a father, I'd provide well for my family. So that's what I did. When Jeannie complained, I felt she was expecting too much out of me. It seemed I could never do enough to make her happy. And to be fair, she liked having the house in Boston's Back Bay, the summer cottage at the Cape. I couldn't manage both a demanding career *and* pay attention to my family. Or maybe I just didn't think I could."

Marnie listened without saying anything. She didn't need to say anything. All this personal reflection had to be exhausting, grueling, but so beneficial. Like cleaning out an infected wound so that it could truly heal. When Brynn arrived in Chatham, and then Bear, Marnie had known that God must be up to something, but she hadn't thought that "something" had extended to Linc. Clearly, it did.

"Being around Bear these last few days," Linc said after a long pause, "I see so much of myself in him. Maybe history is repeating itself. Maybe I'm more like my father than I could've ever imagined. It wasn't all about providing for my family. I didn't value relationships. Bear doesn't seem to either." He exhaled. "It's been a harsh reminder of the kind of man I've been."

"Was," Marnie said softly. "That was the old Lincoln Hayes. There's a new one in town."

He gave her hand a squeeze. "I don't want Bear to look back on his life from a hospital bed and think of all the missed opportunities he's had." A wistful look covered his face. "I should've taken Bear fishing. Every summer, he would ask me if we could go. I meant to, but we never did. Should've built sandcastles. Caught crabs at low tide. Played ball." He released Marnie's hand and lifted his arm to rest his head on his forearm. "I should have done a lot of things with him. I let him down, over and over."

"Have you ever told him about your regrets?"

He let out a defeated sigh. "It's not easy to talk to Bear."

"What about your cancer? Does he know?"

Linc shook his head. "I don't want his pity."

That kind of thinking made Marnie so frustrated. Families should be talking, parents and children, not tiptoeing on eggshells around each other. Too many important conversations didn't take place that needed airing, even if doing so created conflict. She knew that firsthand, after not telling Dawn that she'd had surgery for breast cancer. She'd tried to protect her daughter and ended up making it worse for her.

He misunderstood her silence. "Marnie, I don't want you to tell him."

"It's not my place to tell Bear anything." Nor did she want to! "But it is yours. If not now, then when?"

"Timing has always been our problem." Linc gave one shoulder a slight shrug. "Besides, I think it's too late to change very much."

Oh no. Marnie wasn't buying that. "I think that maybe now . . . he might be willing to listen." Truthfully, she wasn't as sure as she sounded. She had no idea how to lure Bear back to the hospital. Bear needed to hear from his father. For his own well-being, he needed to forgive him. Without forgiveness, the brokenness continued.

"What can I do?"

"You have to talk to him, Linc. I hope you don't mind my saying so, but the Hayes family doesn't talk enough."

"No, we never did." Then, slowly, a twinkle lit his eyes. "And that is something the Dixon family will never be accused of."

A laugh burst out of Marnie and her spirit soared. Linc was on the mend. That, and realizing what he had said about the Dixons was true, but it wasn't always that way. Marnie and Dawn used to have a strained relationship. After Philip died, and especially after buying the ice cream shop, they had learned to accept each other, to appreciate their differences—which were significant ones. Those first few months of getting the Creamery on its feet were pretty rocky between them. Marnie thought back on Dawn's obsession with getting vanilla ice cream just so. And now she was churning out all kinds of flavors, every single day. Experimenting, too, when she had time. And Marnie was working on her weak muscles, like staying focused. Avoiding distractions.

These days, Marnie and Dawn had a very good working relationship. Even better, they enjoyed each other's company. But none of it had come overnight. Still, with time, it had come.

Little more was said for a long stretch, and Marnie started to wonder if she should leave to let Linc sleep. Just as she was about to say goodbye, he started on another ramble of reflection, and she didn't mind a bit. She was finally learning about Lincoln's life before she knew him. Whenever she had tried to find out more, . he would deflect questions, like he just didn't want to churn up memories. He was happier in the present than the past.

"Bear doesn't want my name. Did I already tell you that? He had his surname changed to his grandfather's name. DeLima. I'm not sure if he had it officially changed or if he just goes by it." Linc's eyes closed, then opened again. "Doesn't really matter. He made his point."

Ah. So that was where T. D. DeLima came from. "DeLima . . . is that . . . ?"

"Portuguese. Long, long ago, whalers from Azores ended up

on Cape Cod." He yawned. "A large Portuguese population is still here."

"So that's where Ashleigh's and Bear's dark eyes and olive skin comes from."

He nodded. "Twins, but different in every way. Ashleigh resembles Jeannie. Short and, well, ample. Ashleigh's always taken after her mother's side of the family. Bear is more of a Hayes." His eyes drifted shut.

Marnie thought he might have fallen asleep but with a start, he opened his eyes. "The doctor said I need to go to cardiac rehab after I get released. They said that people who go to post-cardiac rehab have a better outcome. They made it sound almost like a support group."

"Community."

His brows lifted in a question.

"Community is so important, on so many levels. As I recall, that's how you and I met. You kept badgering me to go to the Cancer Support Group." She reached out to give him a light tap on his shoulder. "And look at that outcome."

He gave her a smile, then it dimmed. He was growing weary, fading fast.

"Are you hungry? I'm leaving now to relieve Kevin at the Creamery, but before I go, I could bring you something delicious from the hospital cafeteria."

"That's an oxymoron," he mumbled.

She burst out with a loud laugh, surprising him enough that his eyes opened wide and he started to laugh, then he cringed and put a hand on his ribs. "Hurts to laugh."

"I'll bet it does. The nurse said you were lucky that your ribs weren't broken during CPR. It happens a lot, she said." She bent over to give him a gentle kiss. "You rest. I'll be back this afternoon. Text if you want me to bring you anything."

"I already know. Bring ice cream. Any flavor."

Right. To a patient in the hospital for a heart attack. It would be considered contraband and she would be escorted to the exit by security.

At the door, she turned to say goodbye. Linc was out cold.

● ● ●

Dawn invited Brynn to come over after church to have a bite to eat and to show her their new old house. She'd just finished giving Brynn a tour of the house and ended in the kitchen, apologizing for the temporary flooring of pressboard. "Kevin found wide pine planks in the attic and plans to pull them all up to replace the rotted flooring in the kitchen. Those wide planks are a treasure," Dawn said, as if Brynn had asked. "They're cut from gigantic trees. First growth pine, it's called. Not like today, when trees are harvested after ten to fifteen years." She took a box of square nails off the windowsill to show Brynn. "These are called cut nails or square nails. See how they're wedged with a blunt edge? Kevin's going to install the planks with them to match the flooring in the rest of the downstairs. They're hard to work with, but he's determined. He doesn't like any disconnect between old and new." She set the box back on the windowsill. "Oh! I forgot to point out the windows! See the wavy glass? The pits? They're original."

While she was chattering away, pulling some salad makings out of the refrigerator, Brynn sat down at the kitchen table and set her purse on the floor. Dawn had sensed her lack of enthusiasm in the house, which was a little disappointing. It might not be much now, a hodgepodge mix of time periods and shoddy updates, but eventually, it would be restored to its former colonial-period glory.

And that was when Brynn dropped a bombshell. "Dawn, could you just sit down for a minute? There's something I need to tell you."

Curious, Dawn pulled out a chair and sat down.

"Last Thursday, you sent me to the library to meet with Bear

Hayes. So I did." Brynn took in a deep breath, then let it out. "And that was when I discovered that Bear Hayes and T. D. DeLima are the same person."

Dawn's eyes widened in disbelief. She stared at Brynn, shocked speechless. Her breath caught in her throat. "Bear . . . TD . . . he's . . . who?" She sputtered for words. There *were* no words! "Tell me everything, one more time. Go slowly this time. So you saw Bear"—she shook her head as if to clear it—"you saw TD at the library and . . ."

Brynn repeated the scene, from start to finish, her voice expressionless and oddly measured, as if she'd revisited this scene one too many times.

Yet it was still hard for Dawn to get her head around it. "How is this even possible? You met in Las Vegas one weekend and you both ended up here, in Chatham, the very next weekend. And that's only half of it. Think of all the overlapping relationships you have in common. Mom and Linc. Me and Linc. Callie and Linc. Kevin and Linc. I mean . . . it's . . . it's . . ." She lifted her palms. "Honestly, I don't know what it is."

"Your mom called it a miracle."

That sounded like something Mom would say. If she couldn't explain something, then she dubbed it a miracle. Dawn wasn't nearly so mystically minded, but she couldn't deny that this was a weird, one-in-a-million coincidence. She shook her head. "What are the odds? I mean, what are the chances?" She let out a nervous laugh and said, "Man, Brynn! You should've stayed in Las Vegas and bet the house."

Dawn meant it in a lighthearted way, but Brynn didn't lighten up. In fact, the look on her face was pretty serious. Too soon for Dawn to joke about this.

"Well, here's another way to look at it. Maybe there's a gift in this revelation."

Brynn's eyebrows lifted in a question.

"Actually, the more I think about it, the more of a gift it might be. Now you know, for sure, that TD is not the guy you thought he was. If anything, the interactions you've been having with him should make you all the more determined to dissolve the marriage. I mean, how could you have any doubts?"

But Brynn didn't seem quite so doubt-free.

"Knowing his true identity shouldn't change anything." Dawn was using her best debate-team tone. "If it helps, we've all had a negative impression of Bear Hayes. Including Mom."

Well, maybe not Kevin or Cowboy Leo, but they were guys. Women could sense these things. "So first thing tomorrow morning, I am going to find a lawyer for you and get this taken care of. It's moving to the very top of my to-do list. Sound good to you?"

Dawn waited, but Brynn didn't answer.

Why was she so quiet? So subdued? If Mom were here, she would tell Dawn to ease off a little. She'd remind her that this was Brynn's problem to fix. But this was so important! "Brynn?" Dawn stared at her in bewilderment. "You do want this marriage to be dissolved, don't you?"

Brynn was fiddling with her coffee mug, swirling the last few sips of coffee around and around. She no longer appeared to be listening.

It was strange how much could be said without words.

Back in her freshman year in college, Dawn had taken an entry-level communications class just to knock off a general education requirement, yet she'd learned more from that class about reading people than any other. It went something like this: Nonverbal communication said much more than spoken words. One study found only 7 percent of a speaker's communication was verbal.

Dawn, a very literal person who took people's words at face value, had been shocked by that statistic. In fact, she probably remembered it only because it *was* a number. She loved numbers. What she got out of that class was how critically important it was to listen well, to read cues from body language. She wasn't particularly good at that kind of thing, so she tried to put into practice what she'd learned from class. For a while, she worked hard at listening. And it was hard work! After a while, the whole concept was put on the back burner and soon forgotten. She hadn't even thought about the importance of nonverbal communication until this very moment. It hadn't been easy back in college to listen to nonverbal communication, and it wasn't easy now. In fact, the whole topic made her feel inadequate. Bothered. Slightly queasy.

"Brynn?"

Slowly, Brynn lifted her eyes.

On her dearest friend's beautiful face was pure and naked longing. *That* was the nonverbal cue Dawn had completely missed, until this very moment. Brynn was in love with the horrible Bear Hayes.

● ● ●

Monday, July 4

With Lincoln laid low and with her friend Maeve too busy to talk, Marnie turned to Bruno. He was an excellent listener. He often heard things that weren't spoken aloud. And quite frankly, as a clinical psychologist, he was the most qualified to untangle the knots that faced everyone right now.

She texted Bruno and asked to meet at the beach for an early morning walk. She knew it was a daily habit of his, to watch the sunrise and experience what he called a holy moment. An experience that filled him with awe. Bruno, who studied happiness, felt seeking moments of awe was beneficial to one's well-being. Everyone's.

Marnie made a point to arrive ahead of Bruno so that she could spend a few minutes soaking up the deserted beach. Chatham's personality was constantly changing, and the beach changed with it. On a typical summer morning, joggers and their dogs would be the first to hit the sand. Midmorning, people of all ages started to arrive for the day, lugging chairs and coolers. Sunbathers stretched out on towels, reading novels, oblivious to their reddening skin. Children would build sandcastles, teens would play volleyball or throw Frisbees. Dusk was Marnie's second-favorite time, right after dawn. The sand had cooled, the bright sunlight softened to a rose hue, and a kind of peace settled all over Chatham.

But today wasn't a typical summer morning. It was the Fourth of July, and the beach would remain fairly quiet this morning because of the town parade that started at half past nine. Touted as one of the oldest parades in America, it was well attended by locals and tourists. Later tonight, around nine o'clock, fireworks on the Veterans Field would cap the day. Tomorrow, many would go back to their jobs and resume their lives. Including Bear Hayes.

Bruno arrived right when he said he would and tipped his head to indicate that they could walk and talk. As Callie often pointed out, Bruno didn't like to use more words than were necessary. Marnie wasn't sure how much time she had with him, so she jumped right in, explaining the whole Linc–Bear aka TD–Brynn story, start to finish.

Now and then Bruno's thick eyebrows raised in surprise, then dropped again. Mostly, he just listened. Marnie didn't usually let herself ramble on and on, because when she did, she often had cause for regret. But without any interruptions, she let everything spill out. She sort of wished Bruno would interrupt, but he never did. He was a champion listener.

After Marnie had run out of things to say about the topic, they walked along the beach in silence for what seemed like a very long time. "What's interesting to me," Bruno finally said, "is that both Brynn and Bear came from similar backgrounds. Privileged, but with very distracted parents. And they both have a vision for what they want for themselves. It's probably what they recognized in each other—a longing to correct mistakes from their own childhoods. But there's a gap between the vision and their ability to get to it. They keep people at an arm's distance. They've built moats around themselves. Sounds like they haven't even had much practice at day-to-day relationships." He seesawed his hand in the air. "Brynn has had more practice than Bear because of her friendship with Dawn."

Yes, Marnie thought. The girls' friendship had been a gift, for both of them. But they also depended heavily on each other, which never allowed much room for other friendships to deepen. And their roles seemed very defined. "Sometimes I've wondered if Dawn has acted like a sort of surrogate older sister to her."

He nodded. "Like Callie's doing now. I've noticed how accommodating Brynn is."

Exactly! "See? That's what I mean. Dawn has steered Brynn in directions that she thought were best for Brynn. But she's always steered her away from some things Brynn might've been interested in pursuing. Like baking full-time." She sighed. "Like matters of faith."

Bruno glanced at her. "Dawn has faith. So does Kevin."

"Yes, now, but Dawn's faith was dormant for about a decade or so. Those college years, and post-college years. Her faith woke up after we moved here."

"It took a crisis." He said it like a fact.

"It did. It took Philip's death. It took Kevin calling off their wedding—the first one."

"Crises can play a significant role. They can prompt a needed pivot."

At this point Bruno spun around to turn back, and Marnie worried he was ready to go off to his holy moment. She wasn't quite ready to let him go. Quickly, she said, "So what about Brynn and Bear? They're facing a crisis of their own doing."

"They're two hurting people."

"Yet they're both so successful. So competent."

Bruno smiled in that gentle, knowing way he had. "You'd be surprised at what people hide."

"At the bank, Nanette overheard Bear discuss a plan to insist on estate planning for Lincoln."

"Would that be so bad?"

"Not if Lincoln were on board with it. Bear is doing everything behind Linc's back. From what Nanette heard, he wants limitations placed on Lincoln's ability to access his money. Like, two signatures on every check." Bear, Marnie was pretty sure, would insist on being the second signature.

"Lincoln seems pretty young for that."

"I agree. But Bear is convinced that we are trying to bleed Lincoln's fortune dry." She thought Bruno would be shocked at that, but he hardly reacted. Maybe he'd heard this kind of thing before. Or maybe this was just Bruno's way. Shockproof.

For several yards, they trudged along in the sand without talking. "Money is the noise," Bruno said at last. "The tension."

"For what?"

"For his father's attention."

"Oh no. Bear won't have anything to do with Linc."

"Most likely he thinks we are taking his dad away from him."

"But nothing could be further from the truth!" A seagull flew right in front of them, and Marnie watched it soar over the surf. "What really bothers me is that Bear seems like a man who cannot forgive others. He won't forgive Brynn, and he certainly doesn't seem to have any plans to forgive his father."

"Forgiveness is an essential ingredient for any meaningful relationship." Bruno stopped to stare out at the waves beyond the bar.

Marnie sensed her time was up with him. "So you think I should stop encouraging Linc and Brynn to keep trying with Bear? Accept the reality of their situations?"

"You know this as well as I do, Marnie. 'Nothing is impossible with God.' And I have found that God can surprise you, often when you least expect it." Bruno patted her on the shoulder and turned, wordlessly, to head off to his holy moment.

Marnie watched him go. Nothing was impossible for God, she believed that. But she knew God respected a person's free will. She didn't know what it would take to break through Bear Hayes's hard, unforgiving heart. Nanette had overheard Bear make an appointment at the bank for first thing Tuesday morning, as soon as it opened, to start the process of estate planning for his father. With Linc in the hospital, along with his attitude of "avoid all conflict with Bear because it might push him away," she sensed that his financial independence was soon to disappear. Linc's money was Linc's business. If he allowed circumstances to relinquish control of it, then so be it. But giving control over to Bear would not bring Linc what he wanted, which was his son's forgiveness. He wanted a relationship with Bear. And that wasn't going to happen.

• • •

Dawn couldn't stop thinking about Brynn. She had so many mixed emotions battling inside her: Guilt over how she had badgered Brynn in college to not give up engineering when she wanted to go into baking full-time. Pride in Brynn for making decisions for herself despite the fact that Dawn thought they were terrible decisions. *Terrible.* Sorrow that Brynn had finally risked loving a man, and that man ended up being the horrible Bear Hayes. *Horrible.* Anger at Bear for not realizing what he was losing in Brynn. Anger at Bear for accusing the Dixon family of taking advantage of Linc. Anger at Bear for not visiting his dad in the hospital.

Anger won out.

Kevin had left to meet Brynn at the bakery to do an inspection, and Mom wasn't picking up her phone or responding to texts, so Dawn didn't have her usual posse to vent to. The more she thought about Bear, the more plumes of resentment rose up. She felt she needed to defend Brynn, and Mom, and Callie, as well as her family's reputation. Linc too. She shouldn't forget about Linc. She felt strangely, ridiculously protective. Such feelings felt foreign to Dawn. Off-kilter. She wasn't prone to experiencing strong emotions. Big feelings belonged to Callie. Medium-big feelings belonged to Mom. Dawn was the modest-feelings one in the family. Rational, levelheaded, logical.

It was a beautiful summer morning and here she was inside, stewing, getting more upset with Bear Hayes with each passing minute. She needed to get dressed and go outside to let her brain fill up with fresh air. Fresh thoughts. She wandered through some small cut-through streets, enjoying the blooming red geraniums in window boxes, the cheery flags hanging from front doors. Everyone was setting up for the parade along Main Street. It wasn't long before she felt back to her old, rational self. It felt great to simultaneously breathe in the salty sea air and bask in the warm summer sun. *So smart*, she told herself. *So smart to change up the scenery as a way to break my funk.*

And then, in the distance, she spotted Bear Hayes crossing the road that led to the beach, Mayor trotting beside him. A switch clicked in Dawn. Emotions she hadn't even realized she felt started to fly past her, one right after the other. She bolted down the road, full of shaky fury, shouting at Bear to stop.

She was a crazy woman . . . and she didn't care.

● ● ●

Linc
Are you coming to the hospital this morning?

Marnie
I see you talked the nurses into giving back your phone!

Took some persuasion, plus a borrowed

charger from another inmate. So are you coming?

Yes. Leaving soon. Need anything?

I'm craving ice cream. Can you bring a pint of Dawn's Double-Fold Vanilla?

How about a pint of zero fat yogurt?

Skip it.

Chapter
TWENTY-FOUR

When everyone has let you down, you still have ice cream.

—actor Keegan Allen

Brynn had left the bakery with better news from Kevin than she'd expected. The kitchen equipment was old, but it worked. There was dry rot around each of the windows, which would be costly to repair, but no evidence of termite damage. The roof could last another year or more, Kevin said, if they had a mild winter. And the beehive oven was sound! It was missing a door, but Kevin thought he might be able to scrounge one up somewhere. Bottom line, for a very old building, it wasn't in terrible shape. Touring it from top to bottom, which only took a few minutes, Brynn decided that she could live comfortably upstairs, the way Marnie lived above the ice cream shop. She liked small spaces and was used to them.

Kevin offered to give her a ride back to the Creamery, but she wasn't needed there until it opened at ten o'clock. Besides, Main Street was lined up with parade goers. It would've taken longer to drive around town to avoid Main Street than to just walk. The morning was so beautiful that she decided to go sit on the beach with her yellow pad of notes and start working on her plans. She had much to do in a very short amount of time. She had a life in Boston to untangle and a new life in Chatham to weave together.

And then there was Bear. That would take untangling, too, but she had no second thoughts about leaving the dissolution of the marriage to him. She did wonder, though, how things between them would unroll. How quickly he would be able to annul their marriage. Pretty fast, was her guess.

She turned a corner and saw Dawn crossing the street to come up from the beach. She called to her and Dawn turned, then stopped abruptly. Brynn hurried to her, noticing how she looked. Satisfied. Victorious, like she had just climbed Mount Everest. "Are you okay?"

"I am," Dawn said. "In fact, I feel great. I just read Bear Hayes the riot act and I have to say, it felt really good."

Brynn whipped around to look for Bear on the beach, but she only saw small clumps of people or kids tossing balls. "You did *what*?"

"Now I can understand why my mom does the things she does."

"Dawn, you've always been terrified you'd wind up like your mom."

"But when someone deserves their comeuppance, it feels good to blast them."

"Did you actually use the word 'comeuppance'? Who are you? What is happening to you?"

With that, Dawn paused and pressed her palms against her forehead. "Oh wow. I am sounding like Mom. Stop me if I start wearing maxi dresses."

"Dawn, tell me what you said to Bear."

Dawn's fire was dying down. "He just makes me so mad. He's been terrible to you and to Mom and to Linc."

"Is that what you told him?"

"I saw him jogging." Dawn pointed to the beach. "All morning I'd been mentally rehearsing what I'd like to tell him and then . . . I saw him and it all burst out."

"What? What burst out?"

"My thoughts! All of them. But they probably came out mixed up. I was too mad to link them."

"What are you talking about? What kind of thoughts?"

"How Lincoln had changed after he had cancer and how he was trying so hard to fix the relationships he'd damaged and how Bear didn't even give him a chance. Look at Ashleigh's over-the-top wedding, I said. Look at how his dad had bent over backward to give her the wedding of her dreams. Look at how Bear's mother just kept raising the bar, making everyone jump through hoops, all because she wanted to stick it to Linc. He's trying so hard to make amends and everyone just wants to make him pay and pay and pay. They stressed him out so much that they gave him a heart attack. That's what really infuriates me. He's trying. They're not."

"You said all that?"

"And more! I told him how Mom was a cancer survivor, too, and that was how they met, and Mom was the best thing in Lincoln's life and he was so kind to her and she made him so happy and they loved each other and he shouldn't be messing with them." She finally stopped for a breath.

At least, Brynn hoped, Dawn had kept the rant focused on the Dixons. "Anything else?"

"Lots more. I told him that the Dixon family would never cheat Lincoln Hayes out of anything because we all love him dearly. And that if Bear didn't get his butt to the hospital to go visit his father before he left town, then . . ."

"Then what?"

She actually looked a little embarrassed. "Then he was even worse a human being than I imagined him to be." She looked over at an empty bench. "I need to sit down. I feel a little dizzy."

Brynn followed her to the bench. "So how did Bear respond to your crazed-woman rant?"

"Never said a word. He just watched me like he was at an aquarium, staring at a strange sea creature."

Brynn had to swallow a smile. She knew that look of Bear's. Stone-faced, but seething.

Dawn leaned her head on the back of the bench and closed her eyes, basking in the morning sun. "I'm not accustomed to going on tirades. They take a lot out of you."

"Well, sounds like you got everything off your chest."

A long moment passed before Dawn whispered, "There might've been one more topic I covered."

Brynn jerked her head up. "What do you mean?"

Dawn lifted her head, but her eyes were fixed on the tops of her sandals. "I told him how lucky he was to find you and if he let you go on a technicality—"

"A technicality?"

"Yes. Leaving him because you freaked out. I would call that a technicality. I told him that I thought marrying a man after knowing him just a few hours might be the stupidest thing I've ever heard of, but that Brynn Haywood is not a stupid person, so there must be something good she recognized in him because I certainly can't see it." She stopped for another big breath.

Brynn squeezed her eyes shut, horrified.

"So if he lets you go on a technicality, then he doesn't deserve you. And then . . . I told him that you still loved him."

A sick sensation hit Brynn in the pit of her stomach. "Dawn, why would you say such a thing?"

"Because it's true. And that man needed someone to tell him the truth."

Brynn vaulted to her feet to face Dawn. "How could you! How dare you interfere like that? When you and Kevin were having trouble, you were adamant that I stay out of it. How many times did you tell me to keep out of it? And I did!"

Dawn looked up at her. "That was different."

"How so?"

"It . . . I . . . it just was."

"Dawn! What is the matter with you?"

Dawn lifted her hands in a plea. "I was helping! I feel protective of you. And Mom. And Linc."

"You've just made everything worse."

"Well, if it makes you feel better, the more I think about it, I doubt he heard a word I said."

"Just because he didn't say anything doesn't mean he didn't hear you."

She shook her head. "He had AirPods in his ears." She blew out a puff of air. "My first rant and it felt so good. But it was totally wasted on him."

Brynn frowned at her. Not a chance.

• • •

When Dawn told Kevin about her rant at Bear, she expected a little support. Maybe not a pat on the back because Kevin was a Bear fan, but definitely some understanding. Instead, he gave her a dose of arctic air, a look as if appalled. "What is wrong with you?"

"Wrong? Nothing! If anything, I was doing everybody a favor."

"A favor." He said it with unmasked disgust. "Why do you have to control the narrative for everybody?"

"How was that an attempt to control anybody's narrative? I was trying to help."

He scowled. "I highly doubt that Lincoln, your mom, and Brynn would consider your interference to be helpful."

"Someone needed to tell Bear Hayes the truth."

"Maybe Bear Hayes has a different truth than what you think. You don't even know him, Dawn."

"And you do?"

"I'm getting to know him. And from what I can tell, he's a good guy. I'll bet you've never even asked him a single question."

He was right. She hadn't.

He pointed at her. "Why can't you just let things alone? Trust that things will work out for the best?"

"I do."

"Really? Because the fertility clinic in Hyannis called the land-line to confirm your appointment on Wednesday."

Aaaaand that took the wind out of her sails.

"You weren't going to tell me about that appointment, were you?"

"Kevin, that's a completely different conversation that we can discuss later." She was too tired and upset to think straight.

"Oh no. This is the same scenario. The exact same thing. You are trying desperately to control something that you just can't control. Leave this with God, Dawn. Leave Brynn with God. Leave Bear with God. Stop interfering with everything and everybody."

Now she was mad. "That is *not* fair!" She stomped to the stairs, one hand on the wooden block that was a placeholder for a missing Newell post, and turned toward him. "I'm *trying* to help everyone." She bolted upstairs and threw herself on the bed. She should've just stayed right there, in bed, all morning. Kevin could just go to the parade by himself.

And then she realized what time it was. Mom had asked her to open up the Creamery because she wanted to get to the hospital. With the parade going right along Main Street, the ice cream shop would be packed, all day long. Brynn and Callie offered to help too. But it wasn't even ten o'clock in the morning and Dawn was worn out. Emotional outbursts were exhausting.

● ● ●

Now that Lincoln had been moved out of the ICU, one visitor after the other kept appearing at his hospital door. On the good side, it was sweet to see what a popular guy Lincoln was. On the downside, visitors wore him out.

Mrs. Nickerson-Eldredge had just left when Cowboy Leo, wearing a Chatham Anglers baseball cap, poked his head around the doorjamb. Marnie, sitting in a chair beside the bed of a dozing Lincoln, patted the empty space next to her, and he crossed the room to join her.

Solemnly, he said, "Is he dead?"

"No, he's not dead. He's just sleeping."

"Is he going to be okay?"

"Yes. Even better than okay."

"Then why can't he go home?"

"They're just checking to make sure his heart is beating normally." The doctor explained they were watching for reperfusion arrythmia. More new vocabulary for Marnie. She was doing a lot of googling lately.

"What's a convention?"

"A convention? Where'd you hear that?"

"The nurse said that Lincoln must be having a convention in here."

Marnie nearly laughed out loud. Nurses, she had quickly learned, did not like herds of visitors. They would come into the room to check on Linc, frown at the visitor, and tap their wristwatch to indicate that it was time to leave, but their obvious displeasure didn't seem to discourage anyone.

Leo cuddled up close to her, and she thought of how nice it might have been to have had a little boy like him. It wasn't the first time she'd thought it.

"Is your dad out in the waiting room?"

Leo shook his head.

"Callie?"

"Nope."

"Then how'd you get here?"

"Bear. He brung me." He shifted to face her. "Did you know that Bear hates to eat anything green except dill pickles?"

"Like you."

"Just like me. And did you know that he wanted to be a baseball pitcher but then his arm got hurt and he couldn't pitch anymore?"

"I didn't know that. Are you wanting to be a baseball pitcher now? Not a cowboy?"

"I haven't decided. Bear says not to worry, that I have plenty of time to decide. He says being a kid goes way too fast so I shouldn't rush growing up."

"Bear?" Linc had been listening.

"Where is he now?" Marnie said, hoping he hadn't just dropped Leo off and left.

Leo shifted on the chair. "He's getting candy bars from the machines."

Marnie caught the look of disappointment on Linc's face and knew exactly what was running through his mind. Bear wasn't planning on coming in.

Leo wiggled out of Marnie's embrace to stand next to Linc. "Bear said you liked Baby Ruth candy bars best of all."

Linc smiled. "I did. I still do."

"Good to hear." Standing at the partially opened door was Bear, holding up two Baby Ruth candy bars.

Marnie jumped up. "Come in. Take my seat. I was just going to take Leo for some delicious cafeteria food."

"Oxymoron." Linc and Bear said it at the exact same time in the same deep tone of voice, then they looked at each other in surprise and smiled. Not big smiles, not everything-is-fine smiles, but they were definitely smiles.

Marnie grabbed Leo's hand and pulled him out of the hospital room.

● ● ●

Dawn
Where are you? I thought you were coming to
help me at the Creamery this morning.

Callie
Running behind!

How far behind? Longest line I've ever seen at
the shop. Parade traffic!

Didi is stopping by the cooking school and
wants to rehash before she leaves town.

Rehash. Seriously?

I'll text Brynn to come early. She said she'd help
too.

Well, actually . . . she's here too.

TWENTY-FIVE

Even if ice cream is cold, it has the power to melt away
a frozen heart.

—Unknown

Tuesday, July 5

Early the next morning, Brynn went down to the beach for a run
near the Chatham Lighthouse. The tide was out and waves lapped
gently on the beach. A soft salty breeze blew across her face as
gently as a caress. Fishing boats were already coming in with
their catch; dozens of seagulls hovered over them, squawking
and chattering. The beach was deserted. Summer mornings at
Chatham had to be about as close to heaven as a person could get.

Later today, Brynn planned to head back up to Boston to start
the process of dismantling one life so that a new one could begin.
She had no qualms about what she was undertaking. None at all.
The Cookie Shop was going to open, one way or another.

As she hit the end of the sandy strip of open beach, she turned
around to start jogging back to the lighthouse. Light pastel clouds
hung over the ocean like cotton candy. She loved being here. As

often as possible, every day, she wanted to get to the beach and face the vast Atlantic Ocean. As big and mysterious as it was, it was also soothing and calming. Maybe, she thought, watching the waves crest, maybe the ocean gave a peek into the nature of God. Overwhelming, yet comforting, all at once.

And, suddenly, charging full blast toward her came Mayor, and running behind him was Bear. She stopped and crouched down so the big dog didn't topple her with enthusiasm. He surprised her by dancing for a moment on hind legs, then sitting and mopping the sand with his tail, waiting for her to pat his head. Silly pup. Stroking the dog's red head, she waited until Bear approached, spirals of anxiety rolling through her stomach. After yesterday's unpleasant encounter on the beach, she had assumed she wouldn't be seeing him again.

"Hi, Brynn," he said softly.

She rose to a standing position. "Hi."

His eyes were stark, his body motionless. As if he realized how vulnerable he seemed, he turned away quickly to look at the sandbars that protected this small elbow of land from the pounding Atlantic Ocean. "Chatham is the easternmost town of Massachusetts. Did you know that? Maybe that's why it always felt so far away from the rest of the world."

"You love this place, don't you?"

"I do. I'd forgotten how much. Once I drive over the Bourne Canal, I can smell the salt in the air. Everything starts to change. Even the very color of the sky. Everything just feels . . . different."

She waited for him to elaborate, but he didn't. "I didn't think you'd be at this beach." In fact, that was why she chose it. Far, far away from the Hayeses' cottage.

He swung around to face her. "Actually, I stopped at the Creamery and Marnie said you'd come here. She said you were heading out today. I needed to talk to you before you leave."

This was about the annulment. He'd probably found a lawyer or a judge or whoever would do it fast. She knew this was coming, but it still made her feel overwhelmingly sad. She braced herself, clenching her fists as if to prepare for a blow. "I'm heading back to Boston today."

He nodded. "Same here. Back to real life."

"Not for me. This is my real life now. I'm just going up there to sort things out. Then I'm moving back down here." *Let's just get this over with.* "So you can send the paperwork to the Creamery. Marnie will make sure I get it."

"Paperwork? Oh . . . you mean . . ."

"Yep. Paperwork." Not really knowing what else to do, she took a few steps and he followed along, matching her stride. He didn't say anything, but something seemed different. Softer. He didn't seem on edge like he'd seemed all week. Even his dark eyes had lost that eye-of-the-tiger glint.

"Brynn, there's something I need to ask you," he said, measuring his words. "Why did you panic?"

That was the last thing she expected from him. "Why did I panic?"

"Yes. Why did you panic?"

With a sigh, Mayor flopped down on the sand in front of them, as if he knew this conversation was going to take longer than he had hoped.

"It's a question I should have asked you when I first saw you that day in front of the library."

Was that just a few days ago? It felt like months had passed.

"I felt so offended that you'd left—"

"And you had every right to feel offended. Hurt. Betrayed. Abandoned." All of it. More. It was a terrible thing she had done. "You trusted me and I violated that trust. Trust is such a fragile thing."

He opened his mouth, about to say something, then closed it, as if her words had stopped him. "What I was saying was that I felt so offended you'd left that I never stopped to think about it from your point of view." Staring at her soberly, he took a step closer to her. "So why did you panic?"

"Because," she started slowly, still trying to understand it herself. "Because I thought you'd wake up and regret marrying me."

"What made you think I'd regret it?" His face wore an expression of deep tenderness. "I was the one who asked you to marry me."

"Meeting and getting married the way we did . . . in the cold light of day, the whole thing seemed so . . . reckless." More than just reckless. Imprudent. Unwise. Downright foolish.

"So you jumped before you were pushed."

Slowly, she nodded.

"It might've been improbable, but I didn't wake up regretting asking you to marry me." He smiled. "I only wish I weren't such a sound sleeper. I would've reassured you before you packed up and left." He turned to face the ocean, crossing his arms against his chest. Parallel, side by side, it was easier to talk that way. "Your friend Dawn went all postal on me yesterday."

See? She knew he had heard Dawn's rant. "She's been a little"—she made a circular motion with her hand—"overzealous lately."

"To give you the edited version, she told me I was a merciless lout, and that if I didn't learn how to forgive people—especially when someone has asked for forgiveness—I was going to end up a coldhearted, lonely, bitter old man."

Ouch. And that was the edited version? "You really don't know Dawn, but that outburst was so out of character for her. She's normally quite mild mannered. Vanilla ice cream, all the way."

"I may not know her, but she seemed to know me. It wasn't comfortable to listen to her, but she was spot-on about . . . everything. She told me some things I didn't even know. Like, my father'd had cancer." He put his hands on his hips. "So I went to the hospital yesterday afternoon and had a long talk with my dad."

Brynn's head jerked up. She could hardly believe her ears. *Bravo, Dawn!* She'd have to apologize to her later for accusing her of interference. "A good talk?"

"Very good. Long overdue. Dad and I . . . we're going to get some counseling together. Actually, Bruno suggested it. I had a long talk with Bruno yesterday too."

That was it. That was the *something different* about him. Something was easier in his spirit. A wound had started to heal. She smiled. "I'm glad."

Two shrieking seagulls dipped and swirled overhead, waking Mayor from his nap and spurring him off on a chase after them.

"A lot happened yesterday since your friend let loose on me."

Brynn cringed. Dawn's normally tight filter had gone missing.

"I took my mom to visit my dad at the hospital. He had asked me if I could do that for him, before everyone left town. It took some persuading—I don't think my parents have said more than a few words to each other since the divorce—but I finally got Mom to agree to go. I stayed out in the waiting room, thinking this would be a quick visit. But they talked for over an hour. Mom didn't tell me everything, but she said Dad wanted her to know he was sincerely sorry for the kind of husband and father he'd been. He said that apologies don't have expiration dates."

She liked that. *Apologies don't have expiration dates.* She'd have to remember to tell that to Marnie.

"Brynn, in the hospital parking lot on Saturday, you asked me to forgive you for running away. I didn't give you an answer. I don't think I could've given you an answer until your friend clubbed me on the back of the skull with her verbal two-by-fours." He took in a deep breath and let it out. "Yes, I forgive you."

Brynn studied him. She couldn't be sure, but she thought he might have shuddered involuntarily, as if that admission came from deep inside him, as if it shook his very soul. "Thank you."

"But I'd also like to ask your forgiveness for being such a . . . complete and total jerk."

"What?" A laugh burst out of her.

"Don't laugh. I was a jerk. Especially when it came to the Dixons." He turned to her, and one side of his mouth curved up unevenly. "I can't believe I actually accused Marnie of siphoning off Dad's money. He can do what he wants with his money." He shifted on the sand to face her. "But to you, above everyone else, I was a jerk above all jerks."

"It's okay. I understand."

"Actually, I don't think you do. Do you remember when I told you that I thought you had a way of making people better versions of themselves? That's what this week has been for me. I've had to face some things that I'd kept bottled up. It's been such a strangely . . ."

"Coincidental. Providential. Pivotal."

"Exactly. Such a strange time." He scraped a hand over his jaw. "As I talked with Bruno last evening, it became clear that I had no business getting married. Not yet. There's a lot of things that I need to work through."

Here it came. The thanks-for-everything and have-a-good-life talk. She inhaled a big breath, held on to it as if to gain strength, and let it out slowly.

"We did everything backward, Brynn." He covered his face with his hands, then dropped them. He didn't say anything for at least a minute. "But I don't regret a minute of it. Meeting you, spending the day together, even getting married. What I'm trying to say, to ask, is that . . . maybe we could just set everything from this last week aside—and start dating."

Stunned, for a moment everything stood still, and Brynn replayed his words over and over in her mind. "You mean, just . . . date and get to know each other like two normal people?"

"Yeah," he said, a smile playing at the corners of his mouth. "Like two normal people who happen to be legally bound to each other." His eyebrows lifted. "We could take it slow and steady."

She liked that idea. But she didn't want a second crash-and-burn with Bear. She couldn't handle that. "What about the distance? I live here and you live in Boston."

He shrugged his shoulders. "Not so far. I could come down on weekends." He glanced around the beach. "I've always thought of Chatham as my home away from home." He grinned. "There's a saying among Cape Codders—'I'll call you when I cross the canal.' Maybe that'll be us."

Needing time to respond, Brynn slowly started walking again toward the water's edge and he matched her pace. There was still something holding her back. Something big. Close to where the waves lapped the shore, she stopped and turned to him. "Bear, do you have any faith?"

"Faith, as in . . . God?"

She pivoted to look at his eyes, to see if he was mocking her, but he wasn't. His eyes looked sincere. She didn't know what he thought about such things. Last week, it didn't even occur to her to ask. This week, it seemed like the most important question in the world. "Do you ever go to church?"

"Sometimes. Christmas and Easter, like most people."

"No." She shook her head. "*Not* like most people. I'm not talking about a check-the-box religion. I'm just a beginner, but I think there's something more to this."

"What is *this*?"

She turned toward the Atlantic. "Just ten days ago, we didn't even know each other. There must be a reason we met in Las Vegas. There must be a reason we both ended up here, on the same weekend as your sister's wedding. A week ago, I would never have imagined buying a bakery in Chatham, yet here I am. Maybe there's even a reason your dad had the heart attack exactly when he did."

His face scrunched in confusion. "Like . . . there's a master puppeteer in the sky?"

"I'm serious about this. All these coincidences . . . they're not random. I think we were destined."

"So you honestly think God burst into our lives with this masterful coordination of events?"

Ten days ago, she would've voiced the same question. Why

would God care about two self-sufficient, fairly self-centered people who paid him little mind? Why would those two people matter to him enough that he would steer their paths together? A good path, one that led toward healing and wholeness. "I'm not really sure. But I do know it feels like there's some higher power at work. I have this incredible, hard-to-explain peace about buying that bakery and moving here. And everything that's happened in the last ten days makes me want to know more about God."

Mayor came back to them, shaking himself off in a way that made them turn to shield their bodies. Brynn thought the interruption might give Bear a chance to end the God conversation, but to her surprise, he picked it right back up. "I don't deny that the last week seemed almost . . . orchestrated." He brushed drips of water from Mayor's shake off his legs. "To answer your question, yes. I do believe in God, but I haven't been much on speaking terms with him. There's a reason for that."

Curious, Brynn waited for him to explain.

"I think I told you I played baseball. Played it all through my childhood, all through high school, then was lucky enough to be recruited to play in college. My love for it started because my dad liked baseball. He followed professional baseball avidly. During the summers, when he was in town—which wasn't often—he would take me to the Chatham Anglers games. Those were some of my happiest memories. Just me and my dad. I remember exactly where I was sitting on the bleachers when I made a promise to myself that, one day, I would play for the Anglers. Someday, my dad would be sitting in these bleachers and watch me.

"My first summer after my freshman year in college, I was here, playing for my dream team. I was the starting pitcher, and Dad had promised he'd come. I remember praying he'd make it. Just this one game. I told God I would never ask for anything else. I was having one of those incredible days as an athlete. It was the seventh inning, and we were winning . . . and then I threw a pitch that blew my shoulder out. I ended up at Cape Cod Hospital that afternoon, needing surgery for torn ligaments. I never pitched again. And my dad missed it all. He never made it to the game. Something had come up, like it always did. I felt so let down. By my father, by God."

Brynn was sobered. Sorrow for a boy's lost dreams filled her, as well as something else: empathy. She wondered if *that* was the moment that had hardened him, turned him cold. For some reason, an image of Dawn in the Creamery's kitchen came to mind, rushing the soft ice cream from the machine straight into the freezer. She was hyperconscious about the right conditions for the ice cream to become solid rock. Linc missing his son's game became the right condition for Bear to freeze solid. But ice cream tasted better when it softened up a bit again. Bear would be better if he softened up too.

"So I kept my promise to God," Bear said. "I never asked him for anything else. And quite frankly, I didn't think God even noticed I'd stopped talking to him." He turned to her and she saw a gloss of tears in his eyes. "Not until this week."

Brynn's eyes were fixed on him. There was a vulnerability in his face that she hadn't seen before, a defenselessness.

"Yesterday, my dad said that he felt responsible for stealing my faith in God. There's a tagline for it, almost like a syndrome. Absent father, absent God. This last week, he said . . ." Here his voice became rough and dropped off. He cleared his throat, paused, then began again. "He said that he kept seeing himself in me." He swallowed. "And it troubled him. Mostly, because I had no faith. Not in God, and definitely not in others." He turned to Brynn. "So if you're asking me if I have faith in God, the answer is yes. If you're asking me if I would be willing to learn more about God, then the answer is still yes. But I think what you're also wondering about is if I'm able to have faith in you."

Slowly, she nodded. As soon as he said it, she knew that was what she wanted to know. Needed to know.

"I want to have faith in you, Brynn." His voice was low, hoarse.

"I want to believe that you're in it for keeps. I really, really want that." She felt his gaze on her and lifted her eyes. "What do you think? Would you be willing to give us a try? Start over from scratch?"

What did she think? Start over from scratch? The truth was, she didn't want to erase their wedding. Yes, it was impulsive. Reckless, imprudent, foolish, unwise. All that and more. But there was something right about it—she had trusted her instincts about Bear. As Marnie would say, she listened to her heart. She was starting to think her heart might just give excellent advice. She shielded her eyes from the morning sun to look up at Bear. "Funny that you would use the phrase 'start over from scratch' while talking to a baker." She smiled. "Same ingredients. Better outcome."

A smile started in his eyes and spread across his face. "That's exactly what I'm hoping for."

She took a few steps along the water's edge, then turned slightly toward him. "I don't suppose you might have a little spare room in your car for a girl to hitch a ride to Boston today?"

Still smiling, he joined her. "I think I just might," he said, and they started to walk together. Their hands brushed against each other, and then their fingers caught. Caught and held.

Epilogue

Nothing brings people together like an ice cream shop.

—Marnie Dixon

Eight months later

Dawn looked in the mirror at the dark circles under her eyes, at her long, tangled strawberry blond hair drooping in her face, desperately needing a shampoo. *Is that really me?* She saw a face that looked much older, much more worn out than a woman just thirty-one. When had she last had a shower? Nights and days were blurring together.

How could a little seven-pound baby turn life upside down? And when would it ever go right side up again? Fighting a yawn, she slowly brushed her teeth. Why didn't Mom tell her how hard it was? Pregnancy, childbirth, nursing, sleeplessness. And a colicky baby! She spit in the sink. Life was brutal.

Kevin knocked on the door and pushed it open. In his arms was their sleeping newborn daughter, Charlotte. Forget every complaint Dawn had just made about newborns and pregnancy and sleeplessness. Her heart melted at the sight of their beautiful, precious baby. Charlotte was worth it all. She wondered how soon they should start thinking about trying for the next baby.

"Callie stopped by."

Dawn's shoulders dropped. "Don't tell me. Baby Olivia has started to read."

"Olivia is one month old." Kevin gave her a *look*. "Callie brought us a casserole. I stuck it in the freezer."

"Is she downstairs?" She took a few deep breaths and tried to reassemble the woman she used to be. Quickly, she tried to comb out her hair with her fingers.

"Nope, she was just here for a minute."

Oh, phew. Thank goodness. Her long hair hung limp down both sides of her face. Not a good look. She tucked it behind her ears. Not much better.

"She jogged over with the baby in the stroller and hurried off to meet Bruno and Leo on the beach."

Aaaand that was Callie, four weeks postpartum. Dawn looked back at the mirror. *Aaaand this is me, four weeks postpartum.* Everything sagged or leaked.

"Motherhood is not a race," Kevin said, reading her thoughts. "Hop in the shower. You'll feel better. A hot shower is a miracle drug." He closed the door to give her a little privacy.

How did Callie do it? Do everything? She sailed through life's challenges while Dawn doggy-paddled. As the water for her shower warmed up, Dawn's thoughts rolled back to that momentous Fourth of July weekend last summer. To Ashleigh Hayes's extravagant wedding, to Linc's frightening heart attack, to her crazed tirade at Bear Hayes, landing on the moment when she came clean to Kevin.

Swallowing her pride—which wasn't easy for Dawn—she had finally admitted to Kevin that she'd been wrong to start the process of fertility testing without his knowledge, but that she was *that* desperate. *That* frightened about never being able to conceive. And that his passivity only made her dig her heels in more, because she felt like she was all alone in this troubling concern.

He had listened to her, his face pained, and he remained silent for a very long time. He rubbed a hand through his hair, raised his head, and looked at her with frank, blue eyes. "I still don't know why you can't have a little more faith about this, but I recognize that a man might never understand how a woman feels if she thinks she can't get pregnant." He reached out for her hand. "I'll go with you on Wednesday. You're not alone. We're in this together." With that, she sank into her husband's arms, wrapping hers tightly around him. She stayed there for a long, long time, colossally relieved.

The appointment started out with the nurse handing Dawn a small plastic cup and sending her off to the bathroom. "Just a routine pregnancy test," she told Dawn. "Leave the cup on the shelf and go wait in the exam room with your husband. The doctor is running a little behind."

Fifteen minutes later, the nurse opened the door to the exam room. "We work quick here," she said with a big grin. "The test was positive."

"Pardon me?" Dawn turned to her, wide-eyed, not quite hearing. "What does that mean?"

"Honey," the nurse said, "it means you're pregnant."

Dawn heard a high-pitched little gasp escape from her own throat. Then she burst into tears. There was more emotion bubbling around inside her than she could hold back.

Same for Kevin. He had let out a loud whoop. He jumped up, grabbed Dawn's hands, yanked her to a standing position off the exam table, and whirled her around the tiny exam room.

Later, Mom cried when Dawn told her she was pregnant. A little smile broke out on Brynn's face. She said she wasn't going to mention it, but Dawn had been rather moody lately. Touchy and emotional.

And then there was Callie . . .

When Dawn told Callie that she was pregnant, Callie and Bruno exchanged a sly look. Then out of Callie burst, "So are we!"

Same due date. The exact same due date. How was that possible?!

That meant Callie had taken on the catering of Ashleigh Hayes's lavish wedding, the planning and execution of feeding two hundred guests, the general bossing around of everyone, the schmoozing with Deidre Klassen and *The Knot* . . . while Dawn could hardly stay awake. Could hardly fight down the clot of nausea that kept threatening to undo her.

Unlike Dawn, Callie breezed through her pregnancy. No morning sickness, no fatigue, no stretch marks. She delivered a day ahead of Dawn (of course!) without any anesthesia. She had a daughter, Olivia, who weighed exactly one pound more than Charlotte. Unlike Charlotte, who resisted sleep, Olivia was a champion sleeper. Callie was already back at work—the highly successful Intuitive Cooking School had blown up since *The Knot* featured Callie on its wedding website.

Dawn, on the other hand, was barely functioning. As the hot water washed over her, she couldn't remember if she'd shampooed or conditioned her hair and thought she might have done it backward, so she started all over again.

Kevin knocked on the door. "Dawn? You okay? You've been in there a long time."

"I'm fine." She had to take a moment and appreciate that there was finally a door on the bathroom. She had warned Kevin she wasn't leaving the hospital unless there was a bathroom door, and he had installed it that very day. Baby Charlotte's birthday.

He knocked on the door again and popped his head in. "Maybe you can start thinking about getting out of the shower? I need to finish up those plans for Brynn's bakery and drop them off at the permitting department."

"Today?"

"Yes. We talked about this."

Did they? "I don't remember."

"Just this morning, I reminded you. Mrs. Nickerson-Eldredge said that if I can get them in today, she'll make sure they get looked at right away. And as soon as they get approved, construction can start. I want to keep the crew busy."

Kevin and Linc's preservation architecture company had gained steady momentum this last year, enough to be able to hire two full-time construction workers. Brynn's project, if approved, would dovetail nicely between two big jobs. The Cookie Shop wasn't adding square footage, but Brynn wanted to update the retail space, renovate the kitchen and the upstairs bathroom, and get a new roof. After a very rainy autumn, the roof came first.

Kevin knocked again on the door. "Dawn? Have you drowned?"

Over the water she called, "I was just wondering if dropping off the plans might make us late to the wedding."

"We're not going to be late unless you don't get out of the shower."

Dawn let the water rinse through her hair, thinking about how proud she was of Brynn. The Cookie Shop was a success from the start. Dawn had been full of doubts. She thought Brynn should start expanding her product line immediately, that customers would grow bored with just cookies. Brynn remained firm that she wasn't going to start expanding with more products unless she needed to. Apparently, she didn't need to. Customers liked cookies. They walked in off the street and bought bagfuls. They ordered decorated ones for events. Brynn trusted her instincts. And Dawn's instincts had been wrong, wrong, wrong. Happily wrong. About a lot more than cookies.

Have I learned nothing in the last few years? Facing the showerhead so the water washed over her face, she squeezed her eyes shut, thinking back over the unexpected twists and turns of life. *I can't fix everything. I don't need to fix everything. God can handle it, all of it. Every worry, every insecurity, every unknown.* What was that Bible verse that Kevin had taped on their closet mirror last summer after they found out Dawn was pregnant? *"Trust in the Lord with all your heart, and lean not on your own understanding."*

"Lean not on your own understanding." That was Dawn's biggest character flaw. She was always, always leaning on her own understanding. Thankfully, God overrode. He'd turned her life completely around in ways she never could've imagined. Mom buying the Main Street Creamery on a whim when Dawn brought her along on the groomless honeymoon. And then, Kevin returning to her life in the most remarkable way and their relationship becoming better, deeper, stronger than it had been before the canceled first wedding. She put a hand on her still-jiggly tummy. And now they were parents of a beautiful baby girl. *Amazing.*

God was still surprising Dawn with the unexpected, still reminding her that he had a better view on things. Who would've thought Bear Hayes, down deep, was quite a good guy? Brynn did. Kevin did. Bruno did. Leo did. Eventually, Mom did.

Dawn still felt protective of Brynn and constantly cautioned her to take things slow with Bear. Little by little, Bear was winning Dawn over by his steadfast wooing of Brynn. He drove down every weekend to see her, often spending it at The Cookie Shop with an apron tied around his waist. Brynn assured Dawn that although she and Bear had rushed into their relationship, they were giving it the time it needed to grow. To bloom.

And today . . . well, today was a miracle. Bear Hayes was the best man in this afternoon's wedding, to be held at the Main Street Creamery.

Kevin knocked again on the door, louder this time. "Dawn, you've got to get out of the shower. You don't want to miss your own mother's wedding, do you?"

"Coming!" She turned the shower handle off. No, this was one wedding she didn't want to miss.

Discussion Questions

1. Think about a recent impulsive decision you've made. Looking back, was it a mistake? Or was it the right choice?

2. A hunch. A funny feeling. An inkling. We've all had intuitive moments. Sensing danger, for example. The official definition of *intuition* is the ability to understand something or instinctively feel it without the need for conscious reasoning. Do you pay attention to your intuition? If the answer is no, why not? If the answer is yes, how much does intuition play into your decisions?

3. Brynn and Dawn might not realize it, but they both struggled with fearfulness. Dawn tried to manage fear by control. Brynn tried to manage fear by avoidance. Which approach resonated with you? Why?

4. Which character in this novel did you identify with the most and why?

5. What does Brynn learn through her relationships with the strong women around her (Dawn, Callie, Marnie)? What strong women have influenced your life? How so?

6. Dawn said that nonverbal communication reveals more than words. One study found that only 7 percent of communication is actually verbal. What are your thoughts about that? How well do you read body cues?

7. How many times did Brynn nearly collide paths with her twenty-four-hour groom prior to Ashleigh's wedding? At what point did you guess his identity?

8. The big decisions these characters have made/are making became defining moments for them. Why is it that crises cause so many life changes?

9. "Forgiveness," Bruno said, "is an essential ingredient for any meaningful relationship." Where do you fall on the forgiveness scale: Is it easy for you to forgive others? Is it difficult?

10. Asking for forgiveness started the ball rolling in this novel toward a character's ability to heal from invisible wounds. Think back to some of those turning points for characters in this novel. Was there one that spoke to you in a touching way?

11. Brynn had a successful life, yet she felt a longing for something more. Something, she said, that glimpsed possibilities far beyond fact. Have you experienced a similar longing? Marnie Dixon would say that it's a yearning for God. If so, what's the next step you can take to explore (or deepen) faith in God?

TURN THE PAGE FOR *a sneak peek* AT THE FIRST IN A NEW NOVELLA COLLECTION FROM
SUZANNE WOODS FISHER

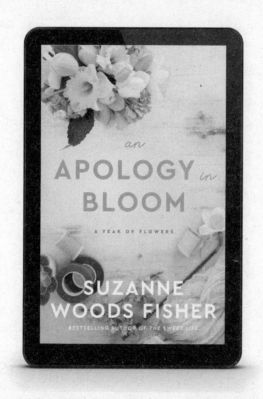

AVAILABLE NOW

Jaime Harper stepped back to examine the bridal bouquet she'd created for the Zimmerman-Blau wedding. She had to get this bouquet right today. Did it seem balanced? Was anything sticking out? A bridal bouquet was the most photographed floral piece of an entire wedding. Nail it down and everything else would fall into place.

This was the sixth mock-up. All previous ones had been shot down by the mother of the bride. These mock-up meetings were critical steps in the planning process. And Mrs. Zimmerman was a critical customer. She had a way of making Jaime feel like a rooster one day and a feather duster the next.

The Zimmerman-Blau wedding was going to be the highest-profile wedding yet for Epic Events. Sloane, the project manager, reminded her that it was such an important wedding that Epic's owner Liam McMillan was leaving an initial design consultation with a prospective client to be at this flower mock-up with Mrs. Zimmerman. "Liam asked me to make lunch reservations at his favorite restaurant," Sloane said. "A congratulations lunch," she added, crossing her fingers. "Today's the day." Final approval from Mrs. Z, she meant.

"Let's hope so," Jaime said, but she wondered. She'd been tinkering with the arrangement all morning. Her mind kept wandering, and she had to keep tugging herself back to the here and now. When she was distracted, she missed things. When she missed things, bad things happened. She knew that for a fact. "Do you think it's too, too . . ." Too much? Too little?

Sloane rolled her eyes. "Stop sounding so pathetic."

"I can't help it," Jaime said. She had a better sense of the terrible things that could happen in the world than most people did.

"Hurry and finish and clean up your workshop!"

Jaime looked at her and sighed. "I don't know why y'all are always in a rush."

Sloane turned from the door and winked. "My little Southern belle, have you still not realized we have only one speed? Express."

Jaime listened to the sound of Sloane's staccato heels doing their fast-walk down the hallway. Why did New Yorkers go through life like their hair was on fire? And for what? She got the same results by taking her time.

In the mirror, she examined the bouquet one more time. Was it as good as Sloane said? She hated that her first thought was no, that she never thought her work was good enough. She didn't know what took a greater toll on her sense of well-being—her own self-deprecating thoughts or high-maintenance clients with way too much money. Something was still cattywampus with the bouquet, and Mrs. Zimmerman would notice that indescribable *something* and reject, yet again, the design.

For most weddings, flowers took about 10 to 15 percent of the total budget. Clients were delighted to cut down on costs and waste by letting the ceremony flowers do double duty at the reception space. The welcome arrangement from the ceremony could be reused at the table seating display. Or the bridal bouquet could be put in a vase and used as the sweetheart table arrangement. But there was no such skimping for the Zimmerman wedding.

Flowers, Mrs. Zimmerman insisted, were to be the main décor for her daughter's wedding. She loved flowers and wanted lavish displays to fill every space in the venue, the New York Botanical Garden—a beautiful oasis in the middle of the Bronx. All in all, the flower budget for the Zimmerman wedding came to a staggering sum. That was the reason there was such heightened concern at Epic Events to get Mrs. Zimmerman's approval on the flowers. Sloane couldn't start billing until Mrs. Z signed off, and Jaime couldn't order the flowers without paying a sizable deposit up front. So today was the day. She had to get the mock-up bouquet right today.

She took a picture on her phone of the bouquet and sent it to Liam. A minute or two later, Liam texted back *Subtract*, and of course he was right. He was always right. Jaime had a tendency to jam-pack so that blooms competed for space as they expanded in the heat of the day. What looked to be a perfectly balanced floral arrangement in the cool of the morning would look stuffed and tight by evening. So she subtracted by pulling stems and removing materials, until she thought it thoroughly resembled Liam's recipe.

That man had some kind of superpower in how he could read his clients' minds. He was able to visualize and articulate what the clients wanted even if they didn't seem to know themselves. This was the sticky-floral-tape thought for Jaime: How to put into reality the creation Liam had imagined. That was the secret sauce for everyone at Epic Events—to think like Liam McMillan thinks and execute like he executes. He *was* the brand.

She went over to the mirror again to hold the bouquet low against her belly, the way a bride would. She rotated the bouquet to see it at every angle, examining different viewpoints to make sure it looked balanced. Photographs exaggerated the depth of field, so it was wise to note whatever might jut out.

Everything looked good. Better than good. Jaime exhaled a sigh of relief. Time to stop. Knowing when to stop was critical.

Jaime taped the stems and set the bouquet in water in the walk-in cooler to keep it as fresh as possible for the meeting.

Before closing the cooler, she breathed in deeply the perfume of fresh flowers, letting their scent calm her nerves. Whenever she paused to soak up the fragrance of flowers, she was instantly transported to the sweetest, happiest time of her life. Back in high school, working afternoons and weekends in Rose's Flower Shop in a tiny town in North Carolina with her two best friends, Claire and Tara. Mentored in the art of flower arranging by Rose Reid, the shop owner, who had the patience and kindness and generous nature to teach the three girls everything she knew. Flowers were the business of happiness, Rose had often reminded them. They brought joy and comfort to people.

Rose Reid had been on her mind all morning. She was the reason Jaime felt as if tears kept threatening. The reason she felt emotionally wobbly. It was hard to squeeze shame back into its box. Even harder to keep it from spilling out again.

When Jaime had arrived at work this morning, a registered letter was waiting for her. Instantly, she recognized the elegant handwriting, the pale pink stationery. She hurried to the workshop and sat right down on a stool, her chest stinging with pain. How had Rose found her? It was the first time there'd been contact between them since that terrible August day. She cringed at the memory she'd tried so hard to forget. Hands trembling, Jaime skimmed the letter once, twice, then read it again more thoroughly. *All is forgiven*, Rose wrote. *It's time to come home.* And then she outlined a plan for Jaime to return to live in North Carolina, to run Rose's Flower Shop.

Run a little flower shop in that off-the-beaten-track Southern town? Was Rose serious? After all that had happened between them, that offer took gumption. But did she really think Jaime would give up all *this* . . . for *that*?

Because *this* included quite a bit. A floral dream job led by a remarkably creative boss. And when it came to Liam, there was potential for romance written all over their relationship. Well, sometimes it seemed to be written all over it. Scribbles, maybe. They had "moments" now and then that made her think something was brewing. She hoped so. Oh boy, did she ever hope so.

Then again, so did most every female who worked at Epic Events. So did every female client.

Jaime closed the cooler door—pushing with two hands because it had a tendency to stick—and grabbed a broom to clean up the stems and leaves and petals strewn over the floor. As she gathered the excess flowers to return to the cooler, she glanced at the large wall clock. An idea had been tickling in the back of her mind for a unique bouquet—a contemporary take on a cascade style. Why not? She had time. Sitting in the cooler were leftover Zimmerman flowers, plus some unusual flowers she'd picked up on a whim this morning at the New York City Flower Market.

First, she began with a dense center: clusters of color for focus. The showstoppers. Café Latte roses, Cappuccino roses, Café au Lait Ranunculus as big as roses. She built intensity by adding pops of color: Black Parrot tulips and Hot Chocolate calla lilies. The black tulips were the color of an eggplant (Mother Nature doesn't make truly black flowers), petals glossy with a dark luster, tops fringed like feathers—hence the name parrot tulips. The calla lilies were a deep chocolate burgundy bloom.

She brought in texture with trailers of creeping fig woven in through the roses. Next came gradients, accent flowers to bridge the colors—mini Epidendrum orchids, ruffly Lisianthus. Then foliage to fill the gaps. A light hand, though.

She stood back to assess. It felt like it still needed more, but she hesitated, thinking of Liam's text: *Subtract!* A phrase from Rose popped into her mind: *"Let the flowers speak."* So Jaime added layer upon layer, letting the flowers do the talking. She stood in front of the mirror, just as she had done with the Zimmerman bouquet, and felt a deep sense of satisfaction.

The door opened and Sloane stuck her head in. Her mouth opened, closed, opened again, then stopped. Her eyes and attention were on the bouquet. "Jaime, it's an absolute stunner." She took a step into the workshop. "It's like an oil painting." Adding in a warning tone, "But . . . that's *not* the bouquet that Liam wanted—"

"No, no. Don't worry. This isn't the Zimmerman bouquet. That's in the cooler."

Sloane crossed the room to examine the bouquet in Jaime's hands.

"Sometimes . . ."

"What?"

"Sometimes . . . I wish I had your job."

Jaime's eyes narrowed in surprise. Sloane was a phenomenal project manager. So smart, so capable. She kept the team on a strict timeline. "I thought you liked doing what you do."

"I do. Sure I do. I mean, if I want my own company one day, this is the best path. But there's just something about flowers."

Sloane bent over to inhale deeply from the bouquet and Jaime understood. There *was* just something about flowers. "I'll tell you *what*! After the Zimmerman wedding, maybe I can teach you some flower basics."

Sloane smiled. "I'll tell *you* what." She liked to mock Jaime's Southernness. "You're on." She tipped her head. "Are those black tulips?"

Jaime nodded. "Tulips symbolize eternal love."

"Get a picture of that one. I want it for my wedding." Sloane rolled her eyes upward. "If Charlie will ever get over his allergy to commitment." They'd been engaged for seven years. She pointed to the large clock on the wall. "I just heard from Liam. They're on their way."

More than on their way. Through the large warehouse window, Jaime could see an Uber pull into the parking lot, followed by Mrs. Zimmerman's white Tesla. She took a few steps over to the large window, watching Liam, her heart humming like a contented cat. She enjoyed observing him unawares. Stolen moments, she thought of them.

"Checking out Mrs. Z's latest ensemble?"

Not hardly. Jaime's eyes were on Liam. He hurried over to open the door on the Tesla for Mrs. Zimmerman. *Such a gentleman.*

Sloane came up behind her to join her at the window. "What's she got on today?"

Mrs. Zimmerman, somewhere in her late sixties, had memorable taste in clothing. Today, she wore an orange pantsuit—radiation, glow-in-the-dark orange—and her hair was hidden under a yellow and purple scarf, its tail resting on her shoulder. Sloane whistled, long and low. "I'm still amazed that the flowers for the wedding are subdued colors."

"She wanted everything in pink, all shades, especially hot pink, until Liam told her that pink was requested all year long."

Sloane coughed a laugh. "He's got her figured out. Mrs. Z wants nothing more than to stand out from the crowd." She gave Jaime a pat on her shoulder and started toward the door.

Jaime was barely aware of Sloane's departure. Her eyes were still glued on Liam. Mrs. Zimmerman was giggling at something he was telling her. Mothers of the brides seemed especially vulnerable to Liam's charms. Maybe it was his thick Scottish brogue. There was definitely something mesmerizing about it. Or maybe it had to do with the way he looked at you when he spoke, as if you were exactly the person he was hoping to see and he just couldn't believe how fortunate he was to find you. She wondered if that characteristic might be true of all Scotsmen . . . or if it was just part of the Liam McMillan magic.

Add to that musical accent his good looks—finely chiseled features, his deceptively casual appearance—and females became captivated. Jaime, especially. If he were tall, he might have been an imposing figure, but his below-average height for a man only added to his appeal. He was so approachable, so inviting. Today, Liam was dressed in a black merino sweater and olive trousers, Ferragamo loafers. Jaime caught herself calculating how much money his outfit cost—easily between one and two thousand dollars. Right in the range of hers, though everything she was wearing today had been purchased at an upscale consignment store for a fraction of its original cost. It was one of the perks of living in New York City—lots of one-season-wear castoffs.

With that thought, her stomach started turning again. This, she knew, was the core of her insecurity. Pretending to be someone she wasn't.

With a start, she hurried over to the walk-in cooler to switch the bouquets. She pulled at the door with her free hand, but it wouldn't open. "Stupid cooler!" She rued the day she'd bought this cooler. It was a smoke screen—it looked new but broke down regularly. She yanked and yanked, but she'd need two hands to open the stuck door. She spun around to find a place to set the cascading bouquet and there were Mrs. Zimmerman and Liam, staring at her with wide eyes.

Acknowledgments

Thank you is never enough.

Lindsey Ross is my first-draft reader for manuscripts, and that is no small thing. First drafts are pretty messy—no chapters in place, lines are single spaced, typos are rampant. Despite the mess, Lindsey has an amazing ability to spot missed opportunities for characters. I always look forward to her feedback. It gives me a boost of energy to revise and improve the manuscript. I have to give her a lot of credit for why I have a reputation for providing "clean" manuscripts to my editors.

Jane Womack, nurse extraordinaire, was such a help in providing specific details about a patient's experience with a cardiac arrest in a hospital setting. She brought that scene of Linc in the ICU to life. After interviewing Jane, I realized that a hospital is the very best place to be if you're having a heart attack. "Door to needle in ninety minutes," Jane said. In other words, get to a hospital immediately.

Thank you to the Revell A-team for all the ways you've supported me. What a blessing to have had the same remarkable Revellians working on behalf of my books since the very first one was published! A rare experience for an author. A shout-out to

Andrea Doering and Barb Barnes, editors extraordinaire. Karen Steele, Michele Misiak, Brianne Dekker—publicity and marketing maestras. And, of course, Laura Klynstra, the artist behind the eye-catching covers of the Cape Cod Creamery series. These covers just call out to the reader, *Read me!*

Speaking of readers . . . thank you, each one of you. You're the best. I value your input and feedback and encouragement.

Above all, my gratitude goes to the sovereign Lord, who is continually at work in our lives to move us toward healing and wholeness. As Brynn noted, God is like the ocean. Vast and mysterious, calming and comforting. All together, all at once.

Suzanne Woods Fisher is the award-winning, bestselling author of more than forty books, including *The Moonlight School*, *Anything but Plain*, *The Sweet Life*, and *The Secret to Happiness*, as well as the Three Sisters Island, Nantucket Legacy, Amish Beginnings, The Bishop's Family, The Deacon's Family, and The Inn at Eagle Hill series. She is also the author of several nonfiction books about the Amish, including *Amish Peace* and *Amish Proverbs*. She lives in California. Learn more at SuzanneWoodsFisher.com and follow Suzanne on Facebook @SuzanneWoodsFisherAuthor and Twitter @SuzanneWFisher.

Welcome to Summer on Cape Cod

"This story is uplifting and inspirational, emphasizing what is important in life. The small-town setting, humorous banter, colorful characters, and healing make for a wonderful story."

—No Apology Book Reviews on *The Sweet Life*

"Memorable characters, gorgeous Maine scenery, and plenty of family drama. I can't wait to visit Three Sisters Island again!"

—IRENE HANNON,
bestselling author of the beloved Hope Harbor series

Following the lives of three sisters, this contemporary romance series from Suzanne Woods Fisher is sure to delight her fans and draw new ones.

Revell
a division of Baker Publishing Group
RevellBooks.com

Available wherever books and ebooks are sold.

Connect with SUZANNE

SuzanneWoodsFisher.com